Assassin's BLOOD

MARINA FINLAYSON

FINESSE SOLUTIONS

Cover design by Karri Klawiter
Editing by Larks & Katydids

Published by Finesse Solutions Pty Ltd
2019/10
ISBN: 9781925607055

Author's note: This book was written and produced in Australia and uses British/Australian spelling conventions, such as "colour" instead of "color", and "-ise" endings instead of "-ize" on words like "realise".

A catalogue record for this book is available from the National Library of Australia

1

I had contemplated murder once or twice before, but never as seriously as now.

Lily Brenfell, princess of the Realms and heir to the throne of Faerie, had only been staying with us for two weeks, but already I wanted to stab her in the face with a fork. It turned out that in real life, fairy princesses weren't the ethereal creatures of love and beauty that the stories made them out to be. They were actually right royal pains in the arse.

Oh, she was beautiful all right—if you were prepared to ignore the sullen look she perpetually wore on that flawless face—but on the inside? Let's just say that her personality left a lot to be desired.

I stopped in the doorway and surveyed the long oak dining table, with her planted at the head of it like some poisonous spider splayed over its web. Like she had a right to claim the head of the table in someone else's house. "You know," I said, "if it wasn't for that stupid curse that protects your family, someone would have bumped you off by now."

She looked at me down that long, straight Brenfell nose, as if wondering what dark hole I'd just crawled out of, and a frown of confusion creased her perfect brow. "Bumped me off? You're speaking gibberish, Sage."

Our pampered princess wasn't up with the human lingo, having spent her whole life being cosseted in the palace at Whitehaven—whereas I'd spent the years since my exile from the fae Realms learning everything I could, trying to fit in with the humans all around me.

"Killed you. Murdered you. Ended your pathetic, whiny existence."

"They wouldn't dare."

"Wouldn't they? Let's not tempt fate, princess. Maybe that curse is a crock of shit after all. Do you really want to find out?"

I'd started having breakfast earlier so I could enjoy the peace of the garden. In the way of Spring architecture, one long side of the room was open to its greenery, and the gentle trickle of the fountain and the chirping of birds was a much nicer soundtrack to my meal than her whining about how badly she was being treated. But here she was, already seated, though it was barely seven o'clock, demanding that Zinnia serve her fried eggs.

Poor Zinnia was not equipped to deal with someone like Lily. She was too soft, both in appearance and nature, with sweet brown eyes and hair like corn silk loosely braided. Her lips were usually curved in a friendly smile, but at the moment she looked flustered, and I could tell by the number of plates with barely touched meals on them that this wasn't her first attempt to placate Princess Bitchface.

"Not like that," Lily said sharply. "Not with the eggs touching the bacon."

"Sorry, Your Highness." Zinnia nudged the offending egg away from three strips of crunchy bacon, but there were still eggy smears left on the meat. My mouth began to water at the smell, and I headed for the sideboard to serve myself from a covered platter. I had a big day ahead, and I needed the energy.

"Zinnia, why are you even bothering?" I asked as I heaped my plate with strips of bacon and mushrooms perfectly fried in butter. "You know she'll only take two bites and say it's not as good as the eggs at Whitehaven."

Nothing here was as good as it was at Whitehaven, apparently, and the exiled princess was more than happy to remind us of that fact at least twenty times a day.

Lily shot me a filthy look. "The servants were certainly better at Whitehaven. They at least knew how to serve a meal properly."

Unmoved by the royal displeasure, I sat down at the other end of the table, as far away as I could get, and began shoveling food into my mouth. "See, you have two problems there. The first is that you've mistaken Zinnia for a servant."

One perfectly arched black eyebrow rose even higher. "She *is* a servant."

"No. Here in the mortal world, we don't have *servants.*

Zinnia is staff, and her job is to cook, not to wait on you hand and foot."

Zinnia made a small noise of protest, as if she could think of no better reason for existence than waiting on the king's daughter hand and foot. I ignored her.

"And the second problem?"

I gave Lily a greasy bacon grin. "The second problem is that you assume anyone gives a crap about your comfort or your precious princess feelings."

Her nostrils flared as she breathed out in a huff. "My father will hear of this."

My grin turned into a laugh, which made her fume even more. "Your father is number one on the list of people who don't give a crap about your feelings, honey. You'd still be in your beloved palace otherwise."

King Rothbold had sent his errant daughter here, not just to be a pain in our necks—though she was certainly achieving that—but to experience the human world. And to learn a little humility. The king had specifically asked us to treat her as an equal, and I was more than happy to dispense with the bowing and scraping.

Lily wasn't quite as keen on the arrangement. She was the archetype of everything that was wrong with your average stuck-up fae—so much so that sometimes she felt more like a caricature than a real person. Every time she treated Zinnia like dirt, or looked down her long nose at me, I half expected her to laugh, as if it was all a great joke.

But she was for real. She really did think she was better than literally everyone else and deserved special treatment. I shuddered to think what the Realms would be like with her on the throne. Rothbold could live forever, as far as I was concerned. He was hoping that it wasn't too late to change his daughter's character—she was only twenty, which was pretty young for a human, much less a fae—but we had our work cut out for us.

That was, if we could resist the urge to kill her. I didn't like our chances. Willow was a little more patient than me, but if this was how things stood after two weeks, I wasn't sure how much more we could take. Thank the Lady I wasn't on princess-sitting duty today. A whole day without her snide comments and bitchy looks—heaven.

I glanced at Zinnia. "Why are you even here, encouraging her bullshit? Wait, are you *crying*?"

Zinnia scrubbed at her flushed cheek and glanced nervously at Lily. "The princess needed—"

I cut her off. "The princess needs to learn some goddamn manners." I stood up. "Give me those."

Uncertainly, Zinnia offered me the dish of eggs and backed away. Lily said nothing, only pressed her lips together in a clear sign of displeasure, turning back to her breakfast as if she thought ignoring me would make a difference.

"Want some more eggs, princess?" I asked as I strolled the length of the room.

"No."

"See? There you go again with the manners thing. You mean *no, thank you*."

"I said what I meant."

Lady save me. Why couldn't the king have found someone else to turn his daughter into a decent person?

Admittedly, people he could trust were kind of thin on the ground lately, and Willow and I *had* helped save his life and his throne, but still—this was one honour I could have done without.

I reached her side. The golden globes of the egg yolks wobbled slightly in the middle of each perfectly fried white circle, ready to ooze their saffron goodness at the first touch of a fork. "Then you have a problem. If you don't apologise to Zinnia immediately for making her cry, I'm going to dump these eggs all over you."

Storm clouds roiled in her eyes as she put her cutlery down and braced herself against the table.

"Uh-uh. If you push that chair back, you get egged. If you don't say sorry in the next three seconds, you get egged." I hoisted the dish over her head. "Really, there's only one path that leads to you getting out of here egg-free."

Lily's eyes narrowed. "You insolent halfbreed. I will bury you."

"Not with Earth magic, you won't." My hands clenched on the dish, resisting the urge to dash the eggs in her face. Noble fae always resorted to the *halfbreed* insult in the end. After all these years, it shouldn't have bothered me as much as it did. "You took the hearth vow, so no nasty attacks for you."

"The vow binds you as well," she pointed out, triumph in her tone.

I laughed. "Neither of us are allowed to harm the other while we are under Willow's roof—but I don't think a little spilled egg counts as *harm*." I tilted the plate, letting the eggs slide closer to the edge. "Tick tock, princess. Zinnia is waiting."

"Sage, please," Zinnia said. "It was nothing. Please don't—"

She had her white apron bunched in her hands, gazing at me imploringly from the other end of the table. Zinnia had been through enough lately, with the attack on the sith and the death of Nevith. She didn't need some stuck-up princess lording it over her and giving us all indigestion.

"It's not nothing. You're no less deserving of respect just because you wear an apron and she wears a crown. You go have your own breakfast. I'll deal with this."

"What are you dealing with?" a new voice asked.

Willow stood in the doorway, her considerable curves on display in tight jeans and an even tighter top. Her wild red curls were pulled back this morning, confined—barely —in a loose ponytail, giving me an uninterrupted view of her frown. She looked at the eggs, then back at me in clear exasperation.

"Just explaining the local customs to Lily."

"Perhaps you could do it without wasting a plate of perfectly good eggs. I'm hungry." She strode the length of the dining table and tried to take the plate from my hand. I held on.

"She needs to apologise." We glared at each other over the plate. "She made Zinnia cry."

Zinnia, never keen on confrontation, chose that moment to slip from the room.

"Looks like Zinnia doesn't want an apology," Willow

said. "How about we cut Her Highness some slack? She's been through a tough time lately."

"So has Zinnia," I said. "Nevith was like a son to her."

And a good friend to me, though I didn't add that. And now he was dead, caught up in the power struggles of the nobility through no fault of his own. Slaughtered by assassins who'd used him to gain entrance to our sith. We'd found his body in our neighbour's garden, cast aside as thoughtlessly as an apple core when all the good parts had been eaten.

"Sage."

I held her gaze for a long moment, then sighed. "Fine."

I let go of the plate and stalked back to my own cooling breakfast, my temper frayed. I crammed the last of the bacon into my mouth and washed it down with a gulp of coffee, trying not to listen to the long list of complaints Lily was laying before Willow. It would only stoke my anger again, and I'd given our errant princess enough of my attention for one day.

But it was hard not to listen as Lily's voice rose. Willow didn't normally have a high tolerance for bullshit, but she'd been making a special effort with our unwelcome house guest. In my unkinder moments, I wondered if that was because Willow herself was nobility, the heir to the Realm of Spring. She had a keener sense of what was due to rank than I did.

But I could tell even she was reaching the end of her tether when she snapped, "But what do you need a maid *for*?" Lily launched into an explanation, but Willow cut her off. "I'll speak to your father tonight and see what can be arranged."

"You're going to Whitehaven tonight? Take me with you!"

I couldn't resist a jab. "You're not invited, princess."

The royal eyebrow arched once more. "Invited? To what?"

Willow shot me a furious look, and I remembered belatedly that we'd agreed not to mention the ascension to Lily.

She sighed. "To the ascension."

Tonight, Allegra would swear allegiance to the king and be formally recognised as the new Lady of Illusion. Illusion's gain was our loss; her new life had left a big hole in ours. It was a pretty sucky trade, actually—Allegra for the princess. We'd definitely gotten the raw end of the deal there, and we'd had to knock back a couple of gigs, since it was impossible to play without a lead guitarist. Finding a new one was a top priority, but no one could replace Allegra in our lives, however skilled they were as a musician.

Lily's hand fluttered at her throat. "That's tonight? But —but the royal family always attends ascensions."

"The king and queen will be there," Willow said, "and all the Lords. That's enough."

Allegra wasn't the only one taking their place among the Lords tonight. Merritt would become the Lord of Summer at the same time. I certainly wasn't looking forward to seeing him as much as I was Allegra, but of course, Lily had different priorities.

"But I must be there to see Merritt's ascension! We are practically engaged! Surely my father doesn't really mean to exclude me."

Whatever she felt for the new Lord of Summer, I was pretty sure he didn't return the feeling. He barely seemed to notice her when they were together.

"I think that's the problem, Highness," Willow said. "Your father doesn't approve of the match."

Lily pushed her chair back and grabbed Willow's arm. "Take me with you! This is outrageous. My whole family will be there and not me?"

I wiped my mouth with a serviette and stood up, too. "Family is so important to you all of a sudden? You didn't even realise your own uncle was an imposter."

The man who'd been warming the seat of the Lord of Summer for the last twenty years—the queen's brother, supposedly, who'd held a position of such power that he'd nearly succeeded in ousting the king—had in fact been an Illusionist, wearing another's appearance all these years.

She stilled, then turned a frigid glare on me. "He may have been an imposter, but he was the only uncle I ever knew. And now he's dead. I need to be there when Merritt takes his place. This will be a difficult time for him."

"I'm afraid that's not possible," Willow said, more gently than I would have. "The king's instructions were quite clear on that point."

"But what about me? What am I supposed to do while you're all off at the ascension?"

"What *about* you?" I snapped. "We're not a troop of dancing monkeys employed to keep you entertained."

Willow glared at me before addressing the princess. "Rowan is coming over to keep you company."

Rowan was the drummer in our band and wrote all our original songs, but he was never happy in the limelight. He would seize on any excuse to miss a grand gathering such as this—despite the honour of having been invited—and was prepared to forgo Allegra's big moment, even if it meant being saddled with a grumpy princess.

"Rowan?" Her lip quirked in an expression of distaste. "A deerkin with no conversation? What am I supposed to do with him?"

"He's going to take you to the supermarket. Zinnia has a shopping list."

She drew herself up. "A *shopping* list? You expect me to run errands like a scullery boy?"

My blood heated again. Errands had never been beneath Nevith or me, or even Willow. What made her think she was so special?

But Willow just shrugged and pushed her plate away. She'd barely touched her breakfast, but Lily had a way of ruining people's appetites. "It's no skin off my nose what you do. Stay here and count flower petals, if you'd rather."

I followed her out of the room, relieved that Lily would be someone else's problem for a few hours tonight.

"*No skin off my nose?*" I asked once we were out of earshot. "Where did you hear that one?"

We'd been collecting odd bits of human slang ever since we'd arrived in the mortal world. It was something of a competition to see who could find the most outlandish examples.

She shrugged again. "Don't know. TV, probably."

"What does nose skin have to do with anything? What does it even mean?"

She grinned at me, seeming as relieved as I was to be away from Princess Killjoy. "It means that humans are crazy."

"No wonder we fit in here so well."

I doubted that Lily ever would.

2

Say what you like about the fae, but they sure know how to throw a party.

For this occasion, it was standing room only in the throne room. I'd never seen it so full before, with the strip of white carpet leading from the doors to the dais the only clear space in the massive room. The dais rose out of the glittering crowd like an island of calm in the midst of a swirling sea. So many jewels in hair and glittering at throats and on fingers. So many sparkling dresses, in all the colours of the rainbow. Perfumes of every flower imaginable filled the air, and the whole scene was lit by globes of fae light bobbing overhead, casting warm tones of rose and gold on the assembly.

Willow and I forced our way through the crush to join the Spring contingent, who had slightly more room in a place of honour near the front. Willow greeted her mother and father while I hung back, trying to disappear into the crowd. I had no wish to socialise with Lord Thistle and

Lady Feronique, and doubtless they felt the same. We weren't exactly best buds, since Lord Thistle had been the one to exile me from the Realms. Luckily for me, I now enjoyed the king's favour, and Rothbold's approval had reopened doors for me that Lord Thistle had shut.

Across the aisle, a tall, dark-haired man nodded hello, and I nodded back without smiling. When I'd last seen him a couple of weeks ago, Raven had been laying on the charm pretty thickly, and I wasn't ready to be one of his conquests, however attractive the third son of Night was.

"Raven scrubs up well," Willow said, waving at him. He stood with his parents and two older brothers. All three sons had the Lord of Night's black hair and eyes. Lord Nox must thank the Lady every night for so many strong sons —children were rare among the fae, and three male heirs was virtually unheard of. He'd certainly hit the jackpot when he'd chosen his bride.

All the nobility were here for this historic occasion— well, all except Princess Lily, of course. Glancing at the queen's cool expression, I wondered if she was bitter about that. It was hard to tell with Queen Ceinwen. Impossibly beautiful, even for a fae, her white-blond hair and pale skin made her look like something carved from a block of ice, and she usually acted as if her heart was frozen solid, too.

At the queen's side, in contrast to her rigidity, King Rothbold sat easily on his golden throne. He looked a lot like Lily, with dark brown hair, a thin face, and those striking Brenfell blue eyes—except without the perpetual whiny expression that marred Lily's looks. Tonight, he appeared to be enjoying himself. A smile played around his lips, and he often spoke to one or other of the knights arrayed around the twin thrones. The Lion stood right beside him, and the Dragon behind. I frowned at the sight of him. I wasn't sure I'd care to have him at my back—his sudden return when everyone had thought him dead seemed just a little too fishy for my taste.

The Hawk wasn't among the knights tonight. I barely had time to wonder where he was when there was an intake of breath from the crowd. Turning, I saw three glowing lines in the shape of a large gateway appear in the air above the white carpet. In a moment, mist formed and began billowing out of the opening, followed by the gleaming point of a sword.

That was unusual. Normally, gating wasn't allowed within the palace grounds, much less inside the throne room itself. But Allegra was one of the king's favourite people, and he must have decided the security risk was worth it for the sake of honouring her. It still made me twitchy, considering how active the Night Vipers had been lately. Nothing killed a party vibe like having a bunch of assassins suddenly appear in your midst.

"Trust Allegra to make an entrance," Willow whispered to me.

The Hawk soon followed his sword. As soon as he was through, he sheathed it and stood at attention as a small blonde stepped through the gate.

Allegra looked every inch the Lady of Illusion tonight, wearing a shimmering dress made entirely of rainbow drake skin, which caused an audible gasp to ripple through the crowd. It must have cost more than every other dress in the room combined—even the queen's, which was studded with enormous pink diamonds.

"Nice dress," I whispered back. "Do you think she's making a political point?"

Drake skin was Illusion's great wealth, but it had also been its downfall. Access to the drakes and possession of their lucrative skins had been the whole reason behind the vicious Night of Swords, when Summer had invaded and virtually wiped the Realm out of existence. A small group of Illusionists had been in hiding for twenty years, and now, due to the bravery of Allegra and the Hawk, their Realm was restored to its rightful place with Allegra, the lost heir, at its head.

"Undoubtedly," Willow said. "She wants to show Illusion's greatness and remind everyone how much wealth they have at their disposal."

I glanced across at the contingent from Summer. Lady Brona stood surrounded by her advisors, awaiting the arrival of her son. She stared at Allegra without expression, but her hands were clasped in front of her with such force that the knuckles were white.

"Probably doesn't hurt that she gets to rub Summer's noses in the fact that they've lost their lucrative trade in skins, either."

A small party of Illusion's people followed Allegra, including Morwenna and Tirgen, who'd been the de facto leaders of Illusion during its long years of exile. When the last person was through, the gate snapped shut and dissipated in a final swirl of mist.

The Hawk took his place among the knights on the dais, and Allegra and her followers arrayed themselves before it. As if that was a signal, the great double doors were thrown open with a boom, revealing Merritt, Summer's new Lord, posing in the opening.

He was resplendent in sky-blue silk, his golden hair cascading over his shoulders like something out of a shampoo commercial. I barely stifled a laugh. He could have had a marching band and a dancing elephant, and his arrival still wouldn't have been as impressive as Allegra's. As if he knew that, he stalked up the aisle in solitary splendour, a dour expression on his face.

What did Lily see in him? I'd never heard him speak more than three words at a time, so it couldn't be his sparkling personality. Maybe it was his looks. He had the same deathly pale skin and pale blue eyes as his aunt, the queen, but that whole dead-fish aesthetic didn't appeal to me.

"Your friend looks happy," Willow's mother said.

I started; I hadn't noticed her move to stand beside me. Lady Feronique wore a velvet dress the colour of milk chocolate, which matched her large eyes exactly. Coupled with her long, thin face, it also had the unfortunate effect of making her look rather like a horse. The mare I'd learned to ride on had been that same shade of brown.

I looked for Willow, assuming the lady must be addressing her daughter, but Willow was on the other side of Lord Thistle. Lady Feronique was watching me, waiting for me to acknowledge her comment.

"Why wouldn't she?" I finally replied. "She has all the

power she ever wanted, a Realm to rule, plus a hot guy in love with her." Once upon a time, we'd all thought Allegra was a changeling—a mortal child brought up in the Realms—who had no power at all. Next to her, I'd felt strong. And look at her now.

"You sound as though you envy her."

I stared at Lady Feronique, bemused. She hadn't spoken to me in years, and suddenly she was all buddy-buddy? "Why are we having this conversation?"

Steel flashed momentarily in her eyes, like the woman I remembered. She wasn't used to such blunt speaking. But after a moment, the practised smile reappeared. "It was merely an observation. It's been a long time since the two of us have had the opportunity of conversation."

"And whose fault is that?" The gall of the woman, acting as if that was just some unlucky coincidence, when she'd been directly responsible for the fact.

The king had started a speech of welcome, but his words washed over me, focused as I was on this quiet exchange.

"You banished me for someone else's crime." My father had tried to kill Willow in his endless quest for dark magic. His betrayal had been just as much of a shock to me as it was to everyone else. "Spring was all I'd ever known, and you threw me out with nowhere to go."

"That wasn't my idea."

I gave her a straight look. "That's not how I remember it."

Her need to get rid of me had been almost hysterical, her desire to rid her home of this spawn of her daughter's attacker every bit as vehement as her husband's angry shouting. Never mind that I'd actually *saved* Willow. That hadn't seemed to count at all.

She had the grace to look abashed. "Maybe at first. But after I'd calmed down, I realised you weren't at fault."

"You mean after you realised Willow had sided with me over you." I hoped she'd felt sick with horror when she'd discovered her beloved daughter gone and worked out what had happened.

"Then you have had your revenge, haven't you? You took my only child with you and kept her from me all these years."

"I didn't take her—she came of her own accord. If you think anyone can make Willow do anything she doesn't want to do, you don't know her at all."

"Well." She made a visible effort to put her feelings aside, though the heightened colour in her cheeks hinted at the turmoil of her emotions. "None of that matters anymore. You are held in high regard by the king, and my husband's banishment is ancient history. I'm glad you're back."

She was *glad*? "Really. We could have had this conversation any time these past five years. You knew where we were. You could have called us home if you'd wanted to."

"You think what *I* want has any bearing on anything?"

"Of course it does. You're the Lady of Spring." She'd ruled my childhood from her throne like an all-powerful goddess. Just as cold and unapproachable as a goddess, too.

She gave me a long look, and I thought she would say

no more. This was already a longer conversation than any I'd had with her in all the years I'd spent living in her house. I turned my attention back to the ceremony in time to see the king settle a golden circlet onto Merritt's head. He and Allegra were both kneeling before the throne.

"I am the fourth Lady of Spring that my Lord has taken," Feronique said, her voice barely audible. "You can be sure there would have been a fifth if I hadn't been the one to produce a child, something my predecessors never managed. Do you really think I have any power there? I belong to Spring only by marriage. Whatever power I hold is granted by my husband's grace."

And he could take it away again on a whim. She didn't say it, but I understood.

For the first time, I felt a stirring of sympathy for the woman. Lack of power was something I could totally relate to, as the offspring of a mortal woman and one of the most powerful fae in all of Spring. If I'd taken after my father, I could have had almost as much magic as any pureblooded fae, but my mother's genes had proved too strong. So, I'd spent my whole life watching other people perform wonders, while the most I could manage was a faelight or a tiny bit of Glamour.

Not that that had made me bitter. At all. I mean, my father had ruined my life—not once, but twice. The least he could have done was compensate me with some decent magic.

From my point of view as a child thrust upon Feronique's Court, she'd seemed to hold all the advantages. Just one more glittering, magic-wielding fae in a world full of them. With the benefit of hindsight, I wondered if her cool manner had been the barrier put up by a woman far from home, if she'd been as alone in her way as I'd been in mine—though I'd had Willow, of course.

As had she. Maybe that was why she'd clung so tightly to her only daughter. Willow was the one person in Spring who she felt truly belonged to her. And perhaps that explained why she'd never warmed to me—she'd seen me as a rival for Willow's affections.

I didn't look at her. This sudden rush of understanding didn't change the fact that she'd been the adult and I'd been the child entrusted to her care.

"It doesn't matter," I said. "You still should have tried."

And then I moved away. I was here to see my friend's ascension, not to rehash old arguments.

Now, at last, it was Allegra's turn. The king lowered a golden circlet onto her blond hair, then clasped both her hands between his as she recited the vow of fealty, pledging her Realm to the Crown for as long as she lived. The look of pride on the Hawk's face as he watched made my eyes prick with tears. Maybe one day I'd find a man who looked at me like that.

When she'd finished, Rothbold drew her to her feet and kissed her formally on both cheeks.

"Behold our new Lady of Illusion," he said, turning her to face the crowd.

There was a polite round of applause, more enthusiastic from some quarters, rather less so from others. Raven put two fingers in his mouth and gave a piercing whistle.

The rest of the Night contingent shared his delight, if not his lack of decorum. Lady Brona of Summer clapped like a marionette, her movements jerky and forced.

Many of the nobles were undecided about the newest member of their ranks. She had the king's favour, which made her automatically desirable, and yet, where had she come from? Not so long ago, they'd believed her a mere changeling, and the taint of that association still lingered in their minds.

Still, there were others here who were wholeheartedly on her side. The Illusionists owed their Realm's reinstatement to her. Even Morwenna, who'd been the leader of the Illusionists in exile, clapped and cheered her new Lady with gusto—though I noticed the sidelong glance she threw at Lady Brona and the new Lord of Summer as she did so. Who cared if it was a performance put on for their benefit? They deserved to have their noses rubbed in Illusion's restored status.

Allegra held up her hands for silence. "Tonight, the thirteenth Realm rejoins the kingdom, a Realm in its own right once more."

A stirring near the doors caught my attention. Someone was pushing through the crowd, creating little eddies of disruption. Allegra was saying something about Illusion's borders being open to all, and how we could all work together to make it great again, but I was transfixed by glimpses of a tousled brown head and a T-shirt that was definitely not Court attire.

A sinking feeling lodged itself in the pit of my stomach. A quick glance around the vast throne room showed that I wasn't the only one whose attention was divided. The Hawk was frowning at the intruder, one hand hovering near his sword hilt. I caught Raven's eye, and he nodded as if that had been a signal, beginning to work his way through the crowd to intercept the new arrival.

Little murmurings of displeasure and affront drifted to me along with a familiar voice. *Excuse me, excuse me, sorry, sir, excuse me.*

Willow's head turned just as Allegra was reaching the pinnacle of her short speech: her dream of a revitalised Illusion, where all would be welcome. "Is that—?"

I nodded, and we turned as one and began pushing back through the crowd, too. We reached him at the same time as Raven.

"Rowan," Willow said in a fierce undertone. "What are you doing here?"

I dragged him behind the nearest pillar, where the three of us confronted him. His long hair was loose around his shoulders, and he wore the same AC/DC shirt and holey jeans he'd had on when we left. His outfit was drawing scandalised glares from all sides.

"We could all save a lot of money on Court attire if you start a trend with that," Raven said in his slow drawl.

I gave him an impatient glance. Everything was a joke to that man.

"I didn't know what else to do," Rowan said, his face a picture of misery. "The princess is gone."

3

———

"Gone?" Willow snapped. "What do you mean, gone?"

"Vanished, run off, disappeared." Rowan glanced between us and swallowed hard. "Do you need me to draw you a picture?"

Willow opened her mouth again, and I put a hand on her arm. Rowan was a good friend and the best drummer any band could hope for, but not the most reliable person I'd ever known. He was also easily rattled.

"Let's not jump straight down each other's throats," I said. "How could she disappear if you were with her the whole time?"

"I'll jump down his throat if I want to," Willow hissed. "It's my arse on the line, here. I was the one the king entrusted with the safety of his daughter."

"That's right." Rowan seized on this eagerly. "It's not really my fault. You should have been watching her yourself."

"Oh, I am *not* taking the blame for this. Rothbold couldn't have expected me to watch her every minute of the day myself. I have a life, and you are a grown man, Rowan. Why does shit like this always seem to happen around you?"

"What do you mean, shit like this always happens around me? This is the first time I've ever lost a princess."

Raven choked back a laugh, and I shot him another glare as the courtiers around us hissed at us to be quiet. This wasn't funny.

"Remember the time Allegra nearly got killed by some chick you picked up at the pub who just happened to be an assassin?" There was a note of triumph in Willow's voice, as if daring him to get out of that one.

That annoying half smile tugged at the corner of Raven's mouth again—he never took anything seriously. I forced myself to stop looking at him, to focus on what was being said. The Hawk had been furious over that incident. Rowan was lucky he hadn't felt the knight's magic sword instead of just the sharp edge of his tongue.

"Well, how was I supposed to know she was an assassin? She didn't exactly announce it when she introduced herself."

"Maybe if you had an ounce of common sense ... or even if you didn't go around hitting on everything that moves—"

But I wasn't listening to their bickering anymore.

The word "assassin" brought back bitter memories. I hadn't forgotten Nevith, but it seemed as if everyone else had. As if the fact that he was no one special made his death forgettable. But I'd never forget his kindness, or the way he sometimes laughed until he hiccupped—especially when he had a few on board. Nothing was ever a trouble with him. He'd even come with me when I bought my first bike, though the metal beasts—as he called them—made him uncomfortable. Then the assassins had come and used him to access our otherwise-impenetrable sith, slitting his throat afterwards, and the bright spark that had been Nevith was snuffed out forever.

Why were these assassins allowed to continue operating, their existence the worst-kept secret in all the Realms? Why had nobody stamped them out, like the insidious evil that they were? Why had kings and Lords allowed them to remain, a cancer on the Realms' existence, while innocent people died? The whole idea of being able to order someone's death was abhorrent to me. Presumably, anyone with enough money could have anyone at all killed for whatever reason, or even no reason at all. How was that just?

I looked up as the royal party processed out of the throne room. King Rothbold had the queen on his arm, and he was followed by Allegra and Merritt, each walking alone, their new circlets glittering in their hair. What was the point of all these Lords and Ladies—what was the point of a king—if they couldn't guarantee that their people wouldn't be murdered just to satisfy some rich man's whim?

The noise levels rose abruptly as the king left the room, and people broke up into chattering groups. More than a few eyed us curiously.

The Hawk joined us. "Is there a problem here?" His

eyes were the colour of honey, but there was no sweetness there now, only a wary watchfulness. Tonight, he wasn't just Allegra's cool new boyfriend but a Knight of the Realms, one of the king's own Chosen, and nothing was more important to him than the king's safety.

"We need to speak to the king," Willow said.

"He is about to host a banquet for the great and mighty of the Realms. This is not a good time."

"Lily's missing."

The Hawk didn't miss a beat. "Wait here."

He disappeared into the crowd, and Raven laughed. "Cheer up, Rowan. The king *probably* won't have you boiled in oil."

"Ha, ha."

"What happened?" I asked.

"I'd rather not go through it more than once, if you don't mind," Rowan said. He looked so miserable. "Let's wait until we see the king."

That didn't take much time at all. The Hawk was an efficient man, and one who had the ear of his monarch. In a few moments, he had us ensconced in a small, private chamber off the ballroom. Soon after, he returned with the king.

Rothbold's blue gaze raked over us as we sank into obeisance, then settled on Rowan. "Well?"

"Your Majesty, I'm so sorry—"

"Never mind that, just tell me what happened."

Poor Rowan looked like a dog that wanted to slink under the table because it had been caught stealing food from the plates. "We were in Coles. That's a—a supermarket." He glanced at Willow, looking for support, but she gazed impassively back. She could hardly take up the story when this was the first time we were hearing it, too, and she clearly felt no urge to help him out. "A place to buy food."

"I know what a supermarket is," the king replied frostily.

"Willow gave me a shopping list and said I could take Lil—Princess Lily with me."

"You said you wanted her to experience the mortal world, sire," I said. "As an equal."

Rowan's hangdog expression was just too much for me. He shot me a grateful look, but the king only nodded.

"So, we had a trolley full of stuff," Rowan continued, "and we were waiting at the checkout when I realised I'd forgotten the steak. So, I told the princess to wait in the queue, and I ran back to the meat section."

Willow drew in a deep, exasperated breath through her nose, and he glanced nervously at her. I could understand her frustration. Hell, I shared it. He'd left her alone?

"It was only for a moment," he said, as if I'd spoken out loud. "She was barely out of my sight. But when I got back, she was gone, and the trolley ... the trolley was full of rocks. She'd Glamoured all the food. The checkout chick glared at me like I'd just robbed a bank and asked me if I thought I was being funny bringing a bunch of rocks through her checkout. I didn't know what to do."

"I *hope* you went looking for my daughter," the king said, still in that icy tone.

Rowan's head bobbed in a nervous nod. "As soon as I

could. After security threw me out and told me not to come back."

I wondered what had happened to the Glamoured groceries. They'd probably been thrown out into the carpark, where they would have rotted. What a stupid waste. Seemed like a dick move by the princess. Doing a runner was one thing, but why mess with the food? Just to slow Rowan down? He was hardly a threat to her, anyway. The antlered fae were nearly as gentle as the deer they resembled.

"Presumably, you're here because you couldn't find her."

"Yes, sire."

The king sighed, pinching the bridge of his nose between thumb and forefinger. "Any reports, Kyrrim?"

"No, sire," the Hawk said. "She could have gone to Summer."

"She could," he agreed, "but my daughter lacks subtlety, so let's try the obvious first. Come with me."

He strode from the room. We lingered, unsure if he'd meant us, but hurried in his wake at an impatient gesture from the Hawk. The king led us through narrow corridors I'd never seen before—servants' ways, probably—far from the eyes of his other guests.

After ascending a narrow spiral stair that echoed hollowly with every step, we came through a plain wooden door into a wide and sumptuous hallway. Clearly, we were back in the public areas of the palace. Thick white carpet muffled our footsteps, and blue-eyed Brenfells gazed down their long, painted noses at us from the walls as we passed.

The king opened a door covered in golden leaf carvings without knocking. "Lily? Are you here?"

The chamber we entered looked just as I had expected the princess's rooms to look. Pink and white velvet draped the tall windows; overstuffed lounges were upholstered in deep pink velvets, their arms and legs gilded within an inch of their lives, and cushions were everywhere—more cushions than any normal person could ever need in a lifetime. A strong scent of lavender hung on the air.

A door in the far wall opened, revealing an equally pink bedroom, and Rowan let out a sigh of relief when the princess emerged.

"Yes, Father," Lily said, a defiant tilt to her chin. She wore a white satin ballgown with tiny pink roses encircling the hem. Her hair was around her shoulders in a dark cloud, only partially pinned up. "Fennery will be done with my hair directly, and then I'll be ready. I'm sorry I wasn't here for the ceremony."

"That's quite all right, my dear, since you were not invited."

His genial tone contrasted oddly with the hard look in his eyes. She quailed a little under that unflinching gaze, but straightened her shoulders, prepared to brazen it out. Irresistible force, meet immovable object. This was going to be good.

"It's tradition for the whole royal family to be present for such occasions," she said, managing to sound as though she were gently reminding him of something that might have slipped his mind. "And Merritt is family."

She made no mention of the abortive engagement, but

we all knew her interest in the new Lord of Summer wasn't cousinly.

Her father stepped forward and took her hand. "It's also traditional for subjects to obey the king's orders. Even if they *are* family."

She tried to tug her hand free, but he refused to let go. A golden glow grew around their joined hands, and the princess stiffened.

"What are you doing?"

"Removing your ability to open gates between worlds. You will stay where you are put, young lady, until I say otherwise."

Tears started in her eyes. "Why are you punishing me? Is it a crime to love someone?"

Rothbold sighed. "I'm not punishing you, Lily, I'm saving you. Maybe when you're older you'll understand the difference."

He nodded at the Hawk, who drew his sword and opened a gateway. Then he offered his free arm to the princess with a courtly bow. "Your Highness?"

Her lower lip trembled, but she laid her hand on the knight's muscled forearm with as much dignity as she could muster. "Am I not even allowed to say goodbye to my mother?"

"The less time you spend with your mother and her family, the better." The king sounded tired. "I have hopes that the mortal world and these fine people can show you a better path. Off with you, now. Rowan, you, too. And Kyrrim—stay until Willow and Sage return, please." It almost sounded like a request rather than an order. "Just in case. Let's have no more incidents."

The Hawk nodded, then stepped through the gate, Lily on his arm. He would be sorry to miss the rest of the evening with Allegra, but he'd always been one to put duty first, and he was technically on duty. Lucky Allegra. It was as if the king was a third wheel in their relationship. I was glad I wasn't the one having to try to make that work.

"Surely you're not expecting trouble, sire?" Willow asked as Rowan followed and the gate closed in a puff of mist behind them.

My mind immediately went to assassins again—being attacked in the dead of night in the sanctuary of your own home can focus your mind wonderfully on threats, I'd found.

"I daresay she can't get into any trouble," the king replied, showing that his mind wasn't quite as paranoid as mine. "But Rowan is clearly not up to the task of managing her alone."

"Sometimes I wonder how Rowan ties his own shoelaces," Willow muttered.

The king smiled. "I'm sorry to put this burden on you. Is there anything I can do to make it easier? Any boon you would have of me?"

"Actually, sire," I said before Willow could open her mouth, "I've been meaning to ask you about the assassins."

"The Night Vipers? What about them?"

"Well, are we just going to leave it at that? They broke into our sith, and killed my friend to do it. Why are they allowed to carry on without consequences? Can't you punish them? Destroy them, even?"

He considered me for a moment, as if the request had caught him by surprise. "Unfortunately, Sage, assassins are like weeds. No sooner do you kill one than three or four more pop up in their place—only then you're on their hit list. And they are dangerous enemies to have."

"Then let's bring on the weedkiller and burn them out. Why should such an organisation be allowed to continue?"

"I don't know if it's possible to ever stamp them out completely. They've been around as long as the Realms have, and, like weeds, they serve some purpose in our ecosystem."

"But we can try, right?" I struggled to contain my outrage at his live-and-let-live attitude. They served a *purpose*? Sure, if you were rich and ruthless. I bet if his precious daughter had been in the sith the night of the attack, he'd be singing a different tune. But because Nevith was a nobody, his death didn't matter. "They can't be allowed to kill whoever they like without us at least *trying* to do something about it."

He looked as if he was regretting his generous impulse, but if he was handing out boons, this was the one I wanted.

"I'll have someone look into it. They are notoriously hard to find." He glanced at Raven, who nodded almost imperceptibly. "But I make no promises. I fear it is an impossible task."

4

___

"*M*ay I have this dance?"

Raven appeared out of the crowd in the ballroom, black eyes gleaming, and extended his hand with graceful courtesy.

I eyed it wearily. Playing in a band meant I was used to late nights, but it must be almost dawn by now, and I was ready for my bed. "Actually, I'd rather sit this one out. My feet are killing me."

He adjusted smoothly, drawing my hand through the crook of his arm and leading me towards an alcove where there were a few empty seats. "You don't wish to ease the ache?" he asked.

Of course I did—that was why I wanted to sit down. It took me a minute to realise what he was really asking.

"You mean why haven't I used my magic to soothe my feet?" I glanced at the whirl of bodies going past. Of course, the fae never suffered from sore feet. Why suffer when you had magic at your fingertips? "You forget, I don't have magic to burn like you purebloods. I'd rather save up what I have in case I really need it later."

Not that there was a lot I could do with my magic, anyway. Daring rescues and superhero feats were well beyond my reach. I could make faelight, but then, so could any fae child; I could regulate my own body temperature and do some small self-healings—but when it came to magic that could affect the world around me, I was no better than any mortal.

That had used to really burn me when I was a kid. When your father is one of the most powerful Spring fae to have ever lived and all you can do is create little balls of light when you snap your fingers, you feel like genetics has really screwed you over. My father had said that sometimes happened when fae mated with mortals, as if the mortal blood was so powerful it completely overwhelmed the fae. He'd said he still loved me just the same.

Well, we all knew how that had ended up. Mostly, I was reconciled to my lack of power, but occasionally some careless comment like Raven's would awaken that deep longing in me again. I would give anything to be able to perform wonders without any more thought than I gave to snapping my fingers. Still. I took a deep breath and returned to the present with some effort. Sore feet were hardly the worst thing that could happen to a girl.

"Allow me?" Raven laid a hand over mine where it rested on his arm, and I felt a warmth grow under his touch. A feeling of wellbeing spread up my arm and out through my whole body.

My feet tingled as I gazed up into his coal-black eyes.

Now, they felt good as new, and I almost regretted turning down another dance.

"I didn't know you were a healer." Most fae could only use their magic to heal themselves. It was a rare person indeed who could affect the wellbeing of others.

"Hardly a healer. That's about the limit of it." He gave a careless shrug and drew me down onto a padded seat with a low back, barely wide enough for two. The warmth of his thigh against mine radiated through the thin silk of my dress. I must have still looked impressed, because he smirked. "One of my many talents."

"Most of them hidden."

White teeth flashed in a smile of genuine amusement. "That's what I like about you, Sage. Such a gilded tongue, so full of compliments. But you should really tone it down, lest I become giddy at the shower of constant praise."

"There's nothing wrong with calling a spade a spade." I drew my hand out from under his. He was a practised flirt —he'd already tried working his charm on me when we'd been working together to help Allegra save Arlo—and I had no intention of becoming another notch on his bedpost.

"Of course not. Your interest in spades is only one of your many delightful qualities. It's rare enough in fae circles to be quite refreshing. Would you like a drink?"

"Sure."

He signaled a passing waiter, who offered a tray of icy cool wines and cocktails in improbable colours. I chose a pink champagne, which proved to be sweet and refreshing. Raven took a small glass full of some thick, dark liquid.

The orchestra was playing a lively tune. We could almost have been in some European palace, watching a sea of beautiful dresses and graceful bare arms whirl past, were it not for the occasional wings or horns among the throng.

Raven himself looked fully human tonight, though if I glanced at him from the corner of my eye, his fae wings, black as any real raven's, rose powerfully from behind his back. He was a true shapeshifter—Allegra had seen him transform completely into a raven—which was rare among fae. I hadn't been kidding about his hidden talents.

Above us, fake rainbow drakes made of pure magic, their jewelled skins flashing, cavorted against a dazzling blue sky—equally fake, but no less impressive. It was as if the ballroom had no roof, and we sat outside, an impression only heightened by the giant oaks that circled the edge of the room. Their greenery was likely meant as a hat tip to Summer, just as the rainbow drakes were to Illusion.

"What are you drinking?" I asked, watching the dark liquid ooze back down the side of his glass after he'd taken a sip. "It looks like mud."

"Far nicer." He offered me the glass, but I shook my head. "It's a chocolate liqueur. Bitter as my soul, but rewarding for those brave enough to try it. Are you sure I can't tempt you?"

He put a slight emphasis on the word *tempt*. Did this man never let up?

"I'm not big on giving into temptation." I put as much discouragement as I could into my tone. Raven's mercurial ways were well known, and this sudden interest in me was nothing new for him.

He had a reputation for seeking new conquests, charming women into love with him, then losing interest once he had them eating out of his hand. But he was the son of the Lord of Night and, as such, would be expected to make a political marriage. I could never be more to him than a passing fancy, and I had no intention of letting him break my heart.

Still, I wasn't made of stone. He was as gorgeous as all fae were, and I was afraid that if he kept up this assault for too much longer, I might give in to it.

"Aren't you a guitarist in a rock band? I thought that was the whole point—sex and drugs and rock 'n' roll?"

"The whole point is the *music*." He should understand that. Fae loved music. Almost all of them played at least one instrument.

He trailed one hand down my bare arm, leaving a shudder of gooseflesh in his wake. "But surely you must let your hair down sometimes? Life can't be all work."

"Spoken like a true fae. What do you know about work? You're a Lord's son. Work takes on a whole new meaning when you live in the world without magic." *Ask me how I know.* I pushed his hand firmly back into his lap, pleased that I still could. "And you may not have noticed, but my hair is too short to let down."

"Oh, I've noticed." His dark eyes were mesmerising. "I've noticed everything about you."

I dragged my gaze away with some difficulty and watched the dancers swirl past. My glass was nearly empty; perhaps I shouldn't have drunk it so fast. A pleasant buzz was stirring in my veins. I should leave, before he actually started making sense.

The Dragon danced past with Lady Brona in his arms, and I pulled a face. "I'm so glad to see Sir Ebos hasn't suffered any ill effects from his near-death experience."

"You sound bitter." Raven's arm lay along the low back of our couch, and his fingers stroked the short hair on the nape of my neck, sending all kinds of odd thrills through my body. "Surely you don't imagine our noble Dragon is lying?"

"What is the king thinking?" I burst out, moving to shrug his hand off at the same time. "Of course he's lying! He turns up right at the crucial moment, when everyone thought he was dead, and takes Summer's side against Allegra. How can the king still have him as a knight?"

Raven lips twitched in a sardonic smile. "You can be sure he backpedaled fast enough once he realised the lay of the land. He told the king some sob story about being lost in a healing coma for days after being nearly killed by trolls."

"Kyrrim said that according to Allegra's description of that fight, he should hardly have been bothered by that blow. He's a dragon, and they're tougher than other fae."

"They also have gilded tongues. The king seems convinced."

"But the way he popped up just in time to support the Lord of Summer's argument couldn't have been a coincidence. That had to have been planned. And that whole trekking into Fire through the mountains of Winter in the first place—what did he say about that? Seems to me like he was *trying* to get them attacked by trolls."

"He was very apologetic about that. Said he was so sorry to bring Lady Allegra into danger, but he was afraid of his brother's reaction if he had turned up directly at the gates of Fire."

"My bullshit meter is pinging like crazy."

He smiled. "Apparently, he had mentioned to the king that it would be a problem when he accepted the job of escorting Allegra to Fire in the first place, so the king's isn't."

"Well, I wouldn't trust him anymore after a stunt like that. I don't know how the king can have him around."

"It's hard to un-knight someone, you know," he said mildly. "The bond between the king and his Chosen can really only be severed by death."

"Maybe the king should hire his precious Night Vipers, then, and get rid of him. After all, he seems so convinced that the Vipers are *serving some purpose in the fae ecosystem.*"

"Now, now, don't be bitter," Raven chided. "Rothbold has asked me to see if I can locate them. Me and my little birds. Maybe if you're very good, I'll tell you what I find."

"Maybe if you tell me what you find I'll let you keep your ball sack in one piece."

"Threats, Sage?" He laid a dramatic hand on his chest and opened his eyes wide. "When all I've ever done is try to help you?"

"No one wants to help me. Even Willow won't tell me what she knows about the Vipers. Says she doesn't want me doing anything stupid."

He smiled. "Willow has more sense than I thought."

"Oh, come on, I'm not an idiot." I held up a finger when he opened his mouth. "*Don't* argue. I'm not going to take on an ancient bloody assassins' guild on my own. I just want to know that *something* is being done about them. Nevith and all their other victims deserve that much, at least."

Raven watched me, his usual mocking expression missing for once, replaced by a more serious light in his dark eyes.

"Truly," he said at last, "they are a blight on the Realms. If I find anything out, I will tell you." His sudden seriousness was enough to make me wonder if he'd lost someone to the assassins himself. Then he grinned, his habitual half-smile returning. "The question is, will you be grateful?"

"Oh, I'll be soooo grateful, sugar," I purred, leaning closer and finally letting myself run my fingers down the black silk of his shirt. "I'll get you a box of chocolates and a thank-you card."

His eyes gleamed with amusement as he covered my hand with his own. "Strawberry creams are my favourite."

5

———

"Stop pulling on that," Willow said as Lily got out of the car and tugged on the crotch of her jeans again.

"They're cutting me in half," the princess complained, slamming the car door behind her, a sulky expression on her face. "The seam is going right up my—"

"They'll stretch," I said.

The throb of a bass beat pulsed inside The Drunken Irishman, and my body relaxed into it. The car park was almost full; it looked like a good crowd tonight. Maybe Randall had a band playing. We hadn't been here for weeks, and the darkness, the music, the crisp night air— even flavoured with the scent of the overflowing rubbish skips against the back wall of the pub as it was—felt like coming home.

"Why couldn't I wear a dress? I look like a human."

"That's the idea," Willow said. "Relax. You might even enjoy this."

Lily looked unconvinced, but followed Willow up the back stairs and into the pub. The noise hit like a wall to the face as we went through the doors. Queen was playing on the jukebox, and I bounced to the rhythm of the song as we pushed our way through the crowd to the bar.

"Evening," Randall said, coming to take our orders. The big bartender had some troll blood somewhere back in his family tree, and he was an impressive figure at well over six feet of pure muscle. His son, Tony, on bouncer duty at the front door, was even taller. Between the pair of them, they managed to discourage any unruliness among the patrons. "What can I get you lovely ladies?"

"And me," Rowan said. "Or are you counting me as a lady, too?"

"I don't need to ask what you'll have," Randall said, already reaching for Rowan's favourite beer.

"Two rum and Cokes," Willow said.

"I'll have a beer, too," I said.

"Coming right up."

Randall moved with quick, efficient movements, eyeing Lily curiously as he worked. She wore a Glamour tonight. Not enough to make her look like someone else entirely—she still had blue eyes and black hair—but her features were subtly disguised, so that she was no longer recognisably the Crown Princess of the Realms. It had seemed safer that way, and surprisingly, Lily had made no protest. Being a princess no doubt had its advantages, but it would make it almost impossible for her to experience the real world in the way her father wanted. This pub was a well-known fae haunt, and we didn't need word getting around that we had the princess staying with us.

"I haven't met your friend before," he said as he pushed our drinks towards us.

"This is Lily," Willow said. "She's visiting from Spring. Lily, meet Randall."

"Hello." Lily took an experimental sip of her rum and Coke. Her expression gave nothing away, but she took another, larger one, so first impressions must have been positive. Either that or she was determined to get drunk as quickly as possible.

"Pleased to meet you," Randall said. "Lily, like the princess?"

"Yes."

She could have tried harder to divert suspicion, but she'd insisted that she wouldn't be able to remember a false name. Randall's gaze was speculative.

"Just about every second Spring daughter since the princess was born has been called Lily," I said hastily. "It was a good Spring name anyway, but the royal connection made it super popular. Must be a drag, running into people with the same name all the time."

Randall nodded, and his eyes lost that questioning look. "Are you staying long?" he asked her.

"I'm not sure yet." She turned away to survey the vast room packed with people, signalling her lack of interest in further conversation.

Randall raised an eyebrow but said nothing.

"Who's playing tonight?" Rowan asked.

A band was setting up in our familiar corner, and I felt a pang of loss. I'd rather be up there than babysitting our sulky princess. But at least it was a night out, and maybe Lily would stop harping about how boring it was in the sith for a while.

We really had to find something to keep her occupied, but the thought of trying to find her a job—and getting her to actually do it—was enough to make me shudder. I couldn't imagine our proud princess taking orders from a human, or demeaning herself with actual work. But she couldn't sit around the sith forever. That would only put us all on a fast track to madness.

"New band called Talking Parrots. Screeching Parakeets? Something like that. I haven't had them in before. Don't suppose there's any chance that you guys will be available again soon?"

Rowan shook his head. "Still looking for a new guitarist."

"There's a guy in tonight who might do. He usually does session work, but I think he's between gigs at the moment. You might be able to twist his arm."

"Fae?" I asked.

"Changeling, actually. Kiwi guy, nice fella. Just moved here." He looked around the darkened room then shook his head. "Can't see him right now, but I'll point him out to you later. You staying awhile?"

"Probably," Rowan said. He was already surveying the room, nodding at people he knew and checking out the single girls. A big group of them were clustered around a table at the edge of the tiny dance floor, and a girl with sleek brown hair half-smiled and looked away as he met her eyes.

"Remember what happened last time you picked up a girl here," I muttered to him as Randall moved away to serve another customer.

He rolled his eyes. "I'll make sure to ask if she's an assassin first." He picked up his drink and strolled across the floor in her direction.

"A changeling guitarist?" Willow asked as we watched Rowan's progress. Someone turned off the jukebox, and the familiar sounds of a guitar being tuned struck me with a pang that was almost like homesickness. "It'll be almost like old times."

I nodded, watching the band make their final preparations.

"You'd work with a changeling?" There was a note of horror in Lily's voice.

I bristled. "And why not? What have you got against changelings?"

Lily shrugged. She had borrowed a glittery top of Willow's with a wide neckline, and it had slipped casually off one creamy shoulder. "I suppose they're not as bad as humans, but ..." She trailed off, leaving me to imagine the supposed horrors of changelings and humans.

Being half human myself, I was unimpressed with her fae snobbery. "Stick around. You might even come to like a few of them."

"I find they don't try to kill you half as much as the purebloods do," Willow added in her most sardonic tone.

"You might want to keep an open mind, girlfriend. You'll make more friends that way."

Lily drained her rum and Coke and set the glass back down on the bar with a sharp tap, meeting Willow's eyes with a challenge in her own. "And what do I want with friends?"

I snorted. "Do you have so many that you can't do with a few more? Everyone needs friends."

She transferred that blue gaze to me, something of her father's steel lingering in it. "Brenfells have subjects. We don't have friends."

I snorted. "Sure they do. Don't you think your father sees Kyrrim as his friend? He bloody well ought to, considering the lengths Kyrrim went to in order to save him."

"Who told you you didn't need friends?" Willow asked.

Lily shrugged again. "People who know. My mother. My uncle."

"Right," I said. "So that would be the fake uncle who wasn't even a real family member. Naturally, you should take everything he said as gospel, because I'm *sure* he never tried to manipulate you."

It was kind of sad. For someone in Lily's position, it would be hard to know if people liked you for yourself or for what you could do for them. Even Willow was wary about letting new people into her inner circle, and she was only the heir of a Lord, not a king. Not that I was going to start feeling sorry for our pampered princess, but I was beginning to see why her father was so keen to get her out of the palace. She had a pretty skewed idea of life.

Willow got another round of drinks while the band

started their first set. A few brave souls got up on the dance floor, and I could see Lily's foot tapping against her bar stool.

She leaned over to me in a break between songs. "What kind of music is this?" Her face was flushed with alcohol, and her eyes sparkled in the flashing lights from the dance floor.

"Good old Aussie rock 'n' roll," I said, stifling a smile at the surprise on her face. "It's a little different to what you're used to hearing."

"It certainly is."

Rowan was dancing with the brown-haired girl, spinning her into some wild turns as she laughed up at him, obviously enjoying herself. Rowan was a good dancer. Decades of practice will do that for you. I couldn't tell from here if the girl was fae; she was pretty, though not outstandingly so, so perhaps she was human. Not that Rowan would care. Like most of us who spent the bulk of our time in the human world, he'd lost a lot of the old-fashioned fae attitudes to mortals.

"Hope she doesn't turn out to be another assassin," Willow said, following the direction of my gaze.

I nodded. "I've had a gut full of assassins lately."

"Whoops. Don't look now."

I started, wondering what fresh hell was about to be visited upon us, but she jerked her head toward the door. Raven stood there, talking to Tony, his black hair shining almost blue in the dim light. His eyes scanned the room as he spoke until they alighted on us. With a last word to the bouncer, he began to make his way towards us.

"I reckon he fancies you," Willow said. "He's always turning up lately."

"I doubt it. He throws compliments around like confetti, but they're all just as paper-thin and meaningless."

She gave me a sidelong look. "Don't be so hard on him. He's one of the good guys."

"Maybe."

Sure, he'd come through for Allegra when she really needed him to, but I wasn't sure he was entirely reliable—that playboy reputation worked against him. Plus, some of his methods were kind of extreme. Rowan still hadn't forgiven him for blowing up his garage in an effort to warn Allegra away from her investigations.

Watching him walk toward me, brimming with self-confidence and turning heads as he passed, I couldn't help but feel that I was right to keep a little distance between us. He was so clearly enjoying the attention—was everything just a game to him? He never seemed to take anything seriously.

"Evening, ladies." He gave a half-bow in that usual mocking way of his, so you were never sure if he was actually being courteous or subtly sending you up.

Lily nodded regally, taking it as her due. I said nothing, but Willow nodded a greeting. "Can I get you a drink?" she asked. "I was just about to buy another round."

"No, no, my shout. I insist." He beckoned, and Randall appeared as if on a string. "Another round for the ladies, and I'll have a Scotch on the rocks."

"Coming right up."

He turned to Lily. "Having a good time?"

She shrugged and leaned closer to shout over the music. "It's a bit loud for my liking."

I noticed her foot was still tapping, though. Evidently, Raven saw it, too.

"Perhaps you'd like to dance later?" he asked.

She lifted a supercilious eyebrow. "Dance? Is that what they call that?"

We all looked at the couples on the dance floor, most of whom were merely shuffling, using the music and the darkness as an excuse for a good grope. Only Rowan and his girl could actually be said to be dancing.

Raven laughed. "Maybe it's not quite how things are done at Whitehaven, but you might find you enjoy it." He leaned back and put his elbows on the bar behind him, surveying the packed room with cheerful good humour. "Good crowd tonight. What do you think of the new band?"

"They're all right," I said. Their choice of songs was good, but the singer's voice had an unpleasant nasal twang.

"Not a patch on you, of course."

"Of course."

Our drinks arrived, and he passed me my beer. "Come outside for a minute?"

I took a deep swallow of beer, then licked the foam off my upper lip. "I'm good, thanks."

He leaned closer. "I have some information for you about that matter we were discussing recently. I don't really want to shout it in the middle of a crowded bar."

A thrill of excitement shot through me. Already? It had

only been a little over a week since the ascension. "You move fast."

"That's what all the girls say," he threw over his shoulder as he led the way to the door.

I followed, elbows out to protect my beer.

"How you doing, Sage?" Tony rumbled in his deep voice as I passed him at the door.

"Never better than with a beer in my hand," I said, and he nodded. Beer was serious business to trolls.

Outside, my ears rang at the sudden drop in decibels, though I could still feel the beat reverberating through my body as I leaned up against the front wall of the pub, facing the street. The row of businesses opposite were all tightly shuttered against the night, except for the little Thai restaurant, which was doing its usual roaring trade as delicious curry smells of coconut and spices wafted across the road. A car horn honked further down the street, and over on the highway, the rumble of trucks and the squeal of air brakes could be heard, a deep counterpoint to the music inside.

Raven leaned against a telegraph pole that was plastered with layer upon layer of handbills advertising bands appearing in the pub, so many that the pole bristled with little metal piercings like a punk rocker. I'd stapled a few of those in my time. Humans were so casual with iron. I rubbed my iron ward—a simple silver ring—reflexively with my thumb. Even someone whose fae blood was as weak as mine needed a ward to cope with all the iron in this mortal world.

"Did you miss me?" Raven asked, his dark eyes glittering in the light from the lamp overhead.

"Inconsolably," I replied with cheerful insincerity. "What did you find out?"

He shook his head reprovingly. "Sage, Sage. You must learn to take time for pleasure among the business."

"In this case, business *is* pleasure. Nothing would give me more pleasure than hearing you've tracked down ... the people we're looking for." At the last second, I stopped myself from naming the Vipers. There was no one near apart from Tony, but fae had good hearing. There was no need to flaunt our business all over the neighbourhood. The assassins had enough advantages on us already.

"Then prepare to be pleasured," he said drily. "I have a meeting arranged for tomorrow."

"You do?" I could hardly believe it. "It was that easy?"

"Easy, no. Simple, yes. It's all in knowing how things are done."

"And how *are* they done? Where is this meeting?"

"Right here in Sydney, in the Queen Victoria Building. A little café called Perk You Up."

I smothered a laugh, checking on Tony again. He was on the phone now, so I spoke more freely. "The most feared assassins in the Realms operate out of a café called Perk You Up? Do you get a free cappuccino for every ten hits you order?"

He smiled. "It's just a meeting place. I don't know where they operate from. That is a closely guarded secret. But I made contact, and I got a message back tonight that someone would meet me there tomorrow to discuss the specifics of my request."

"So, what, to get a meeting with them you had to pretend that you wanted someone assassinated?"

"Well, of course. They're not going to sit around and discuss the weather."

"But ..." The obvious perils of such a course hit me, and I drew a shaky breath. This was so typical of Raven. "What if they actually do the job? Who are you going to order a hit on?"

"I can think of a number of people whose removal would make the Realms a better place, can't you?" He glanced down into his glass and swirled the amber liquid so that the melting ice cubes clinked against the sides. "I thought perhaps our new Lord of Summer would be an ideal candidate. What do you think?"

I nearly choked on a mouthful of beer. "Not sure the king would approve of having his nephew targeted."

He shrugged. "Well, this is just a preliminary meeting, where we get to eye each other off and they decide if they want to do business with me. When they name their price, I'll just decide it's too high."

"And then?"

He looked up, his eyes full of mischief. "And then we tail them back to their lair."

6

———

Somehow, plans concocted late at night over a beer or four seemed much more workable than they did in the cold light of day. I walked through from Town Hall Station into the bowels of the Queen Victoria Building, leaning into the gale of homeward-bound office workers streaming the other way towards the trains. It was just after five o'clock on a Thursday night and people were everywhere, enjoying late-night shopping or heading home from a day at work.

Rowan followed in my wake, clearly uncomfortable at the mass of humanity surrounding us. The noise was intense—the thunder of hundreds of feet on the tiled floor, the whistle and grind of trains behind us. The smell of the trains filled the air, too, all hot, dirty metal, buffeted by the winds of their passage through the tunnels below us.

Rowan stuck close to my side, leaning in to be heard above the rage of sound. "What if he recognises us?"

"He who?" I sidestepped a woman with an enormous

54

pram and a toddler in tow. *Good luck getting that on the train, lady.* It would be standing room only at this hour, and the toddler was already whining to be picked up. Her frazzled expression made me thankful I was only going to spy on an assassin. Toddlers were way scarier.

"The assassin."

"Don't be so sexist. Who says the assassin won't be a woman? And why on earth would they recognise us? Who have you been hanging out with lately?"

"We've both been hanging out at Court," he said in a sharp tone.

"So has half the Realms. Relax. That's why I brought you. Me sitting there on my own might look suss. The two of us will just be a couple of tourists chilling together, seeing the sights."

The Queen Victoria Building was a gorgeous old building, all golden sandstone and pale green copper domes on the outside, intricate tiles and woodwork beneath soaring ceilings on the inside, renovated and restored to its former glory. Once a marketplace but now the pre-eminent shopping destination in the heart of Sydney, there were always tourists hanging around, taking photos on the grand curving staircases or posing for selfies outside with the huge statue of Queen Victoria herself.

We took the escalator up from the basement, and the noise levels began to abate. A steady stream of people still headed for the trains, but here the arcade, tiled in old-fashioned patterns, was far wider. On each side, small, up-market shops enticed the passers-by. These were probably some of the most expensive retail spaces in Sydney.

Soon, we found the café. Every surface was sleek and modern, with black leather booths and marble bench tops. We ordered and paid, then took a table by the door. Our coffees came quickly, and I snapped a quick photo of the artful love heart in the foam on top.

"What are you doing?" Rowan asked, frowning.

"Looking like a tourist. See? Isn't it pretty?" I showed him the photo on my phone. "Totally Instaworthy."

"Sometimes I wonder what language you're speaking," he grumbled. Clearly, espionage didn't agree with Rowan. He wasn't usually this grumpy.

"Oh, come on, you're not that old. Don't pretend you don't know what Instagram is."

"I feel like a sitting duck."

"Why? No one's going to buy a hit on *you*. Relax." Maybe a timid deerkin hadn't been the best choice for this little adventure, but who else could I ask? Willow would have been better, but she was too recognisable with her bright copper curls. I had to assume that the Vipers would keep dossiers on all the Lords and their families.

And just imagine if I'd brought Lily! If I thought Willow was too noticeable, I could hardly substitute the princess. The thought made me snort. Being helpful was probably against her religion, anyway.

"I don't like that it's here," he said.

I raised my eyebrows. "In this café? What's wrong with it?" The only thing I didn't like about it was the fact that it had two exits; one to the interior of the QVB, and one to the street. But I'd placed myself so that I could see both.

"In Sydney," he said impatiently. "Don't you think it's a

bit of coincidence that they arranged to meet in Sydney? It's like they know who we are."

"I think it's smart. Much less chance of being spied on in the mortal world. You know most fae won't even come here. They could just as easily have picked Prague. They can gate to anywhere."

"That's what I mean. Why Sydney, out of all the places in the world?"

I shrugged. "Why not? Maybe their base is here."

He lowered his voice, leaning over the table and practically whispering. "Do you think he's here yet?"

"Raven? I don't see him."

"No, the assassin." He caught my glare and sighed. "Fine. He *or she*, I mean?"

"Probably. No, don't look around, you idiot."

"I should have worn a Glamour."

"No, no magic." Glamours were hard to spot, but not impossible. "We don't want to look anything but ordinary."

He fiddled nervously with the saltshaker, spilling white grains on the black marble surface of the table.

I laid a hand on his to stop his fidgeting. "Drink your coffee and try to look like you're having a good time."

He swallowed a sip, managing to look like an extra from a horror movie who just *knew* that the monster was right around the corner. I sighed and scooted my chair around the table so I could sit next to him and put my arm around him.

"What are you doing?"

"Getting comfortable." I laid my head on his shoulder.

"Here's Raven," he said.

It was five thirty, and he was right on time. He strode past, further into the café, without acknowledging us, and I heard his deep voice ordering a long black.

I gave it a few minutes, then picked up my phone, pressing my cheek against Rowan's, angling the camera for a selfie. In the background of the shot, I caught Raven taking a seat at a table where another man already sat. How had he known this was the guy he'd come to meet? There must have been some prearranged signal between them.

I snapped the picture, then showed it to Rowan. "Laugh," I said.

He gave an unconvincing chuckle, so I punched him in the shoulder. Then I studied the stranger caught in the background of the photo.

He was about medium height, with mid-brown hair that fell into his eyes. He wasn't ugly, but he wasn't a head-turner, either. He wore a dark suit, like so many of the men who still passed outside the café, and his tie was a neat, pale grey. There was nothing about him that was more than average, nothing that made him stand out. I couldn't help feeling a little let down. Somehow, I'd expected an assassin to look ... well, less ordinary.

Although, perhaps that was the point.

"Is he fae?" Rowan asked, frowning at my phone screen.

I enlarged the photo, but of course it told us nothing. Just an Average Joe, only bigger and blurrier. He'd been glancing down when I'd snapped the photo, so I couldn't see his eyes. He had nice eyebrows, thick and arched, under that floppy fringe.

"He's probably wearing a Glamour," I said. Fae just didn't do ordinary. By their nature they were extraordinary, larger than life, beautiful as a spring morning, even the least of them. No one looked at a fae and said, *Well, at least he has nice eyebrows.*

"I suppose he doesn't want to stand out too much from the crowd," Rowan said.

"No, I guess not. Being noticeable wouldn't be an asset in his line of work."

"If that even is an assassin. Maybe he's just an errand boy."

"Maybe. Doesn't matter, though. We can still follow him."

"What's he doing now?"

"I don't know. I'm not going to keep looking at him and give the game away. Just sit tight and enjoy your coffee."

Rowan took another sip. "Enjoy my coffee? This is going to give me heartburn."

"You're such a sook, Rowan."

He gave me a stern look over the rim of his cup. "This isn't a game, Sage."

"Oh, I'm well aware." People had died. *Nevith* had died, right outside our front door, surrounded by enemies, while we slept peacefully inside. "And I'm not playing around here."

I put down my cup and picked up the phone again. Would it look too obvious if I took another "selfie"? I desperately wanted to watch the meeting, but it was too risky. I couldn't do anything to draw the man's attention. I forced myself to study the photo again instead, committing every mundane detail of his face to memory. Getting this far hadn't been easy, and I didn't want to blow our chances through impatience.

My restraint was rewarded a few moments later when the man himself passed our table, trailing a faint scent of ironbark behind him. The suit was good quality and cut to show off an athletic body. He checked each way before leaving the café for the bustle of the QVB's tiled cavern, like a man about to cross the road, showing a straight nose and strong jaw in profile.

I waited a breath, then another, before standing, too. "Let's go."

Without acknowledging Raven or waiting to see if Rowan was coming with me, I strode after the man. He had turned left, heading back the way we'd come, towards Town Hall. Large numbers of people still filled the space, some window-shopping, others striding towards the train station. Little knots and eddies formed as people met up with friends or traffic jams started in the doorways of particularly popular shops. A busker had set up his empty guitar case just near the big centre aisle that crossed over from York Street to George, and a young couple had stopped to listen to his rendition of "Stairway to Heaven".

My man moved with surprising speed through the crowds. Without appearing to hurry, he sidestepped around obstacles and made the most of clear paths that formed among all the moving bodies, so that I had to pick up the pace or risk losing him. He might only be average height—just a shade under six feet, by the looks of it—but his legs seemed particularly long.

I'd hoped he was heading outside, but he suddenly veered towards the escalators down to the basement level. Damn. I hurried to close the gap. If I lost him down there, he could end up anywhere—on a train to another part of the city, or coming up one of the numerous other exits from underground into other streets or different shopping centres.

A large group of teenagers, wielding bulky backpacks like battering rams, cut between us at the escalators. I watched in a fever of impatience as he stepped smoothly past the people standing in place on the escalator, while I was too hemmed in by backpacks to move. I tried to shove my way through, but all that got me was a chorus of protests from the teens.

The man looked back as he reached the bottom of the escalator, as if he'd heard the commotion. Cold grey eyes raked across me, and I melted back behind a backpack.

"Don't let him get away," Rowan urged at my shoulder.

"I'm *trying.*" I came off the bottom of the escalator almost at a run.

His head was disappearing into the crowd, being carried further and further off by the inexorable tide of commuters. I managed to shove past the wall of backpacks, only to be brought up short by slow-moving pedestrians dawdling outside the cheaper food shops lining each side of the narrowing passageway, as if a choice of juices was a decision worthy of endless pondering.

The dirty smell of trains and a rush of hot wind from

the tunnels below smacked me in the face as I burst out into a momentary gap in front of the automatic gates of Town Hall Station. Up ahead, my quarry tapped on at the gate, and the barriers slid aside for him. I rushed to follow, but the backpack kids spread out, hogging the gates and generally slowing everyone up.

"Go around to the exit," I told Rowan in a fever of impatience, "in case he walks straight through."

Rowan nodded and forced his way through the crowd to circle around the outside. The man in front of me couldn't get his Opal card to work. I sidestepped smartly and shoved in front of a woman who gave me a filthy look, but I didn't care. My quarry was already at the top of the stairs leading down to platform three.

I hurled myself through as soon as the barrier opened. His lead was widening, and I only caught glimpses of him getting further and further ahead as I was buffeted by the crowds. He was at the bottom of the stairs, and there was a train *right there*, standing at the platform with its doors open. The announcement boomed and echoed, distorted by the tunnels. I caught the word *Hornsby* before the chimes sounded.

Pushing and shoving for all I was worth, I tried to catch up, but there were too many bodies between us. Carried along on the human tide, I was only halfway down the stairs when he stepped onto the train and the doors slid closed behind him.

"God *damn* it." I glanced up at the indicator board. All stations to Hornsby via Chatswood. Not that that meant anything. He could be getting off at the next station.

I turned and fought my way back up the stairs. Had he known he was being followed? He certainly had a thing or two to teach me about evading pursuit—although, perhaps that had been magic at work. A subtle Aversion, maybe, that allowed him more space to move freely than I'd had. I'd been so sure I could track him.

I squared my shoulders. Now I had to go and tell Raven that I'd failed.

7

———

Worse than failing Raven, I'd failed Nevith.

Nevith had been a quiet soul, though he used to get talkative over a beer or two down at The Drunken Irishman with friends. He'd challenged me to an arm wrestle, once, that had ended with him nearly wrenching my arm out of its socket. He'd forgotten I wasn't a full fae and hadn't stopped apologising for weeks afterwards.

But his strength had meant nothing when the assassins came, and now he was gone. I lay back on the grass and stared up at the leaves waving overhead. The assassins continued to thrive. No one could make them pay for Nevith's death if we couldn't track the bastards down.

"I'll thank you not to shred my entire lawn," Willow said.

She and Lily were lounging on chairs by the fountain, enjoying a pre-dinner wine. Lily looked up with interest at the acid tone in Willow's voice. She was like a bloodhound, attuned to the scent of discord. Probably came from living her whole life in the toxic atmosphere of the Summer-dominated Court, where someone else's argument could become your advantage.

I let the stalks of grass I'd pulled fall and sat up. "Sorry."

I was so sick of sitting around, my whole body itching for action. I'd run five kilometres after coming home from the city, but it hadn't soothed my restless energy. I pulled out my phone and opened the photo I'd taken at the café again, studying the assassin's face and imagining that straight nose crunching underneath my fist, blood spurting from his mouth.

I'd studied every line of this face until I could have drawn it blindfolded, but Sydney was a city of four million people. The chances of ever finding him again without a lead were slim—and that was even assuming he'd been here for more than a brief visit. He could be anywhere. London. Munich. Some piddly little sheep station in the back of beyond.

Or, more probably, safely back in the Realms.

"Is Rowan joining us?" Willow asked.

"No. He said he'd had enough excitement for one day. He's just too chicken to face Raven and admit that we lost the guy."

We'd agreed to meet Raven here at the sith at nine, to tell him what we'd discovered. It was nearly nine, and a sick feeling was rising in my stomach. I hated being the bearer of bad tidings.

I threw the phone down on the grass. Lily leaned over to see the photo.

"Is that him in the background?"

"Yes."

She picked up the phone and studied it, then shook her head. "He's not one of the men who came for me."

The assassins had staged a fake attempt on the princess's life a couple of weeks back—one of her so-called uncle's many plots.

"Weren't they all killed by your guards?" Willow asked. She was leaning back, eyes closed, her half-empty glass dangling from one relaxed hand. I wished I could feel so calm.

"No, only one. The other three escaped. I wish they'd killed them all."

I cocked an eyebrow at her. "You sound very fierce, princess."

"It was terrifying. I thought I was dead." She tossed the phone back to me. "Their whole organisation should be wiped from the face of the Realms."

I smiled. "That's the first sensible thing you've said since you got here."

A crunch of pebbles on the path heralded Raven's arrival. He wore black jeans and a black silk shirt, the sleeves rolled to the elbow, showing well-muscled forearms. His dark eyes surveyed our little group as he dropped into a spare chair.

"Can I surmise from the look on your face that the news isn't good?"

I sighed and flopped back into the grass, throwing one

arm over my face so I didn't have to see the disappointment on his. "Surmise away. I lost him at the train station."

There was no sound but the glugging of wine for a moment as he poured himself a glass. When I peeked at him, his head was tipped back, gazing thoughtfully at the leaves overhead. He looked almost as relaxed as Willow.

"Did you learn anything from him that might help?" Lily asked him. "What did you discuss?"

Raven sipped his wine, then closed his eyes with an appreciative sigh. "It was a short conversation. The Vipers have been doing this too long to give anything away. He asked me who I wished to target, and whether I had a preference on the method of dispatch." His mouth quirked in distaste. "Apparently, it's extra for something showy."

"Do people want that?" Willow asked, showing some interest in the conversation at last. "I would have thought if you were hiring an assassin, it was because you wanted a discreet job done."

"It appears that some people like to make a political statement with their murders."

Lily nodded. "Making an example."

"Quite," said Raven. "It's good business practice in some circles, I'm sure. But I said I wanted a standard job and left the method to their discretion."

"Did he give you a price?" I asked, half-intrigued despite my horror. How much would it cost to take out a Lord of the Realms?

"When he heard my target, he said he would have to consult with his superior, though he warned me it wouldn't be cheap."

"Who was your target?" Lily asked.

Raven's eyes met mine for a brief moment, amusement dancing in their dark depths, and I wondered if he would lie. How would Lily take the truth? "Your boyfriend, actually. Merritt."

Not well, as it turned out.

"What?" She sat bolt upright, a look of outrage on her face. "Is this a joke? How dare you?"

"No joke," Raven said mildly.

"You can't order a hit on a member of the royal family."

Raven swirled the wine in his glass lazily, watching the dark liquid. "As a matter of fact, I can. It's just going to cost a lot. 'A huge amount of money' were his words."

"I forbid it!"

A gleam of mischief entered Raven's coal-black eyes. "Must I remind you, princess, that you are in no position to forbid anything? Your father has given my plan the all-clear."

Her face paled dramatically, which was saying something, considering how fair her skin was anyway. "My father would never countenance the assassination of a member of his own family."

And yet she was clearly afraid that he would. I almost felt sorry for her, and had to clamp down on a twinge of sympathy at the naked fear in her face.

Raven relented. "Relax. No one's getting assassinated. But it gives us another chance to track them. He said he would get a message to me with the price and then, if I agreed, we would meet again to hand over the money."

Lily didn't look reassured. "But if you give them the money, they'll do it!"

"I'll give him fairy gold. When it turns back into leaves, they'll void the contract."

"As long as they don't come looking for you to complain about being duped," Willow said.

"I'll take my chances." He looked at me. "But we'll need to work out some better means of surveillance."

I nodded. "This is our last chance. He won't meet you again after you leave him holding a bag of fairy gold."

"Can't you have your birds follow him?" Lily asked, as if the answer should have been self-evident.

"My birds were ready to follow him last time, but they can't go underground—not without attracting a great deal of attention. If he meets us in the city, he could easily escape through the rail system again. It will depend on the place and time of the meeting. Ravens generally aren't active at night, and most likely, he'll pick evening or night for a rendezvous."

"We need more people," I fretted. "I could give them all a copy of his photo, so he doesn't have such an easy time escaping."

"We don't have more people," Raven said. "We can't involve anyone else in this. The king is expecting me to handle this discreetly. And who knows what he'll look like this time? That was a Glamour."

"Damn." So my photo was useless. I chewed at my lower lip, thinking.

"Shame Allegra's too busy with her own affairs,"

Willow said. "That cloak of shadows of hers would come in handy."

I sat up straighter, staring at Raven in sudden hope. "You gave that to her! Can't you make one for me?" Allegra's cloak of shadows only worked for her, otherwise I would have borrowed it in a heartbeat. But if Raven had made one, couldn't he make another?

But he was shaking his head. "No. Those things are rarer than hen's teeth. There isn't another in the whole Realm of Night."

"Then can't you make it accept me somehow?" Allegra had tried to lend it to me once before, but every time I draped the midnight feathers around my neck, the cloak slithered straight to the floor, refusing to stay put. Only when Allegra put it around her own shoulders did it clasp itself and cling tight, turning her invisible.

"I'm afraid that's a negative, too."

"Something else, then? Surely there's something suitably sneaky in Night's box of tricks? You people spend half your lives sneaking around in the dark."

"Way to vilify a whole Realm, Sage," Willow said. "You make it sound as though *they're* the assassins."

Raven just smiled. "It's true that shadow-weaving has given us a bad reputation. A skilled shadow-weaver can bend the darkness around themselves, but it's almost impossible to cloak someone else. And the same goes for light-weaving, although Day magic isn't going to help you at night anyway. What you need is an invisibility potion."

I snorted. Such things were notoriously screwy, liable

to fail at the exact moment you needed them most. "Thanks, but I'm looking for serious suggestions."

"I *am* serious. A truly skilled Earthcrafter could make you something that would work, as long as you remained in contact with the earth."

"There's the rub, isn't it? How much earth contact do you reckon I'd get in the Queen Victoria Building?"

"We don't yet know the location of the meeting."

"You said it yourself—the Vipers have been doing this for a long time. They're not going to be stupid enough to pick a location that gives us any advantages." Still, I eyed the princess. Maybe it was worth having something ready, just in case. If she was half the Earthcrafter her father was ... "Can you make a potion like that?"

"My training has tended more toward statecraft than parlour tricks," she said stiffly.

"Raven just said it wasn't a trick, it was a real possibility." But of course Lily wouldn't want to get her hands dirty helping us. She was good for nothing except whining. I felt the loss of Allegra intensely. Maybe my friend could spare a little time to don her cloak of shadows again for a good cause.

"What about Yriell?" Willow said suddenly.

Hmmm. The king's sister was the most skilled Earthcrafter I knew, even more powerful in her way than the king himself. If anyone could turn a so-called parlour trick into something useful, it would be her.

I heaved myself off the ground, brushing loose bits of grass off my jeans. "Good idea."

Raven raised a lazy eyebrow. "You're going straight away?"

"Why not? No time like the present."

"I haven't finished my wine."

"That's okay. I don't need an escort."

"Nevertheless." He tipped his head back and sculled what was left in his glass. "This is *my* evil plan, and I'm not having you cocking it up without me."

"It's just a visit. Yriell and I are friends."

Raven stood up. "Yriell isn't always as welcoming as she might be."

He was right. Last time the Hawk had called on her for help, she hadn't been in the mood for visitors and had used a localised earthquake to remove him from her front porch.

"So I'll take a bottle of vodka," I said. "She likes that."

"Then you'll need someone to carry it for you." He smiled, pleased to have a bargaining chip.

"I do have saddlebags, you know."

"I'm sure you have every modern convenience. But the king has entrusted this duty to me, and I take my duties very seriously."

"Since when?" I muttered. Raven was no Hawk, selfless in his devotion to duty.

He smiled winningly. "Since they involved escorting beautiful women around the countryside."

I gave up and went to get the spare helmet and jacket, and to change into my own leathers.

He took the helmet, but when I offered him the jacket, he refused.

"That shirt's not going to protect you if you fall off," I pointed out, zipping my own jacket. I liked all my skin right where it was, thank you very much.

His eyes glinted with laughter. "Are you intending to dump me on the road?"

"Of course not, but—"

"Then I'll put my faith in your no doubt expert riding and leave the jacket behind."

"Suit yourself. It's no skin off my nose." A grin tugged at the corner of my mouth. That really was quite a handy phrase. "Just off your elbows, and hands, and arms …"

a tingle of threshold magic washed over me like tiny insect feet on my skin as we exited the sith, leaving our own little bubble of the fae world behind.

From the outside, none of the beauty of Willow's sith was visible. No gardens, fountains, or airy pavilions set in meadows of nodding wildflowers—just a small red-brick house with an overgrown front yard. It was shabby and uninviting, and Willow had chosen it as the place to anchor the entry to her sith for precisely that reason. No one would expect the heir of Spring to live here. And no one would find anything but the dilapidated house if they entered without an invitation.

Outside, the one working streetlight glinted off the shining metal of my motorbike, waiting where I'd left it at the kerb. It was always kind of a relief to see it still there, since this wasn't the nicest neighbourhood. I would have preferred to bring it inside the sith with us, but Willow said it had too much iron in it and flatly refused to consider it. She'd put a minor Aversion on it instead, to encourage humans to overlook it, same as she had on her car. I patted the gleaming chassis as I threw my leg over.

The bike roared to life as Raven settled himself behind me, placing his hands firmly on my hips. It felt weird to have his heat snugged up to my back as we sped through the cool night streets. I didn't often take passengers, but when I did, it was usually Willow. Somehow, knowing that it was a man's body pressed against me, a man's hands holding me so close ... it felt different, and it took me a few kilometres to shake off the oddness and relax into the ride.

I loved this bike. It was a Yamaha SR400 in classic black. Cornered like a dream, and a nice smooth ride. Sure, it was no Harley, but the salary of a part-time receptionist at a real estate agency didn't stretch to Harleys. One day. In the meantime, this bike was my dearest possession.

I could happily have ridden all night, but we only had to go across town, and in less than an hour, we were crossing Audley Weir in the National Park, the bike's headlight sweeping across trees and water. There were no other lights here; even the visitors' centre was dark at this time of night. We passed it and a lone toilet block crouched by the riverside, and I parked under a big old gum at one end of the carpark.

It was very quiet once I'd turned the bike off. I took off my helmet and ran a hand through my short hair, letting the night breeze cool my scalp. Raven looked around with interest as he took off his own helmet.

"Hard to believe we're in the middle of a major city," he said, taking in the dark river and the brooding trees. A few house lights shone through the dark from the slope above the river opposite us, but they were the only sign of human habitation. No streetlights, no traffic noise, just nature and an empty expanse of dirt next to a river.

We found the walking track and headed off into the night. The bush was still, but not quiet. It was never completely quiet. There were rustlings as small animals passed unseen in the darkness, and the shrill, repetitive song of a night bird somewhere deep among the trees. Close to the river, a frog croaked, and I felt my shoulders relaxing. This was almost like being back home in Spring. I'd spent many a night roaming through the forests on Lord Thistle's estate, exploring every quiet shadowed pool and poking into every burrow or hidey hole I could find in search of the creatures that called them home.

The trees filtered the moonlight, creating a soft dappled effect that silvered the white trunks of the gums and cast deep shadows over the leaf litter beneath them. The path we followed was reasonably clear and well maintained, so we kept up a good pace in the low light. Fae night vision certainly didn't hurt—at least my father's genes had come through for me there.

I felt the first shudder of unease as we approached the lightning-blasted trunk that marked the turn-off point to Yriell's house. Her wards were powerful; even before I stepped off the path, I felt a huge reluctance to go any further. Without willing it, my steps slowed.

"Need a hand?" Raven's voice was very close, making me jump.

"Not at all." Of course *he* had no trouble resisting the

Aversion, with his pure noble blood. It was really only meant to turn humans away.

Resenting the ease with which he moved, I forced myself to stride towards the thicket that loomed ahead, blocking our way. It bristled with thorns, seemingly impassable, but I'd been here often enough to know better. I shouldn't have balked. All I had to do was make myself walk straight at them and those thorns would disappear.

Only the fact that I'd managed it unscathed so many times before kept my feet moving when all they wanted to do was turn and take me in the other direction, as fast as possible. Truly, Yriell's Aversion skills were unparalleled.

The thorns dissolved around me, and I let out a sigh of relief as the pressure did, too. Now, I could walk unhindered towards the small cottage that sat in the centre of its little clearing before us. A thin drift of smoke, barely visible against the night sky, curled from the chimney. Yriell always seemed to have a fire going, whatever the weather. There were lights on inside, but the blinds were drawn.

I paused halfway up the path that led to her front steps. Now that we were here, memories of the Hawk's last reception intruded more strongly than they had when I was safely back in the sith. Yriell didn't like being bothered with the affairs of the kingdom. She had made that abundantly clear on more than one occasion. It was the whole reason she lived out here, under a fake name and using a Glamour to make herself look like an old woman and not the fae in her prime that she was.

I hefted the vodka bottle in my hand consideringly. On

the other hand, she also liked to drink. I was hoping that the one would cancel the other out.

"What's wrong? Lost your nerve?"

"Never. I was just thinking that, since you're the self-proclaimed leader of this little expedition, you really ought to go first."

Raven grinned in appreciation of this sally. "No, no, I insist. Ladies first." He sketched an elaborate bow.

"Chicken."

He flapped his elbows like wings. "Bok bok bok."

Taking a firm grip on the vodka, I marched up the steps and onto the veranda. Raising my fist, I rapped three times on the door.

Raven took an ostentatious hold on the veranda post and winked at me. "Just in case she decides to start another earthquake."

I turned my back on him, listening to the sounds within the house. Footsteps approached the door, followed by the sound of a bolt being shot. The door swung open, revealing Yriell's diminutive form, her grey hair wild as usual. A piece of twig was snarled in it just over her ear, and I almost reached out to remove it but thought better of it.

Her eyes, the warm brown of rich soil, lit on the bottle of vodka and brightened. "Is that for me?"

"I thought we might share it."

"Beware Greeks bringing gifts, they say. Is there a price attached?"

"We're not Greeks, and this is a bargain offer," Raven said. "Not only do you get this top shelf bottle of hard liquor, you also get our scintillating company. Two for the price of one, in effect."

She scowled at him. "You're as full of bullshit as your father." But she opened the door wider and stepped back so that we could enter. Then she led the way towards the long kitchen table at the back of the large main room.

Yriell's house looked like a bellbird and a magpie had shacked up and built a home together. Every flat surface was covered with tiny marvels: bottles full of oddly shaped things, bunches of herbs dried and fresh, more books than you could poke a stick at, and containers of every kind and colour. As Princess Orina, sister to the king, she could have had apartments in the palace and a dozen servants, but she preferred her own happy chaos to the upheavals and political drama of the Court.

"Glasses in the cupboard," she said, gesturing with a vague hand at one of the overstuffed cupboards.

Raven opened the door gingerly, lest the contents come cascading down on his head, and extracted three glasses while I opened the bottle.

Yriell plonked herself down in one of the seats at the table and watched us expectantly. "I suppose it's too much to hope that you've come purely for the pleasure of my company?"

"Not *purely*," Raven said, setting the glasses down on the table and taking his own seat opposite her. "Although, of course, your company is a major draw. We also have a kind of two-for-one deal going on. We get to enjoy your marvellous company while also scouring your formidable brain for something that might help us with our current problem."

She groaned. "Of course there's a problem. Has my royal brother sent you? What has he screwed up this time?"

"He didn't precisely *send* us," Raven said.

I poured three generous nips of vodka and passed the glasses out. Yriell lifted hers in salute. "To my useless brother, long may he reign." Then she knocked back the whole lot in one go and pushed her glass toward the bottle again in a not-so-subtle hint for a refill.

I obliged, of course. That was what it was for. "Actually, we're hoping to do something about the Night Vipers."

"That's a ballsy move, girl. You and whose army?"

I glanced at Raven. "Just the two of us, at this stage."

"We're on a reconnaissance mission for the king," Raven said.

Yriell barked a short laugh. "Why, is he sick of you already? Messing with the assassins seems like a fast way to get yourselves killed."

"We're not messing with anybody," I said. "Just checking things out at this stage."

Raven nodded. "It will be up to King Rothbold what he decides to do with whatever information we manage to gather."

She shook her head. "You've got rocks in your head, the pair of you. But go on, I could do with a laugh. What have you done so far?"

We took turns filling her in on our attempts to track down the assassins' headquarters. She grinned appreciatively when I recounted how easily our contact had managed to evade me at Town Hall Station.

"You've gotten soft," she said to Raven. "You're too used to relying on those birds of yours."

"My friends do have their limitations," he said, watching her with those midnight eyes. It occurred to me that he looked rather like a bird himself. His head was tipped to one side, his dark eyes fixed on her face, full of a lively curiosity.

"Well, then, pour me another drink and tell me what it is that you think I can do for you. This should be good."

I took a deep breath. This was the moment. She would either laugh and continue taking the piss out of us but help us, or she'd decide that it was all too much effort and become affronted at our daring in laying yet another burden on her slight shoulders. "I was hoping you knew a way to make me invisible. I can't see how else I can stay close enough not to lose him the next time."

Her eyebrows shot up. "Invisible, is it? Well, at least you're not asking for anything difficult."

Relief washed over me. "It's not difficult?"

She roared with laughter. "I'm shitting you, sweetheart. Of course it's difficult. Otherwise every fae and his bloody mother would be traipsing around unseen, sticking their noses in where they aren't wanted."

"But not beyond someone of your inestimable skills, surely?" Raven suggested, smiling.

Yriell directed a disgusted look at me. "Is he always such a kiss-ass?"

"He thinks he's pretty charming."

Raven drew back, affronted. "I *am* charming."

I held up an impatient hand. I didn't want to listen to his blathering anymore; I was more interested in what Yriell had to say.

"Well, there are potions …"

"Yes?" I sat forward eagerly.

"But they're finicky bloody things. Always some limitation. You have to remain in contact with the earth, or they stop working if someone touches you, or they can only be used at night in a dim light. And what's the point of that? If the light's dim enough, you're practically invisible anyway." She got up and pulled down a thick book with a worn leather cover. It had clearly seen a lot of use; the spine was half broken and several yellowed pages were hanging out of it. She flipped through, muttering to herself. "This one might work. But not if you're meeting him in the city. Too much iron will screw with it."

I sighed. "We don't know where we'll be meeting him yet."

"Well, that's a bummer. Because this one will take me two days to brew." Her finger tapped on the page and she got a faraway look in her eyes. "Unless …"

"Unless what?" I could see our chances for success slipping away here. Yriell had always come through for us before, but she wasn't a miracle worker. Nevertheless, stubborn hope filled me as I watched her think.

"Pour me another drink." She got up and headed for the door that led down to the caverns below her little cottage.

Raven half got out of his seat. "Should I come, too?"

She waved dismissively at him from the top of the dark stairs. "I won't be long."

I refilled her glass as instructed, then topped up Raven's. I couldn't have any more if I wanted to be able to ride when we got out of here. Faint sounds echoed up the stairs—the clinking of glass bottles, the occasional noise of something heavy being shifted. A good ten minutes went by before Yriell reappeared, a triumphant expression on her face.

"Found it! I knew I had it somewhere."

"A candle?"

I'd been expecting something a little more impressive. She set it on the table in front of me—a thick white candle inside a clear glass bowl. The opening at the top of the bowl was just wide enough to allow someone to light the candle. It looked like something you would buy in the home décor section at Target for five bucks.

"What does this do?"

She sat down and drained her glass with obvious relish, then grinned at me, pleased with herself. "It's a light-weaving candle."

Raven sat forward, a gleam of interest in his eyes. I stared at the plain white column of wax, confused. Light-weaving was a skill that some Day fae possessed, allowing them to bend light around objects—usually themselves—to render them invisible. It was an active thing, something you had to perform in the moment. How was this lump of wax meant to perform magic?

"I've heard of these," Raven said, "but I never thought I'd see one. How did it come into your possession?"

Yriell grinned. "That's a long story, involving two chickens, a bottle of rum, and some very bad decision-making by a certain Day fae who shall remain nameless. I didn't think I would ever find a use for it, but there you go. Just shows you should never throw anything out."

I snorted. The candle was probably worth a fortune. As if anyone would throw something like this away. "But how does it work?"

"It's not rocket science, girl. You light the candle, and as long as you're holding it, you're invisible. If the candle goes out, poof! You're visible again. Pretty simple."

I shook my head in wonder. I had no idea how such a thing could be, but I didn't need to understand Day magic to follow those instructions. "Got a match?"

She wagged a reproving finger at me. "Not so fast. This is a one-time use gadget only. Light it when you need it and make sure you don't blow it out too soon, because there's no relighting this sucker."

Troubled, I contemplated the squat little candle in its glass bowl. "What if it blows out accidentally?" I had a feeling that the grey-eyed assassin wouldn't take well to discovering he was being followed.

Yriell shrugged. "Then I guess you're screwed. But that's why it's in a bowl. You should be pretty safe. So, do you want it or not?"

"We want it," Raven said. "It is a princely gift."

"Not so fast, Mr Smooth Talker. Let's think of it less as a gift and more as a payment in advance."

He regarded her warily. "A payment for what?"

"Who knows? Maybe I'll need a big, strong man like

you to mow my lawn. Let's just say you owe me a favour. Both of you." She waved an airy hand. "I'm sure I'll think of something."

I glanced at Raven. He didn't look altogether happy, and I couldn't say I blamed him. Unspecified favours were dangerous obligations among the fae. Even though I trusted Yriell, it made me uneasy to have such a thing hanging over my head. But what else could we do? We were kind of short on options.

I closed my hands possessively around the glass bowl, pulling it towards me. "We'll take it."

9

The raven croaked: a harsh, unmistakable sound. I glanced up into the branches and closed my book with a sigh. I'd been killing time in the gardens of the sith, waiting for Raven to ring me with news of our next appointment with the Vipers.

But of course Raven wouldn't do anything so mundane as use a mobile phone if he could make an extravagant gesture instead. His insistence on meeting in person the other night instead of talking on the phone had been bad enough, but this was ridiculous. And here I'd thought *I* was the paranoid one.

The bird croaked again and fluttered down from its branch onto the grass by my chair. A tiny scrap of paper was tied to one leg.

"How did you get in here, then?" The sith's wards would normally prevent animals from entering, yet I had no doubt that this was one of Raven's messengers. I would have noticed before if we had resident ravens. The wards must have somehow recognised the bird's connection to Raven, who had an open invitation. "Can I have that, please?"

Cautiously, I stretched my hand out toward the bird. Up this close, that beak was enormous, black and hard. A phone call would have been so much better. A text, even. Then I wouldn't have to risk life and limb to get this stupid message.

The black wings fluttered as the bird hopped up onto the arm of my chair. It took a huge effort not to flinch away, and I stared straight into its strange white eye, waiting for my heart to stop pounding. But it stood patiently while I untied the piece of paper as fast as I could, then hopped back to the ground and began picking at the grass, looking for insects, as if it did this every day. For all I knew, it did. It certainly seemed well-trained.

My hands still shaking, I unrolled the tiny scrap. *Circular Quay 9pm. Observe only.* "Only" was underlined several times, and I smiled. Raven had been very particular on that point. One would almost think he didn't trust me.

When we'd said goodbye the night before, he'd put both hands on my shoulders and given me his most serious look. "You only have to follow him. Don't engage. Don't do anything risky. Just follow and see where he leads you."

"I know. We have to report anything to the king, and he will decide what to do," I parroted.

His coal-black eyes searched my face. "You say that almost as if you're a reasonable person—and yet I know you." His eyes softened as one hand lifted. His knuckles grazed across my cheek in a gentle caress. "Not as well as I would like, of course."

I stepped back from the intensity of his gaze, shrugging off his hands. I wasn't quite sure what to do with this Raven. I preferred the mocking one who was never serious. "I can follow orders."

"Really? Just as well as your friend Allegra, I'm sure."

I shrugged. "Well, things turned out all right for her, didn't they?"

He stepped closer again, crowding me up against the bike. We were outside The Drunken Irishman, where he'd told me to drop him. I had no idea where he lived or whether he even had a home in the mortal world. Heavy rock blared from the open door. Randall mustn't be working tonight—that wasn't his style at all.

"She wasn't taking on the Night Vipers though, was she?" Raven pointed out. "Just don't do anything stupid. Please, Sage."

I put my hands against his silk-clad chest and shoved. "You're a fine one to talk. You're the king of stupid decisions and reckless behaviour."

He smiled lazily. "Exactly, and I don't want anyone else usurping my position. Promise me you'll be careful."

"I promise."

He caught my hands in his, checking them both ostentatiously. "Just making sure you didn't have your fingers crossed when you said that."

Then he'd pressed a kiss into one palm and walked away, leaving me staring after him.

Now, I eyed my reflection in the bathroom mirror at

Circular Quay Station, wondering what to make of that kiss. A joke? A bit of light-hearted fun? Or something more?

My own confused brown eyes stared back at me. Raven's moods were as changeable as the wind. How was anyone supposed to keep up with them? I gave a mental shrug. Time to think about that later. Right now, it was ten minutes to nine, and it was time to turn into the Amazing Invisible Woman.

I pulled the light-weaver and a box of matches out of my backpack, biting my lip. Should I be holding the candle when I lit it? How soon would the invisibility take effect? Somehow, something that had seemed perfectly cut and dried around Yriell's kitchen table was no longer so simple. I should have asked more questions—but then, would Yriell have answered? Did she even know?

There was only one other woman in the bathroom with me, which was some kind of miracle, as Circular Quay was a busy station. It was snuggled up to the ferry wharves, as well as being right in the heart of tourist central. The great steel arch of the Harbour Bridge reared out of the night on one side, and the winged sails of the Opera House on the other. There was always a mass of people coming and going, whatever the time of day or night.

I put my backpack back on and checked that my pistol was still settled comfortably in my shoulder holster, hidden under my jacket. Raven would freak if he knew I'd brought it. Lucky I'd be invisible, then. Its weight against my body just made me feel more comfortable, and he'd never have to know. Unless, of course, he went in for a kiss this time when I met up with him later. Best not to think about that possibility.

The light-weaver sat on the plain white sink, and I opened the matchbox with hands that trembled ever so slightly. From excitement, of course. At least, it was better to believe that. I could hear the other woman ripping toilet paper out of the dispenser in her cubicle, so it would be best to get this over quickly, while I still had the space to myself. Witnesses were the last thing I needed. I could just imagine how quickly the assassin would ditch this assignation if people started screaming about magically disappearing women.

The tiny flame fizzed and trembled on the end of the match as I picked up the light-weaver. Holding my breath, I shoved the match into the glass bowl. A moment later, the wick flared into life.

Shit. I could still see the candle. And myself. The match burnt out, and I dropped it into the sink. Behind me, the toilet flushed, and I looked up.

And nearly dropped the light-weaver.

There was nothing in the mirror. No reflection. Well, there was a reflection—of the dryers on the wall behind me—but not of the nervous brown-eyed girl who'd gazed back at me a moment before. I had ceased to exist.

I let out a shaky breath. Well, that was handy. I could still see myself, still see the all-important candle—but no one else could. At least, I assumed so. I waited a moment for the woman to emerge from her cubicle. She walked straight past me to the basins and washed her hands, then inspected her teeth, completely unaware that I was standing within arm's reach. In fact, I had to take a quick step out of the way when she turned towards the dryers.

I let her open the door, then followed her out into the night. Here, I had to keep my wits about me. It proved more difficult than I'd expected to move through the crowds without bumping anyone, since no one gave me any space. Plus, I had to keep one eye on the candle at all times, terrified that it would suddenly blow out and leave me exposed. I wouldn't like to try this in peak hour.

Raven was standing at the water's edge, not far from a busker perched on a box pretending to be the Statue of Liberty. I eyed the busker's fake torch enviously—at least *he* didn't have to worry about it going out.

A ferry had just left, and another was pulling in, creating choppy waves in the black waters. The lights of the Overseas Passenger Terminal and the Museum of Contemporary Art reflected in wide bands of rippled orange and gold on the restless harbour. Everywhere was movement and action: people walking along the waterfront; people dining al fresco in the restaurants there; the deep blast of a ferry's horn; music drifting from somewhere further along where another busker strummed his guitar.

Raven's hair lifted in the breeze, reminding me to tend my flame as I took up a position to his left, hard up against the railings and out of the way. The wind was cool, as it often was on the harbour, and tasted of salt. I was tempted to cup my hand over the top of the glass jar to make sure the precious flame wasn't troubled by the breeze, but I was afraid of stifling it altogether.

A crowd of people had just come off the ferry, and a small knot of them hurried towards us. Raven had his back to them, looking out over the dark water, apparently taking in the view. A man wearing jeans and a dark hoodie broke from the crowd at the last moment and came to stand at Raven's side. Cradling my candle bowl, I moved closer.

It was the same man as before. Now that I had the opportunity to have a good look at him, I could see the faint signs of the Glamour he wore, a pulsing in the air around his face that only someone with fae blood could have picked up.

He rested his forearms on the railing and gazed out over the harbour, not looking at Raven. "You have the money?"

Raven nodded. A backpack rested on the ground at his feet. He nudged it towards the stranger. "It's all there."

In a smooth, efficient motion, the assassin bent down and hefted the backpack, slipping his arms through the straps.

"If it's not, the deal's off."

"I understand." Raven cast a sideways glance at his companion. "I'm surprised you people don't use Swiss banks. That would be easier than lumping gold around."

"We have our traditions." The man never turned his head toward Raven, but his eyes roamed, constantly assessing his surroundings. "You have three days to change your mind. After that, we will begin work. It may take up to a month. Do not contact us again to enquire about progress or anything else—only if you change your mind within the initial three-day period."

He spoke quickly, as if he had delivered these instructions many times before. How many people had he killed? His hands on the rail were slim and elegant—a guitarist's hands, or an artist's. He looked completely unthreatening.

A sudden gust buffeted me, and I glanced down sharply at the light-weaver. The flame bent and flickered but didn't go out. I cupped my free hand more closely over the opening.

When I looked up again, the assassin was staring straight at me. I flinched.

Then I realised his gaze was focused behind me, and he couldn't actually see me. I must have made some kind of noise that had alerted him; it took all my willpower to hold myself, unmoving, until his gaze moved on.

His hearing must be super sharp if he had picked one little indrawn breath out of all the ambient noise, and good instincts to decide from that tiny sound that something was off. But how had I thought him unthreatening? Those grey eyes were as cold as the dark waters of the harbour, and hid dangers just as deep.

"Remember." He looked at Raven for the first time. "Three days. After that, Merritt is as good as dead."

Raven nodded, and the assassin walked away.

Spooked by his reactions, I gave him more of a head start than I'd been intending. He hurried towards the station entry. Damn. Why couldn't he open a gate to the Wilds like a normal fae, instead of running around Sydney's bloody train system? But at the last minute, he changed direction and diverted onto Wharf 4, where the last of a crowd was filing onto a ferry bound for Neutral Bay.

I followed him onboard, moments before the gangway was drawn up and the crew cast off the massive line holding the ferry in place. The engines throbbed and rumbled, the water bubbling furiously as the ferry backed out of the wharf and began its ponderous swing to head out into the harbour.

My quarry took a place on the open deck at the stern of the ship. No one else braved the cold—all the other passengers were inside, protected from the wind. I decided to join them. Unless he jumped overboard, he wasn't going anywhere until we reached the first stop at Kirribilli, and I preferred not to panic over my flickering candle in the wind all the way there. I sank gratefully into a seat by the window, where I could keep an eye on him.

For his part, he remained standing at the stern. From the direction of his gaze, I guessed he was watching Raven, who hadn't moved from his position. As the ferry drew away, Raven finally turned and headed toward George Street. The assassin relaxed, turning to lean his elbows on the stern rail behind him and gazing up at the night sky.

There was a subtle difference to his face, and I realised he'd dropped the Glamour. None of his features had changed dramatically, but his jaw was stronger, his cheeks more sharply defined. Now, he was someone you might look twice at—a male model, perfect in his symmetry. I glanced again at those elegant fingers. Or a poet, perhaps. The dark brown hair tumbling over one eye made him look a little Byronesque.

He stayed out there all the way across the harbour, not budging when people got on and off at Kirribilli, but he started to move as we pulled into the wharf at North Sydney.

When we disembarked, the wind was quieter, though I still kept a careful eye on my candle as I followed him up High Street. North Sydney was a big business hub, full of tall office buildings. It had a little nightlife, particularly in the long stretch of restaurants along Miller Street, but it was quieter than the Quay had been.

Taxis zoomed past as we made our way along Miller Street, muffling the sound of my footsteps, but I took care to give him plenty of room. He was moving at a fast pace, untroubled by the weight of the backpack. Every time we passed a quiet alcove among the buildings, or a narrow alley, I expected him to open a gate and disappear—but every time, he disappointed me. At least he hadn't gone to North Sydney train station.

Finally, he stopped outside one more office building, indistinguishable from all the others we'd passed. Just another glass and steel edifice, its night lights showing a glossy foyer and a bank of lifts. He ran a card over a small sensor plate to the right of the doors, and they slid open.

Well, that was unexpected. No magical breaking and entering? Fancy the assassins being so tech-savvy that they had security passes. I looked up as I followed him inside. The building was called Hampton Court.

He headed straight for the lifts and pressed the call button. Now, I had a dilemma. This building had looked just as tall as all the others that loomed over the streets here. Twenty storeys? Thirty? Even more? How would I know which floor he was going to unless I got into that lift with him?

The thought of being trapped in such a small space with him was terrifying. One wrong move, and I would be discovered. Surely it was enough to tell the king that he'd come here? Someone else could look more closely into the assassins' association with this building.

But what if there *was* no association? He could have stolen that security pass. Maybe he planned to open a gate from somewhere in this building, and these were all just paranoid precautions against being followed.

The lift dinged and the up arrow illuminated. I only had seconds to decide. As the doors slid open, I forced myself forward, my feet like lead weights. He stood slightly to the right, facing the closing doors, so I plastered myself against the left-hand wall, hardly daring to breathe. Fear sweat broke out on my forehead and under my arms—thank goodness the lift already smelled of stale sweat and old coffee, or he might have been on to me—and I clenched the bowl tight against me, concentrating on not moving.

He pressed the button for the twenty-first floor. God, I hoped this was a fast lift. At least no one else got on as we climbed smoothly upward. I watched the numbers slide past, praying for twenty-one. I couldn't even look at him, afraid that, somehow, he would feel my gaze on him and become suspicious.

Finally, the torment ended. The doors opened on level twenty-one, and he stepped out onto soft navy-blue carpet. I followed as close as I dared and found myself in a reception area. *Fraser and Young, Chartered Accountants* was written in a curving script on the pale grey wall behind the desk.

Accountants. Not quite what I'd been expecting. He led the way past the reception desk and down a long hall with offices on either side, stopping at the door to a large meeting room. Through the glass wall, I saw black leather chairs around a massive teak table. Then he opened the door and it all disappeared.

On the far side of the wall, moonlit grass appeared,

and the impression of many buildings. Holy shit. That wasn't the Wilds.

He'd opened the door into a sith, and I had a split second to decide: follow or not?

Raven would say not. *Observe only*, he'd written, with many firm underlinings beneath the word "only". And yet … what a massive opportunity this was. A chance to see inside the mysterious headquarters of the fae world's most infamous assassins. And who knew how long their sith would remain tethered to this particular door in the mortal world? Tomorrow, it might be anywhere.

But tonight, I was invisible and I was right here. Who knew what I might find, what secrets I could uncover?

I nipped forward and slipped through the door just before he closed it behind him, amazed at my own daring. I was so close to him I could have counted every one of his eyelashes, which I couldn't help noticing were long and luscious. That faint scent of ironbark I'd noticed the night before still clung to him. I literally held my breath until he moved away, afraid he would sense me there. But he turned and walked away, moving at a relaxed pace. I guessed he felt secure, now.

After a moment, I let out a long, steadying breath and set off in his wake. An enormous building of grey stone lay dreaming in the moonlight before us, in the middle of massive grounds. Or rather, a set of interconnected buildings. It looked more like a university than the headquarters of a feared assassins' guild, built in a fanciful style. Flying buttresses protruded from one wall. An assortment of towers, some round and others square, rose at intervals from the jumble of stone. It was like walking into a real-life Hogwarts.

I cast a quick glance behind me to check the door we'd come through. On this side, it was a massive set of gates with ornate brass hinges bigger than my head. A high stone wall ran off to either side from the gate and, from my vantage point, it appeared to run all the way around the estate.

Because "estate" was the only word to describe it. A small forest stretched off to the right, a lake on the left, its waters shimmering silver under the moon. In front of us, Killer Hogwarts sprawled. I realised I'd been so busy checking it all out that my assassin had gained quite a lead on me, and I hurried to catch up. My guess was he'd be taking the gold to someone important, and I wanted to see who that was.

As far as I was aware, no one knew who the elusive head of the Vipers was. Imagine taking that information back to the king! A fierce determination entered my heart: I would see him—or *her*—brought down. It was the least I could do for Nevith. All that anyone could do for him now, really, and it was too little, too late. It wouldn't bring him back.

But somebody needed to pay for his death.

My guide bypassed the imposing front entrance and went around to a smaller side door. He was too quick to close it behind himself this time, and I stopped short as the door slammed in my face.

I blew out a frustrated breath and checked my candle. It had burned down to perhaps half its original size, but the flame was still going strong. Plenty of time left. I wouldn't need to be invisible for long once I returned to Sydney; only long enough to leave the office building without trace. I could spend some time here exploring before I had to think about leaving.

I waited a good minute before cautiously opening the door and peeking around the edge. I didn't want my quarry noticing the door opening and closing by itself. Inside, a dim corridor carpeted in red stretched away, with solid wooden doors opening off either side. He was just disappearing around a corner, so I darted inside, eased the door shut behind me, and went scurrying after him.

Wall sconces holding candles were the only illumination. It was cool inside and very quiet, and I got a sense of the thickness of the stone walls around me. The assassins weren't much for interior decorating—there were no portraits on the walls or rustic suits of armour. Just bare corridor, though the carpet was patterned with fading flowers.

No, actually, those were body parts, not flowers. Hands, fingers spread in agony. Severed heads dripping blood. I pulled a face as I turned the corner. They had the creepy mansion vibe down pat.

The assassin mounted a narrow staircase, so I went up, too. The corridor on this level was wider and ran along beside deep windows on one side, giving a view across a moonlit herb garden. It looked pretty, but I wondered how many of those herbs were deadly.

He finally stopped and knocked on a door.

A man's voice called, "Come in."

The assassin paused in the doorway, hand still on the doorknob. Hovering behind his shoulder, I saw a pleasant, book-lined room. A dark-haired man behind a large oak desk looked up as the door opened. He had a sallow pallor to his skin and shadows under his eyes that made him look tired. For a fae, that was practically at death's door.

My gaze caught on a dagger on a stand behind him, looking out of place among the books. Its long blade wasn't straight but had waves in it, unlike any knife I'd ever seen before, and shone with a kind of oily sheen. It was probably the ugliest dagger I'd ever seen—I had no idea why anyone would keep such a thing on display.

"Ashovar," the man said, and smiled. Then the door closed, and I was shut out.

11

I contemplated my candle, thinking. Less than half the wax column remained. Still plenty of time for me to have a good look around before I had to make my escape. I could bring the king back a full report on the setup of the assassins' lair, on how many people were here, maybe even give him a basic map of the layout.

I squared my shoulders and set off down the corridor. I had a lot to do in the next hour or so. Some of the doors were open, showing me comfortable sitting rooms or larger meeting rooms. One looked like a schoolroom, with two neat rows of desks. I wasn't game enough to open the closed doors in case I surprised someone inside. Doors opening by themselves would surely arouse comment.

The corridor took a bend to the right, and doors appeared on both sides instead of windows to my left. I kept going, passing a staircase that led upward. I could come back to that. A man passed me, wearing plain grey clothes and carrying a stack of books. I stepped to the side and held my breath, but he had no hint of my presence. His eyes were fixed straight ahead as he marched down the corridor.

When I had completed my tour of this level, I returned to the stairs and checked out the upper level. There were fewer doors up here, though all of them were closed. The rooms must be bigger, or perhaps the doors led to suites. I stood outside one for long moments, listening hard for any sound of movement, any slightest hint of a presence on the other side. Eventually, I worked up the courage to turn the handle ever so slowly and push the door open the tiniest bit.

Peeking through, I found a comfortable if rather austere lounge or sitting room. Emboldened, I opened the door wider and slipped inside. There was no one here. One wall was lined with bookcases, which held volumes with dark leather spines. Through one door, I glimpsed a bed, its covers tumbled; and through another, a bathroom. Someone's private quarters.

I resisted the urge to go hunting through the papers on the bedside table. What was I expecting to find? Contracts? A map of the sith with all the weaknesses marked? My time would be better spent in checking the place out for myself.

There was one more floor above that one, reached by a narrow, uncarpeted staircase. A series of small rooms were tucked up among the eaves—clearly servants' quarters. I hurried back down to see what the ground level of this labyrinth had to offer.

More grandiose rooms, as it turned out. I found one

that reminded me of the refectory of a monastery I had seen on TV once. Four long, bare tables stretched nearly the length of the room, with hard, backless benches on either side. Perpendicular to these was another, smaller table. This one had chairs along one side, and the one in the middle had a high carved back and arms. It even boasted a cushion of red velvet. The butt that sat in this chair must belong to someone important—perhaps the tired-looking man in the booklined room upstairs. There were no other furnishings in the room. The windows appeared to be stained glass, but since it was dark outside, I couldn't make out the details.

A clatter of pots and pans drew me to the kitchen at the back of the building. It was huge, as expected for a place this size. To my surprise, half a dozen people, all wearing the same plain grey clothing as the man I had seen in the upstairs corridor, were working there in complete silence. I stood in the doorway and watched them for a long, puzzled moment.

Back on Lord Thistle's estate in Spring, the kitchen had been one of the noisiest places; full of people coming and going, full of laughter and the sound of the people who worked there chattering. It had been a welcoming place, and I'd spent a lot of time there over the years. Even in our own sith back home, Zinnia was always singing while she worked, and whenever someone came in, there was conversation and laughter.

Here, there was nothing. A woman was kneading bread, flour puffing up into the air as she pummelled the dough with her fists, but her expression was blank. Even the boy turning the spit—which had to be one of the most boring jobs in creation—stared straight ahead at the meat, barely blinking as his arms moved. No shifting from foot to foot, no impatient sighs. His attention never wandered, and I began to get an uneasy prickling at the back of my neck. There was something wrong with these people. Each of them might have been completely alone. They acted as if their companions didn't exist.

Unsettled, I left the kitchen and headed for the door through which I had entered the building. Outside, a cool wind blew, making me wonder if this sith had originally been part of the Realm of Winter. It certainly didn't have the balmy feel of our own Spring sith. But the sky was clear, and the grounds were well lit by bobbing faelights. I heard the sound of something striking wood and decided to investigate in that direction.

I passed a little cottage and a stand of tall pines. On the other side of the trees, a large, flat area of packed dirt stretched. Two men, their shirts off and their bodies glistening with sweat, were wrestling. Another, a little further on, faced a wooden wall on which were drawn the outlines of human figures. In rapid succession, he drew a series of knives from sheaths concealed about his body and hurled them at the painted figures. *Thunk, thunk, thunk.* Each knife quivered, its blade embedded in the heart of a painted figure. That was the noise I had heard. When all the knives had found their targets, he collected them and performed the same manoeuvre again.

I watched, fascinated. His accuracy was unnerving, though his movements were so fluid, almost languid, that he hardly seemed to be aiming. Each time, the knives found their targets unerringly. Sometimes he varied things and aimed for the head or the throat instead, but every time, the result was the same. He never missed.

The wrestlers finished their bout with the smaller man pinned facedown in the dirt, his arm twisted up behind him. He yielded, and the victor released him, then they both stood and bowed to each other.

The smaller man wandered over to watch the knife thrower. "Nice work, Evandir, but maybe not all your victims will do you the favour of standing still while you throw knives at them."

Evandir cast a cool glance at the other as he pushed blond hair impatiently out of his eyes. He had a hard face that suggested cool glances were not unusual with him. "If you're volunteering to run, I'll be more than happy to put a knife in you."

The first man laughed and buried his sweaty face in a towel. They seemed to be finished their practice—or whatever this was—so I slipped away, conscious of my dwindling candle. There was still so much to see.

I bypassed the cottage, heading for another, larger building. It turned out to be stables, which I realised as soon as I got close enough to get a whiff of that familiar horsey smell. It was the grandest damn stables I'd ever seen—more like a mansion than a place to keep horses. I was sure the horses didn't care if they had majestic columns out front and elaborately carved friezes over the doors.

Resisting the temptation to go inside and check out the

horses, I moved on. The sound of childish laughter led me to a small school where teenaged fae bent over their books, and then on further to where a group of smaller children played on some swings. How many people called this sith their home?

I hadn't considered it before, but I supposed the assassins must have families, and they all lived here together. I didn't like that thought. I was happier imagining them as faceless killers who did nothing else. It was easier to hate killers than people who enjoyed a beer as much as I did, people with real lives. I didn't want to consider that they might have family who would miss them every bit as much as we missed Nevith.

I stopped in the lee of a stone wall where the shadows gathered eagerly and stared, unseeing, at my candle. It didn't matter if they had children. They had chosen this life. No one forced them to go around killing people for money. What kind of career choice was that? Not one that any decent person could make. And Nevith had done nothing to deserve his horrible end. He was as innocent as those children.

Probably more, if they were growing up in an environment where killing was the norm. At least they hadn't had that weird, empty look to them that the servants in the kitchen had had.

My flame flickered, and I jerked upright, adrenaline flooding my body. The candle was only the width of two fingers tall now. High time to make my way home.

I strode back along the paths and alleyways I'd taken, heading for the main building. This place was a real rabbit warren of buildings, as if they'd grown organically, smaller buildings sprouting off the sides of larger ones with winding paths appearing between them. But I had a good mental picture of the layout now, and I'd be able to draw a reasonably accurate map when I got back. The king should be pleased with me.

Hopefully, this would give him the push he needed to do something about the scourge of the Vipers once and for all.

Darkness pooled around the feet of the flying buttresses as I came out into the open space that surrounded the main building. Moonlight lay softly on the short grass and silvered the stone paths. All I had to do was keep going in this direction and I'd arrive back at the gate I'd come in through. I could see it from here, firmly closed against the outside world.

And yet my steps slowed, my feet hesitating. I came to the door that I'd followed the assassin through, and I laid a hand on it, feeling the smoothness of the ancient wood. My fingers swept across the surface toward the door handle, hesitating.

Maybe I should have tried to listen at the door to that conversation between Ashovar and the tired-looking man. He was obviously someone important. But I'd been so eager to look around that I hadn't even thought of it. What if I could have learned something vital to tell the king? The more I thought about it, the more it seemed like a missed opportunity.

My instincts were usually reliable, so I turned the

handle. Just a quick look. I could spare a few more minutes.

I slipped inside, closing the heavy door behind me, and retraced my previous steps. Down the hallway, around the corner. Up the grand staircase. I trailed down the first corridor, checking the view out the windows, noting the better perspective of the assassins' compound this bird's-eye view gave me.

The door to the room where the assassin had met the tired-looking man was still closed. I crept closer, laid my ear against the door. They might not even still be in there.

I strained to hear anything. The door was thick. Was that the low murmur of voices or only my imagination? I leaned my whole body against it, straining to hear.

In that moment, the door was snatched open, and I pitched forward. I sprawled on the carpet and the candle, the precious light-weaver, rolled free. In horror, I lunged for it, but the flame flickered—once, twice—then dwindled and died.

A hand jerked me roughly to my feet. "Got you."

12

Ashovar's grey eyes blazed down at me in fury for an endless moment, then I stamped down hard on his foot with the heel of my boot. At the same time, I drove my free elbow back into his stomach.

To the assassin's credit, his hold on me barely loosened —but it loosened enough that I could twist my way out of his grip. I leapt away, drawing the gun concealed under my jacket in one smooth movement and pointing it at the man behind the desk.

"Stay back or I'll shoot him."

His boss showed no sign of alarm at having a gun levelled at him at point-blank range. Did he not know what a gun was? That seemed unlikely, given his profession, even if fae assassins didn't use them because of their iron content.

The assassin made no move towards me, glancing at his boss for instructions.

The tired-looking man eyed me thoughtfully for a

moment, as if I were a trained seal that had just surprised him with a new trick. "You are unusually enterprising." He actually sounded approving. "But I think you'll find that gun will do you no good here."

"Bullshit." My gun worked just fine in our own sith. He was trying to talk me into giving up without a fight. I had to admire his balls, but I wasn't falling for it.

He sat back in his chair, a small smile on his face. "Go ahead, then. Shoot."

"Do you think I won't? I can't miss from here."

"Whether you will or won't makes absolutely no difference."

This guy would make a great poker player. Arms steady, I held the gun in a firm double-handed grip. The barrel never wavered as I stared him down. "Tell your goon to get out of the way."

I started backing away, sights still trained on him.

He sighed. "She's not going to shoot. Take it off her."

Crunch time. I'd never killed someone in cold blood before, but it was quite clear that if I didn't pull the trigger, my days were numbered. They probably still were, even if I shot them both, since the gunshots would bring others running and I'd be unlikely to make it out of the sith. But there was still a chance, and I wasn't ready to die yet.

I pulled the trigger. I had no silencer, and the sound was overwhelming in the enclosed room. The gun kicked in my hands, but I was prepared for that. The bullet would still find its mark, right in the centre of the smiling man's forehead.

Except it didn't. I was swinging around to take out the

assassin who was now lunging for me when I registered something wasn't right. No impact. No blood.

It didn't matter. My finger squeezed the trigger again, but the assassin kept coming. He ploughed into me like a charging rhino, taking me down in a tackle that any front-row forward would have been proud of. I lost my grip on the gun as his hands closed around my throat. I struggled and thrashed, trying to twist him off me somehow, but he was solidly muscled and outweighed me.

What had happened to my shot? I couldn't have missed at that range, but he wasn't injured at all. I got in a good swipe at his face, but the lack of air was starting to tell. Panic bubbled in my chest as I clawed at his hands. Did he mean to kill me? Had it all been for nothing? Willow would never even know what had happened to me.

"Enough, Ashovar. Let the girl breathe."

Merciful Lady! The pressure on my throat suddenly eased, allowing me to drag in a glorious breath. Ashovar rolled off me as I gasped and coughed, trying to convince my aching lungs to work again.

He hauled me to my feet, twisting one arm up behind my back, his other arm around my still-painful throat. His grip left me in no doubt that he was prepared to break my arm—and probably finish strangling me, too—if the man behind the desk gave the word.

I staggered as he shoved me toward the desk, and then stared, transfixed. The bullet hung in mid-air over it, frozen in space and time. Was this Air magic? It was powerful indeed if it could halt a speeding bullet in its flight.

As I watched, the bullet wobbled, then dropped to the desk with a gentle clatter. The seated man didn't even blink, much less look at it. He ran a dispassionate gaze over me. "She's not much to look at, is she? Not even full fae, if I'm any judge." The man turned a chilling gaze on my captor. "I had thought better of you, Ashovar."

"I had thought better of myself, my lord." The assassin's deep voice rumbled at my back, a note of self-loathing in it.

I began to shake as the initial adrenaline of being caught drained away. Now what? I couldn't bear to think. Something painful and lingering, most likely. I had invaded the inner sanctum of the Night Vipers, and I could expect no mercy.

I clenched my teeth, trying to control my shaking. The face of the man in front of me was a cool mask, giving nothing away. It didn't look like the kind of face that would be inclined to show mercy to enemies.

My gaze slid to the warped dagger behind him. It was more than ugly; there was something unnerving about the way it kept drawing my gaze even though I wanted to look away. It couldn't have said "enchanted weapon" more if it had had a flashing sign. Its cold blade shimmered, almost as if it was moving, as if it were some kind of liquid rather than metal. I forced myself to lift my chin and stare straight back at the man behind the desk instead.

"And what's wrong with being half fae? How many full fae have managed to sneak in here without you knowing?"

He smiled. "You have spirit. Not many, as you have surmised. But as for unnoticed—did you really think our wards were that weak? I knew the moment you stepped into our sith."

If that was true, why had they let me wander around, spying on them? My heart clenched in my chest. The answer was clear—because I was never getting out of here alive. They probably thought it was amusing to let me think I was achieving something, only to snatch my victory away.

"You know I'm not the only one who knows where the entry to your sith is, don't you? If I don't return within the next few minutes, half the Realms will be battering at your door."

The man behind the desk said nothing, merely lifting an eyebrow at the assassin who held me.

"She's lying, my lord. I was sure no one followed me."

"Unless her friends have more of these intriguing little candles," the man replied. "You didn't notice *her*, after all."

There was a hint of rebuke in his tone, and the assassin bowed his head.

The man reached behind him and removed the dagger from its stand. My eye followed it as he laid it on the desk. "Sit down, both of you."

The assassin thrust me toward one of the chairs that faced the desk. Its wooden arm banged painfully into my thigh, and I half fell into the seat. I glared up at him, rubbing my throbbing shoulder and trying to ease the ache. He ignored me, dropping gracefully into the chair beside me.

"That's better. We are not savages, after all, Miss—"

I stared back at him and said nothing.

"Answer when Lord Celebrach addresses you," the assassin growled.

Lord Celebrach picked up the twisted dagger and began to tap the blade against his open palm. Watching the shimmering length of distorted steel was almost hypnotising. Up this close, I could tell it was steel—was it the iron in it that affected me so? But I'd handled plenty of steel blades in the mortal world; I even owned a few. Being only half fae made me much more resistant to iron than the purebloods. No, there was something more about this dagger. Something wrong.

"You must forgive Ashovar. He is understandably upset at his failure. Let me tell you a little story." The man leaned back in his chair, the blade still tapping that hypnotic rhythm on his palm. "When the Realms were new and the Lady still walked our fields and forests, a covert war raged among the fae. Which Realm would be the one to rule the others? This was before good King Agar's time, of course, before the Lords agreed to swear to one high king. Political killings were rife as each Lord tried to claw his way to the top of the pile, but they were messy affairs in those early days. Carried out by amateurs. It became clear to the great folk of the Realms that a better way was called for—a way to keep their own hands clean, while still delivering the desired results. And so, the Night Vipers came into being."

Right. He made it sound like the Vipers were some kind of benevolent public service. He'd have to work harder to convince me that the Lords had *wanted* a guild of assassins.

"A Winter fae was the first Viper," he continued. "His

name was Ishitil, and over the years, he gathered a group around him who were equally dedicated and professional. But, good as they were, the attrition rate among this group was high. Assassination is a dangerous profession, Miss—"

Again, I kept my mouth shut, and Celebrach gave a small sigh, as if my lack of cooperation disappointed him. *Sigh away, buddy. I'm not playing your little game.*

"I could force you to tell me, you know. I'm sure Ashovar would be only too happy to apply a little persuasion."

The grey-eyed assassin levelled a cold stare at me. He'd probably love that, since I seemed to have shamed him by following him in. Not that I was scared of him. But I'd certainly lost any interest in his nice eyebrows or the Byronic fall of his hair over his eyes. In fact, I'd taken quite a dislike to the man.

"Call me Arrow," I said finally. Why make this harder than it had to be? If he wanted a name, I'd give him one.

"Arrow. What a quaint *nom de guerre*." Celebrach shrugged. "Your real name makes no difference anyway. One way or another, that person dies tonight."

A chill shuddered through me. I wasn't scared of Ashovar, but this Celebrach gave me the shivers—him and his creepy dagger. Did he mean to kill me or not? That *one way or another* left a little wiggle room, didn't it?

"As I was saying, *Arrow*, Ishitil found himself running dangerously short of assassins after a few years. The Vipers' services were in high demand, but not all his operatives were as skilled as he. Consequently, he needed to find replacements, but who has the time to train new people? To spread the burden, he instituted a system whereby each Adept would take on apprentices and shoulder the burden of their training."

Ashovar shifted in his chair, and Celebrach's eyes gleamed as he glanced at him. He seemed to find something amusing, though I couldn't see anything funny in what he'd just said. Judging by his sullen look, neither could Ashovar.

"But there was a small problem. How to find these apprentices? Secretive orders such as ours can hardly send out heralds asking for volunteers, and there comes a time when recruitment possibilities from within our own ranks are exhausted. So Ishitil instituted a rather ... eccentric system." He pointed the sinister dagger at me. "You are fortunate that we still follow this system, otherwise I'm afraid you'd already be dead."

I must have blinked, because he smiled.

"Yes, Arrow. Ishitil decided that if anyone could find us, they were good enough to be considered. There have been many attempts over the years. Being a Viper is a position of great status."

Yeah, maybe among psychopaths. Although it was true that a depressingly large number of people would do anything if the money was good.

"Do you wish to be a Viper, Arrow?"

"Who wouldn't?" I replied flippantly.

He smiled. "So, we face a choice. Recruit you to join our number or kill you."

"What if I don't like either of those choices?"

"Unfortunately for you, the choice is not yours. Your fate now lies in the hands of Ashovar."

13

───────

*A*shovar? I glanced at him in surprise. Who'd died and made him God? Why did *he* get the deciding vote? He looked as unhappy as I was at this turn of events.

Celebrach chuckled at the look on my face. "Take her away," he said, waving the dagger dismissively. "Come tell me at dawn what you've decided."

Ashovar's hand closed around my upper arm, and he hauled me bodily out of the chair, propelling me toward the door.

"Let go of me," I snapped as soon as we were out in the corridor again.

He glanced down at me. His eyes reminded me of a shark's—cold, brutal, and utterly devoid of emotion. I thought he would ignore me, but a moment later, his hand dropped to his side. I shrugged my arm, rotating the shoulder a little. Everything was still in working order, thank goodness. I'd taken surprisingly little damage, considering I'd been fighting someone bigger and heavier than me. It was almost as if he'd been going easy on me.

This whole thing had taken such an unexpected turn. Why had I followed him inside? It had seemed like such a good idea at the time—as all the really terrible, bloody *stupid* ideas did. I'd had a few in my time, but this one took the cake. Was I mad? Or had I just let my eagerness to punish the assassins overtake my common sense?

Obviously they would have the very best wards on a sith like theirs. Concealment meant everything to them; it was their stock-in-trade. And there I'd gone, happily waltzing in on the heels of an actual trained assassin, thinking that just because I was invisible, I was undiscovered. I may as well have followed a mountain lion into its den. I glanced at his forbidding profile again. *Or leapt into a tank full of great white sharks.*

"What is your name?" Those hard grey eyes flicked me a cool glance. "Your real name. I'll know if you lie to me."

Oh, yeah? The shark was a walking lie detector as well? My newly awakened common sense warred with my instinct to flip him the bird. Common sense won out.

"Sage." It was a common enough name, even outside Spring. Fae did love their plant names. "And yours is Ashovar."

I don't know why I said that; my brain must have been running on pure adrenaline. This was hardly the time for making conversation. But there's nothing like the threat of imminent death to make a person start babbling inanities.

"Only Lord Celebrach calls me that. My name is Ash."

See? Another plant name. Or maybe it was a cold, grey,

burned-out kind of name. That seemed fitting. "Where are we going?"

He led me through one of the doors on the lower level that I hadn't dared to open during my explorations, which revealed another corridor. At the end of that was a large, airy room full of plants, like a conservatory. He opened a glass door onto the night and gestured me through. "*You* are going to the cells. Where *I* am going is none of your business."

Fear jumped into my chest and took a stranglehold on my lungs. I took a couple of shallow, frightened breaths, just to prove to myself that I still could. *Cells* didn't sound hopeful. Nobody stashed a person they were intending to make their apprentice in a cell. My legs trembled as the fight or flight response kicked in.

Fight or flight? Why not both?

I stepped up to the doorway, caught the door frame, and pivoted into a roundhouse kick straight to his solar plexus. I didn't care how fit he was, that would slow him down a little.

He doubled over, and I heard the grunt as all the air was expelled from his lungs, but I took off running and didn't look back. He had longer legs than me, and I needed to wring every bit of advantage out of this head start.

I burst around the corner of the building and quickly got my bearings. The gate was that way, along the paved path. My boots pounded in a frantic rhythm on the stones. A moment ago, my legs had felt like jelly, paralysed with fear, but new strength flooded my body as the possibility of escape nurtured a tiny flame of hope in my heart.

All too soon, I heard his feet thudding on the path behind me, but the gate was closer. All I needed was enough time to wrench it open and slip through. I felt sure that once I was back in the mortal world, the worst of the danger would be past.

I just had to get to the lift a couple of seconds ahead of him and then I could disappear on the city streets. Assassins weren't the only ones who were good at sneaking around dark alleys. I could even open a gate into the Wilds to escape him if I had to, once I was free of the wards on this place. But it all depended on making it out of here first.

I left the path and pounded across the grass, taking a more direct route. The gate loomed ahead of me, filling my vision. It was closed but not barred, and had a simple latch mechanism. I could do this.

Ash had also left the path in pursuit of me so I couldn't hear his footsteps as well anymore. I risked a glance behind me; that was a mistake. He was far too close, and panic threatened to steal my breath away.

From somewhere deep inside, I tapped a new reserve of strength. I thought I'd been running as fast as I could already, but now I found a new pace. I hoped it was enough to pull away from him and gain me those precious seconds I needed at the gate, but I wasn't risking another look behind me, so I ploughed on, heart thundering, the sound of my rasping breaths filling my ears.

I all but slammed into the gate, not wanting to lose time decelerating. I grabbed the latch and twisted, but it wouldn't move.

Fear clawed at me as I tugged. Shit, shit, shit. What was wrong with it? There was no lock; there was nothing to stop it moving. I heaved at it madly, splinters tearing at my skin.

Moments later, heavy hands caught me by the shoulders and spun me around. Ash towered over me, breathing hard, and at last I saw some emotion in those hard, grey eyes. He was furious.

"Where are you going in such a hurry, Sage? I thought you wanted to be an assassin."

I stared up at him, panting. The true gravity of my situation descended on me, and suddenly, I could barely draw breath as fear crushed my lungs.

I was trapped here. Trapped in the midst of my enemies, with no weapons and no way out.

"You are a fool," he spat. "Did you really think it would be that easy? That the gate would open for *you* as easily as it did for me? Tell me the truth. Why did you come here?"

He said he could tell if I lied. The question was, did I believe him? My body ached, and my heart still pounded. Despair's insidious tendrils snaked around me like the vines of one of Willow's spells. Suddenly, I couldn't have run another step if my life had depended upon it. My legs were heavy, and my feet felt like lead.

What could I say? Might as well go with the cover story that Lord Celebrach had so conveniently supplied. "I came here to be an assassin."

Fury still smouldered in those eyes. "I don't believe you. Why are you running if that's what you want?"

"Because you said you were putting me in a cell. I

thought you'd decided not to take me as an apprentice. The rumours I heard about joining the Vipers never mentioned you might kill me."

"Not everyone has what it takes to be a Viper." The bastard wasn't even breathing hard, though I was still panting. "But there's no point running. You've seen too much—the only choice is to stay or die. Even if you did manage to escape, we'd only hunt you down and kill you."

Awesome.

I faced him, shoulders back, though inside I wasn't feeling so brave. My fate rested in his hands. What would it take to make this man agree to have me as an apprentice? There didn't seem to be any other options—apart from death, which wasn't a choice I could get behind.

If I could convince him to take me as an apprentice and earn his trust, I would be able to get out of here eventually. *Eventually.* My heart quailed at the thought of a long separation from my friends, trapped here among my enemies. Willow and Raven would be worried about me. Hell, even Rowan would worry if I just disappeared without a goodbye. But surely once I was an apprentice, this damn gate would open for me and the problem would be solved. I'd be out of here in no time.

That made me feel better. And while I was here, I had an unparalleled opportunity to explore every weakness of the Night Vipers' organisation and memorise every last detail of this infernal sith. It wasn't all bad news.

But first I had to convince Ash of my sincerity. So far, his claim to be a human lie detector appeared to be spot on. That just meant I had to up my bullshit game.

"So apprentice me. I've been training all my life. I'm only half-fae, as Lord Celebrach so rightly guessed, so I've had to make up in brains and muscle what I lacked in magic. I will be the easiest apprentice you've ever had to train."

He was standing so close I could have kissed him with only the slightest movement of my head. Was that an option? Would that be more likely to advance my case or work against me? I would happily clutch at any straw that weighted his decision in my favour, though trying to fake a romantic moment with this cold man felt like mission impossible. Might as well try to make love to a statue.

"I have never trained an apprentice. I vowed to Lord Celebrach that I never would."

Well, that wasn't good news for me. He gestured for me to start walking, and we headed back across the grass toward the distant buildings. He took no account of the difference in the length of our strides, so I had to hurry along in an undignified trot to keep up with him.

"You don't like apprentices?"

"I don't like people."

Well, he was in the right line of work, then. Getting to kill people every day must bring a smile to his flinty face. No. On second thought, I doubted he ever smiled.

"Couldn't I be apprenticed to one of the other assassins? Why does it have to be you?"

"Because those are Ishitil's rules." He smiled at me, and

I revised my previous estimation. He *did* smile occasionally, but it was a savage baring of teeth and not an expression of pleasure or happiness. "It's a kind of punishment. If you are stupid enough or bad enough at your job to allow someone to track you back to the sith, then the burden of what to do with them falls on you."

"Oh. Do you get many apprentices this way?"

"No. Most of us choose to redeem our shame by killing the intruder." Again, he offered me that horrifying smile. "Unless we are particularly short-staffed, in which case Lord Celebrach strongly recommends that we choose the path of apprenticeship."

But Lord Celebrach had made no such recommendation in my case, which meant they were in no great need of new apprentices. My tongue darted out, licking suddenly dry lips. This was not looking good.

"How many apprentices do you have at the moment?"

"Only one."

He could have been lying to put me off. In which case, it was working. A little desperately, I said, "I'm already skilled with guns, knives, and the bow. I can use a staff, and I'm also pretty good at hand-to-hand combat." As he had seen. I'd managed to take him down, hadn't I? There couldn't be too many people who could say that. If I was honest, my success was probably only due to the fact that I'd caught him completely by surprise, but still, as far as I was concerned, it counted.

"If it comes to hand-to-hand combat, you have failed as an assassin." He gave me a chilly glare. "The aim is to strike at your target without being seen and escape unde-tected. And you won't be using that gun again."

"Usually, they're excellent against fae. They never expect modern weaponry—they're too old-fashioned."

That gun had served me well when his Night Viper friends had broken into our sith, intent on killing us all in our beds. Although this probably wasn't a good time to brag about how many of his mates I'd killed. I changed tack. Might as well try to see what information I could get out of him. If I was still alive when the sun came up, it would be useful.

"Not that it worked so well against you and Lord Cele-brach," I continued after a moment. "How did he do that?"

"You assume he did it? What makes you think it wasn't me?"

"Why? Are you an Air fae?"

He frowned. "You ask too many questions."

"That's because I love learning—and I'm good at it, too. It would hardly take you any time to train me."

We passed the practice ground where I'd seen Evandir throwing knives and the other men wrestling, and he led me into a separate building beyond that. It had no windows, at least on this side. Inside was a large room where wooden practice weapons were stacked in racks against the walls, but he didn't stop there. Men's voices came from further down the corridor, and he checked his stride for the briefest moment.

I glanced at him curiously. Why the hesitation? His expression gave no clue, and he continued on as if the brief moment of doubt had never occurred.

The sound of water running came from an open door just ahead, and the voices echoed inside. I wrinkled my nose; the place had that locker room smell that was common to gyms everywhere.

Evandir appeared in the doorway, clad in a pair of dark pants, his chest bare, towelling his blond hair dry. He must have just stepped out of the shower. His eyes lit up with interest at the sight of us. Up close, they proved to be a startling green.

"What have we here, Ashovar?" he asked.

So much for only Lord Celebrach calling him Ashovar. Judging by Ash's frown, maybe only people who were trying to piss him off called him Ashovar. I'd have to remember that.

"She followed me back."

"Are you going to keep her?" Evandir's gaze ran over me appraisingly and then he called back over his shoulder. "Mezzi, come and check this out. Ash has a prisoner." He reached out to stroke my cheek. "Shame she isn't a pureblood. She's a pretty thing."

I knocked his hand away, glaring at him. Just let him make something of it; I'd be only too happy to wipe the smile off that too-handsome face. They were talking about me as if I were a stray dog, and I'd had enough. "My blood is every bit as good as yours."

"Indeed?" The smile was frostier, now. "Perhaps we'll get to see your blood all over the stones tomorrow. What do you think, Ash? Keep or kill?"

Another man appeared, clad only in a towel wrapped around his waist and still dripping water, presumably

Mezzi. He was the man who had laughed with Evandir after the wrestling match. "Ash won't take an apprentice," he said. "He always swore he never would."

I loved how they were discussing my fate as if I couldn't hear every word they were saying. Did these people have no hearts?

No, of course they didn't. What was I thinking? They were assassins.

I shrugged. "It would be your loss. I'd be the best damn Viper you've ever seen."

Evandir laughed. "She's a feisty one, Ash. She might make a good playmate. That's one thing to be said for apprentices—they're good bed warmers."

"Not everyone is as free with their apprentices as you are," Ash said.

"Why not?" Evandir turned away, as if he'd lost interest in the conversation, and resumed rubbing his hair. His next words were muffled by the towel. "Training an apprentice is extra work, and seven years is a long time. You may as well get some payback for your effort."

Seven years? Would I have to remain here for seven whole *years*? I glanced up at Ash, but his face was the usual cold mask. I could glean nothing from it. *Calm down, Sage, of course you won't.* I'd find a way to get out of here sooner than that. My friends were counting on me.

Water was pooling around Mezzi's feet. "Have you decided yet?"

"I have until dawn," Ash replied.

He tugged me on, and we resumed our march down the corridor. We passed a door bound with strips of iron.

That was an odd thing to find inside a sith. I wondered what was behind it and why it needed iron's extra protection. But a moment later, Ash unlocked a heavy wooden door ahead of us, and I became more focused on my immediate situation.

It was a cell, as promised, and a tiny one, barely big enough to accommodate the thin mattress that lay on the stone floor. A bucket stood in one corner, presumably to take care of bodily functions. There was no window and no other door. It was enough to give a person claustrophobia.

Ash pushed me, not ungently, into the tiny room, and I went because there was nothing else I could do. Should I fight him? And after him, Evandir and Mezzi and every other assassin in this place? And even if, by some miracle, I managed to defeat every one of them, there was still no way out of the sith. Not for me. It made no difference whether I was locked in a cell or not; I was just as trapped.

I turned to face him, and all my bravado fell away. "Please don't kill me. I know you've never had an apprentice and you don't want one, but I'll make it worth your while. I'll be the best damn apprentice anyone ever had. I'll make you proud, I swear. Just please, please. Give me a chance."

He stared at me in silence, that cool gaze giving nothing away. Then he closed the door. The key turned in the lock, leaving me to await my fate in total darkness.

14

Faelight blossomed at my fingertips, then bobbed into the air like a soap bubble, lighting the small cell.

There wasn't much to see, no more than I'd glimpsed from the doorway. Grey stone walls surrounded me on all sides. I rapped a few with my knuckles, but the walls were just as solid as they appeared and cold to the touch. A chill radiated out from them into the small room, and I soon wished for warmer clothing.

The mattress hid no secrets—not that I had really been expecting to find the entry to a secret tunnel underneath it, but it never hurt to look. The whole floor was depressingly solid and as icy as the walls. The only other thing in the room was the bucket which, surprisingly, was bright blue plastic with a white plastic handle, incongruously cheerful and modern in its bleak surrounds. Not exactly what I'd been expecting in the stronghold of the fae assassins. Clearly, they had no objection to utilising modern technology in some cases, even if they turned up their noses at guns.

I slumped down on the mattress. Hands clasped behind my head, I gazed up at my little light bobbing just below the thick beams of the ceiling. I was pretty much out of options here. If the bucket had been wooden, maybe I could have used it as a weapon against the first person who opened the door, but I could hardly beat anyone to death with a piece of flimsy plastic.

Ash had taken my gun, of course—not that it had done me any good. Celebrach had also confiscated my backpack, which held my knife. They'd left me my phone, which was no more than a useless hunk of metal and plastic here. Unlike Willow's comfortable sith, this one wasn't rigged for phone signal. I had the clothes I was wearing and my wallet. Not much to work with.

I lay there for a while, feeling sorry for myself, but it was so damn cold in the cell I eventually had to stand up and pace around just to keep warm. My movement startled a mouse I hadn't noticed, and it skittered out underneath the door. There wasn't even room to pace properly. Three steps one way, three steps back again, bringing me so close to the door my nose was almost touching it. I'd checked it out in my initial examination of the cell, but it was way too heavy and thick to even contemplate kicking my way through it.

And what if I did? I still couldn't get out of the damn sith. If only I had my father's power—why the hell couldn't I have scored a few more of *his* genes? I clenched my fists, the familiar frustration swelling in my chest. What use was being half-fairy if you had no more magic than a baby?

What were my choices? I could wait here like a good girl until my fate was decided by Ash, or …

I couldn't really come up with an alternative. If I could get out, I could go find myself a weapon. At least that way, if it was a thumbs down from Ash, I might be able to take him out before I died. But getting out was the problem.

There was a fair gap at the bottom of the door, perhaps an inch. Plenty big enough for my mouse friend, but no real use to me. Rubbing my cold arms, I crouched down to peek through the keyhole, but he'd left the key in the lock on the outside and I couldn't see a thing.

I rose slowly, my brain racing. *He'd left the key in the lock.* Well, well. Suddenly I had options.

I pulled out my wallet and considered its contents, the cold forgotten. A credit card, a bank key card. Driver's licence, various loyalty cards to the stores I frequented. Not a lot of cash, which was nothing new. I spent it almost as fast as I earned it. A bunch of receipts and one folded piece of paper. Aha! I'd hoped that was still there.

I pulled it out and unfolded it. It was my shopping list from last week, only small, but big enough for my purposes. Now all I needed was something long and thin.

If only I had Willow's long hair; she always had a clip or bobby pin handy. Mine was so short I needed neither. I considered the plastic cards from my wallet. Perhaps I could snap a piece off. But then my eye fell on the bucket and its thin, white plastic handle. Even better. It was the work of a moment to detach it from the bucket, and then I was ready.

Carefully, I smoothed the paper and slid it under the door, leaving only a small amount of it showing on this side. Then I shoved my plastic bucket handle into the keyhole, which was one of those large and primitive ones that took an enormous old-fashioned key. It took hardly any jiggling at all before a satisfying *thunk* from the corridor told me that the key had landed on my piece of paper.

Eagerly, I slid the paper back toward me, and *voilà*! The key came with it. Simple. I fitted it to the lock on this side, and in a moment, I was free.

I doused my faelight and stood listening for a long time, to assure myself that there was no one else left in the building. There were no sounds from the shower room, so I hoped that meant that I had the place to myself. Moving as quietly as I could, I headed for the exit.

Outside, I slipped into the cover of a small stand of trees and considered my next moves. I could go back for my own knife, which was probably still in Celebrach's office. That seemed the quickest way to find a weapon. There were probably dozens—if not hundreds—here, but I didn't know where any of them were kept, and the longer I had to search, the higher my chances of being caught again.

The downside to that plan was that I would have to evade perhaps several people in the main building, and there was no guarantee that Celebrach's office would even be empty. For all I knew, Celebrach himself would still be there, which kind of cruelled my chances of getting my knife back.

Option B was wandering around looking for someone else's weapon to steal. If only all those practice swords and knives on the walls of the building I'd been imprisoned in were real. That would have made my life a lot simpler. But assuming I could find a weapon, what then? Go back to my cell to await my doom, ready to make sure Ash shared it with me if it wasn't good news?

It seemed like a pretty sad plan. I'd much prefer one where winning wasn't defined as taking someone into death with me. *Really* winning would be getting out of here. Ash had warned that I'd be hunted down and killed if I escaped—but he didn't know I had the king as my trump card. The assassins wouldn't be able to hunt me if we hunted them first.

Someone was passing my hiding place, and I held my breath. As their footsteps receded, I risked a glance. It was a woman, dressed in the grey livery of the servants, gliding along the path and staring straight ahead.

And then it came to me. Once I had a weapon, I could pull the same stunt that the Vipers had pulled on Nevith. Talk about poetic justice. All these servants must be able to open the gate to the sith, and presumably, they were servants because their magic wasn't very strong. I should be a match for them. All I had to do was capture one and force them to open the gate for me.

I took a deep breath. I liked this plan much better. If it worked, I could be reunited with my friends inside the hour. I smiled; I did so like a happy ending.

With renewed enthusiasm, I began my search for a weapon. The first cottage I came to was lit up. A peek inside showed a man and woman and two small children seated at a table, eating together. I passed that one by, hoping to find one that was empty.

Further on through the trees, another cottage stood alone, surrounded by tall pines that almost completely cut it off from its neighbours. Whoever lived here obviously enjoyed their solitude. The place was dark but for a faint glow from one window, and I crept closer, careful to make as little noise as possible as I pushed through the bushes and peered through the glass.

The glow came from the small fire that burned in the hearth. The room was a sparsely furnished lounge with only two large wing-backed chairs set before the fireplace, a couple of small side tables, and a long sideboard.

I thought it was empty until someone moved in the armchair that faced away from me.

It was Ash, and he leapt from the chair and strode across to the sideboard, which groaned under the weight of the array of bottles clustered on it. He took a decanter from a tray and poured himself a glass of something that glowed amber in the firelight. Whiskey, probably. He tossed it back as if it were water, then contemplated the empty glass, turning it in his hand.

In a move that shocked me with its suddenness, he hurled the glass into the fireplace. The smash and tinkle of glass was loud in the stillness. What was his problem?

I dragged my gaze from the pieces of glass littered like chips of ice on the bricks and looked at him. His expression was bleak, but that seemed fairly standard for him.

He raked his hair back, the long strands falling forward straight away to shade his eyes again. Then he pinched the bridge of his nose in between thumb and forefinger in a gesture familiar to tired people the world over. Both worlds, in fact.

Was he struggling with his decision? If that was the case, I was even happier that I'd come up with an escape plan. Leaving my fate in the hands of someone else, particularly someone who had no interest in my continued survival, was not in my nature. And if the decision was causing him this much grief, the chances of my living past dawn were looking pretty slim. The only question was why a man like him would feel any remorse at the thought of taking yet another life.

He yanked the door open and left the room in another abrupt movement. A moment later, the front door of the little cottage slammed.

I kept still, flattening myself against the wall behind the bushes, but he didn't come my way. I gave him a good few minutes to get clear, then I slipped around the corner and let myself in. Once inside, I conjured the tiniest faelight, shrinking it down to almost nothing to stop the light showing through the windows. He was bound to have weapons I could steal, but I'd need a little light to find them.

The cottage was small, containing only four rooms—the lounge room I'd already seen, two bedrooms, and a bathroom. No kitchen, which seemed a little odd, but I guessed he took his meals at the main building in the austere dining room I'd seen. Assassins were probably too important to bother with cooking.

I checked the drawers of the sideboard and the cupboards below them but found only papers and yet more bottles of booze. This guy had a serious drinking problem. Did he drink so much to forget the ugly deeds he'd committed?

One of the bedrooms seemed unoccupied. Though the bed was made, there were no ornaments or personal effects around the room, and a peek inside the wardrobe showed it was bare. The other bedroom was clearly Ash's. Furnished in a dark, sombre style, there wasn't much personality on show, beyond a couple of photos in silver frames and half a dozen books stacked on the bedside table. The drawers held only clothes; I felt around underneath them to make sure.

I was coming up blank until my gaze fell on the carved wooden chest that sat at the foot of the bed. Sure enough, when I opened the heavy lid, I hit pay dirt.

The gleam of fairy steel greeted me. Three swords of different types—including one rather exotic one with a curved blade—half a dozen daggers and throwing knives, throwing stars, a garotte, and a couple of other things whose purpose I could only guess at. Gingerly, I picked out a short, straight dagger and drew it from its sheath. The blade's edge gleamed in the soft glow of my faelight. It was a nice weight and fit comfortably in my hand. Hurriedly, I closed the wooden lid and left the house with my prize.

All I had to do was find a servant and take them prisoner. The main building was the obvious place to start, since I'd already seen several servants there, though my heart quailed a little at the thought of going back in there without the protection of the light-weaver candle. I'd have to find and capture one person without being seen by anyone else.

I took a deep, calming breath. No use putting it off; it wasn't going to get any easier if I delayed, and every minute I wasted was another minute in which my escape could be discovered. My watch showed four o'clock in the morning, which meant that dawn was barely two hours away. I had better get cracking.

Moving as quietly as I could, I crept down the path towards the main building. At one point, I had to slip into the trees to allow two grey-clad servants to pass. They were carrying a large box between them and never spoke or even looked at each other. Only their laboured breathing had alerted me in time to leave the path.

After that, I moved even more carefully. Fae had an uncanny knack of making barely any noise when they walked, moving like shadows on the wind. But I saw no one else.

Approaching the building from the rear, I hurried through the large herb garden I'd seen from the window, feeling exposed with no trees to hide behind. I breathed a little more freely once I'd gained the shelter of the building, though my troubles didn't end once I was inside.

The thick carpets that muffled my footsteps also hid the approach of any others, and I was almost discovered by more of the grey-clad servants, two women who were dusting. They appeared from a hidden staircase with barely any warning. It was only because the first one sneezed just before she stepped off the stairs into the corridor that I had any warning at all.

As it happened, a door was within arm's reach, and I thrust it open and hurled myself inside just in the nick of time. Fortunately for me, the room was empty. I held the door open a crack and watched the corridor. I thought I was in luck when the first woman appeared, but then her companion followed her. I couldn't take two prisoners; I needed to find someone on their own.

But perhaps the dusting would take these two in different directions. I waited until they'd gone past, then I eased the door open and stuck my head out, watching their progress.

For once, the Lady smiled on me. One of them opened a door further down the corridor and went inside, while the other kept walking. I waited until she was out of sight, then slipped out into the hallway and hurried to the room the first woman had entered.

She didn't see me come in. The room was a library, and she was standing at one of the windows, one arm braced on the window frame while she stood on tiptoes, reaching up as high as she could to dust along the top of it. I was across the room in a flash and pressed the tip of the knife to her neck in the soft, vulnerable spot just behind the curve of her jaw.

"Don't move," I whispered. "Don't even breathe, or I'll slash your throat."

To my astonishment, the woman continued dusting as

if I wasn't even there. Surprise held me frozen for a second, then I applied a little pressure to the knife so that the blade bit into her neck. Blood welled from the shallow slice, bright against her pale skin.

I grabbed her around the throat and hauled her away from her task. Maybe she was strange, like the people in the kitchen, but surely self-preservation must kick in eventually? "Are you deaf? Do you think I won't hurt you?"

The feather duster drooped to her side, but that was all the reaction I got. I may as well not even have been there.

In desperation, I tightened my grip, and her blood smeared across my skin. "You will open the gates of this sith for me."

"You're wasting your breath." Ash slouched against the doorframe, arms folded across his chest. "She won't take orders from an outsider."

Those damn carpets! I hadn't heard him at all. Had he been following me this whole time?

I hauled the girl around in front of me so that we both faced him, my knife still at her throat. "Then maybe *you* will. Otherwise, I'll slit her throat."

He shrugged. "Go ahead. Servants are easy to come by."

I glared at him, at a loss for what to do next. The girl wasn't even struggling; she stood calmly while I half strangled her, the blade of my stolen knife nipping at her skin.

I made a noise of disgust and thrust her away from me. I was not altogether surprised when she calmly went back to dusting, the smear of bright blood staining her throat and the neck of her dress the only sign that anything had happened at all. Something was very wrong with her.

"Is she under a spell?"

"She is compelled by the Blade."

"Compelled by which blade? Most people would find it compelling enough to have a dagger at their throat."

"We do things a little differently here among the Vipers." He straightened, a frown creasing his brow as he eyed the knife. He held out an imperious hand. "I'll take that now."

"I don't think so." If I couldn't blackmail him by using the knife on the girl, perhaps I could use it on him instead. I eyed his tall, muscled form, sizing him up. It would be a stretch, but I might be able to do it. I certainly had nothing to lose by trying. It still seemed like a better option than casting myself on his mercy. Even if he had been going to take me as an apprentice, this had probably changed his mind.

"That's my knife, isn't it?" The frown became a scowl. "You stole it from my house."

"Yes, I did, and I also booby-trapped your bedroom while I was there." I hadn't, of course, but the idea of him creeping around his own house waiting for the axe to fall amused me greatly.

He sneered. "With what, your mighty magic?"

Low blow. I straightened my shoulders against the familiar sense of frustration. "No, with my brains. I know you fae don't use them much, but you should try it some time. You might find that they're actually pretty handy."

He advanced into the room. There was ice in those grey

eyes, a hard look that promised a world of pain if I didn't immediately fall in with his wishes. Pity for him I wasn't the falling-in kind of girl. "Give me the knife."

"Where would you prefer it? Heart or spleen?"

"Nobody steals from me."

"Well, that's demonstrably not true." I waggled the blade at him tauntingly. If I could get him to lose his temper, I had a better chance in a fight. People in the grip of high emotions didn't fight as well as those who kept their heads. "If you want it, come and get it."

He took a step closer, then another, his eyes never leaving mine. My heart raced at the promise of action, but my body was loose, ready for anything. My hope was that he would assume I wasn't enough of a challenge to bother using magic against me—fae liked to conserve their energy wherever possible, and magic was draining. Then I could make him pay for his fae arrogance.

I watched closely for any sign that he was about to attack—any little twitch, any tell-tale movement of the eyes. He held no weapon, but that meant very little. I'd seen those assassins wrestling outside. Unarmed combat was clearly nothing new to them, despite Ash's insistence that assassins never resorted to it.

"Last chance," he said. "Give me the knife."

Was he going to talk all night or was he going to fight?

"Sure." I smiled and took a step forward, holding out the knife. He relaxed, ever so slightly, and I launched myself at him. Surprise and speed were my best chance.

Well, surprise was on my side, but speed was on his. I

slashed at him, but he danced away, moving faster than anyone I'd ever seen.

Damn. I'd lost surprise, and there wasn't much else in my arsenal.

"You shouldn't have done that," he said in a conversational tone. He flung one hand in my direction, and a blast of icy wind knocked me right off my feet.

Blue light flashed and the clean scent of his magic filled the room. Everyone's magic had an individual smell —Willow's was like walking through a rose garden in full bloom. Mine had the faintest tang of limes, barely noticeable. His smelled like wet grass and the heady aroma of oncoming rain. I rolled across the carpet, only stopping when I was brought up short by something. The servant's skirts. She continued dusting the bookshelves, taking no more notice of me than she had when I'd held my knife to her throat.

Books. I staggered to my feet and snatched a book from the shelf, hurling it straight at Ash's face. I followed that up with another lunge with the knife, hoping to catch him by surprise, but he batted the book from the air almost lazily, then hit me with another arctic blast of his Winter magic, his whole body wreathed in its blue glow. I was more prepared this time and kept my feet, but that was the best I could do. I leaned into the gale, shivering, trying to force my way closer to him.

"You're a stubborn little thing."

"Big enough to take *you* down." Empty threats. I had no comeback against his magic.

He smiled, a lazy smile that said he knew he'd won,

and I saw red. All my life, fae had looked down on me because of my lack of magic.

Without thinking, I flicked the knife straight at his heart. It was a good throw, and it should have brought him to his knees, but the Winter wind sent it spinning through the air. It lodged itself harmlessly in the spine of an old book.

I was shivering so hard I could barely stand, and I definitely couldn't feel my fingers anymore. The rainy scent of his magic filled the air as the wind buffeted me unceasingly, its icy fingers tearing at my skin. I staggered, trying to keep my feet.

It was no use; I was driven to my knees.

He sauntered across to the bookcase and prised his knife from the book as he let the magic fade. "Look what you've done to this book. Fortunately, it's only Foramund's *Treatise on Herbal Remedies*. I never liked that one anyway."

Then, he swept me up from the carpet and into his arms, and carried me from the room.

I was still shivering when we entered Celebrach's study, my teeth chattering uncontrollably. Celebrach sat in a chair by the fire, a book in his lap, and in my present state, that fire looked like the best thing I had ever seen. I wanted to climb right into it, sure that that was the only way I would ever feel warm again.

Celebrach raised an eyebrow as he closed the book with a snap. "Back so soon, Ashovar? You're eager."

"No need to wait until dawn. I've made up my mind."

Ash set me down, giving me a gentle push towards the heat of the fireplace, then closed the door behind us. I stumbled to a stop as close to the fire as I could get and faced Celebrach.

"Don't keep us all in suspense, then," the Lord said. "What is your decision?"

Ash gave me a long, considering look with those hard, grey eyes. I had no clue as to the thoughts that lay behind them. "Apprentice."

A small sigh of relief escaped me, the only sound in the room apart from the soft crackle of the fire.

Celebrach eyed me with keen interest. "Well, well, we haven't had a new apprentice in some time. You are a fortunate young woman. I really thought the decision would go the other way." He transferred his mocking gaze to Ash. "So much for your vow never to take on an apprentice."

Ash stiffened but didn't reply.

"What happens now?" I asked.

Celebrach smiled. "Eager to get to work, are you? You have a bloodthirsty one on your hands here, Ashovar. Best watch your back."

"I always do."

Celebrach laughed, went to the polished bookcase behind the desk, and took down the curious warped blade from its ceremonial stand. "Then we'd better not keep the young lady waiting."

Ash took my arm and urged me across the room to stand in front of the desk. I'd stopped shivering, but I was still freezing. The warmth of his hand felt like a burn. How could he feel so warm when his magic was so cold?

I shrugged him off. "I can walk on my own, thanks."

Celebrach tapped the dagger against his open palm as he watched us both. "I can see you will have your hands full with this one."

Ash's voice was cool. "I don't anticipate any problems."

Celebrach came around the desk, and I eyed the dagger with misgiving. Up close, there was something about it that raised the hairs on the back of my neck.

"Give me your hand."

I glanced at Ash, but his face was an impassive mask. What was this? Some kind of ceremony, I assumed. Were we going to become blood brothers? Unless this was some elaborate ruse to lull me into a false sense of security and then kill me anyway. I kept my hands at my sides.

Celebrach's mocking smile only grew wider. "Not very trusting, is she? Ashovar, if you please ..."

With a muttered oath, Ash took my wrist in a firm grip and held it out to Celebrach. "Keep still," he growled at me.

"What is your name?" Celebrach asked.

"Sage."

"Sage what?"

"Forester," Ash said before I could reply.

I held Celebrach's gaze, willing myself to show no reaction. Why had Ash lied? His body was rigid beside me. I dared not turn my head to look at his face, though I doubted I would find answers there anyway. Did he just not want to admit that he didn't know? Fae pride could be a funny thing.

"Sage Forester," Celebrach said. He took my wrist and turned it over, exposing the vulnerable veins on the underside. "Tonight, you join the ranks of the Night Vipers."

He drew the twisted blade lightly across my skin.

It was so sharp that, for a moment, I felt nothing. Then, a thin line of blood welled in the blade's wake and ice bit into my skin. More Winter magic? Strange. From my previous encounter with the Lord of the Vipers, when he'd stopped my bullet in mid-air, I'd assumed his powers were of Air.

He laid the flat of the blade over the blood, and it felt as if he'd dunked my whole hand in an ice bath. Ash's grip on my arm tightened as I swallowed. He must have felt the involuntary twitch as I tried to pull away from the pain.

Was that a faint blue light coming from the blade? I stared, distracted by voices in the distance. Someone laughed in the corridor outside; someone else was crying softly just on the edge of hearing. My vision narrowed until all I could see was the icy glow of the twisted dagger.

There was a strange ringing in my ears, and the voices grew louder, arguing with each other, but I couldn't make out what anyone was saying. Neither of the men reacted— was I the only one who could hear them?

Then, Celebrach removed the knife and only silence reverberated inside my skull.

Both he and Ash let go, and I rubbed my wrist, which still ached with a bone-deep chill. But there was no mark, no blood, nothing to show where the blade had bitten. I clasped my other hand around my chilled and aching wrist and waited for whatever came next.

To my surprise, Ash held out his own wrist. I flicked a curious glance at his face; there was a strange look there. Not fear, surely? Perhaps revulsion? But he realised I was watching him and smoothed his expression.

I felt sure Celebrach hadn't noticed. He was focused on the taut flesh of Ash's wrist, drawing the twisted knife across tanned skin—slowly, ever so slowly, as if he wished to prolong the moment. Blood welled behind the blade, and there was a flash of blue light. I flinched, caught by surprise, but Ash stood firm, his arm held straight out.

My wrist buzzed with an odd sensation, as if the muscles beneath the skin were jumping. Or as if something was trapped under there—a tiny insect, perhaps, trying to batter its way free on frantic wings. A faint whisper hissed around my ears. Was there someone outside? If Celebrach or Ash heard anything, they gave no sign.

Celebrach turned to replace the blade in its cradle with loving hands, and Ash glared at the back of his head as if he hoped to drill straight through the man's brains with the force of his gaze.

Something stirred in the shadows behind Celebrach, and the whisper came again, but when I looked closer, there was nothing there. Only normal shadows cast by the flickering firelight. And surely no one in their right mind would be whispering in the corridors of the Night Vipers, disturbing their lord and master? Certainly not any of those dead-eyed servants.

I felt a little light-headed, as if the twisted blade had drunk far more of my blood than that little taste, and the ache in my wrist had built up into a bone-deep chill that sapped the strength from my arm.

I'd been awake all night; that was all it was. Simple lack of sleep, combined with the stress of not knowing my fate. It was enough to have anyone jumping at shadows and imagining voices where there were none.

Celebrach turned back to me and offered a cool smile. "Welcome to the Vipers. You will report to Ashovar. Make sure you live up to his high standards."

"Can I have my weapons back?"

The smile broadened into genuine amusement. "Perhaps not just yet. Ashovar has proven his commitment to you, but you still need to prove yours to us. And make no mistake, Sage, disloyalty will not be tolerated. There are no disappointing apprentices among the Vipers. Only dead ones."

The grey light of pre-dawn lay flat across the training field and trees as we left the building. I walked at Ash's side, apparently free, though Celebrach's final words rang in my ears.

"Your boss needs to work on his welcome speech," I said when the silence became too much for me. "*No disappointing apprentices—only dead ones.* Way to make a girl feel welcome."

He bared his teeth in that humourless expression that seemed to pass for a smile with him. "I'm sure you'll enjoy the welcome party later."

"There's a party?"

"No." His voice was flat, as cold as the chill grey light. I could barely make out his profile: the clenched jaw, the downward turn of his mouth. "Do you think you've joined a country club? Or come to Whitehaven? We are the Night Vipers, not a pleasure palace."

I shrugged, determined not to be intimidated by his cold stare. "Doesn't mean you can't have a little fun now and then. All work and no play make Jack a dull boy, as they say."

"As who says? The humans? You'd do well to keep your human ways to yourself as much as possible. Your heritage already works against you."

Hot anger flooded my chilled body. "You may as well save your breath, because you won't make me ashamed of my mother."

A strained silence fell. I wanted to treat him to the cold shoulder, but I could already tell that my silence would be no penance for him. So, I changed tack. I was here for a purpose, after all. Might as well find out as much as I could about the Night Vipers. Any little detail could be the one thing that brought them down.

"Why haven't you had an apprentice before?"

He didn't answer, so I tried again.

"So, what's involved in an assassin's apprenticeship?" Maybe it would be like potions class at Hogwarts, mixing up deadly drops for the poor victims. Although, feeding poison to the client who stooped to hiring assassins would suit me better.

He walked faster so that I had to hurry to keep up with his longer legs. Was he hoping I would run out of breath for talking? He was doomed to disappointment if so. "First, we'll run you through a few weapons and see what you can do."

He made me sound like a car he was taking for a test drive, one that he didn't have very high hopes for. He might be surprised to discover there was no rust on this bodywork. I still remembered all Dandelion's training, back when I was a bored young thing with too much energy in the gardens of Spring and the kindly guard had taken me in hand. It was he who had taught me the bow and staff and how to place a throwing knife exactly where you wanted it. I'd never been able to beat the burly guard in a fist fight, but once I'd arrived in the mortal world, I'd discovered the joys of martial arts, so I might even have a surprise or two up my sleeve for Ash.

"And then?" I prompted when he seemed disinclined to add anything further. Assassins were a tight-lipped lot, that was for sure. I'd be playing Twenty Questions all night trying to get any information out of this guy. "If this is going to be my life for the next however long, I'd like to know what to expect."

He shot me a hard glance without breaking stride. "It's not as though you have any choice in the matter. You'll have plenty of time to learn your new duties."

We marched across the training grounds and into the building from which I'd so recently escaped. Stopping in the front room where all the wooden practice weapons lined the walls, he selected a short sword.

"This should be about the right length for you." He tossed it to me, and I caught it one-handed.

"Swords aren't really my thing."

"I'll be the judge of that," he said without looking at me. He selected a sword for himself and two staves.

I followed him out to the training ground, giving my new sword a couple of experimental swishes. He set the staves aside and took up his own sword, assuming a ready stance, balancing lightly on the balls of his feet. Remembering Dandelion's lessons, I did the same and circled warily as he began to move.

"It's hardly a fair fight, considering how much longer your reach is than mine," I pointed out.

His eyes gleamed, no doubt in amusement at my expense. My new instructor didn't seem to enjoy anything as much as other people's pain. "Life isn't fair. You must understand that if you are to become a Viper."

In the middle of speaking, he lashed out with his sword, and I only just got mine up in time. The wooden blades clashed together, and I felt the impact jar all the way up my arm. He was strong—much stronger than me—and I wouldn't be able to fend off too many blows like that before my arm was completely numbed.

I watched even more carefully for any warning that he was about to strike again. Dandelion had always said that a man fights with his eyes; you must watch the eyes and the rest will follow. But Ash's steel gaze gave nothing away. In an instant, his sword was moving again, but this time I ducked and rolled, avoiding the blow. I bounced back to my feet, pleased that I'd managed to evade him.

"You move well but, in fact, if you end up in a sword fight, you have already failed as a Viper. We work in the shadows, dealing death unseen."

"Then why are we doing this?" I panted as the tip of his sword sailed past a hair's breadth from my face.

"Because you want to be an assassin." He landed a hard blow on my shoulder, and I stumbled back. Already, sweat was gathering in my hair and rolling down between my breasts. I'd thought I was fit, but the man was a machine; he barely seemed to be breathing hard. "And, thus, you must develop lightning-fast reflexes and the fitness of a warrior."

I took my sword in both hands, my arms shaking with the unaccustomed effort, and darted in, feinting a blow to his right. But as he moved to block me, my leg shot out to hook around the back of his.

I wasn't sure exactly what happened. He should have ended up on his back in the dirt, but somehow, it was me lying on the ground, staring up at him with the wind knocked out of me. Again.

He rested his sword point on the ground and stared down at me. "You're right. The sword is not your forte." He walked away and picked up the two staves. "Get up. We'll see how you do with this."

I scrambled to my feet, resenting his dismissive attitude. I'd warned him, hadn't I? My side throbbed where the practice sword had hit me. He certainly hadn't pulled that blow.

I caught the staff he threw to me and twirled it experimentally, getting a feel for its weight. This was one of my better weapons. I settled into a ready stance. This time, I'd wipe the sneer from his face.

He didn't waste any time, coming at me with his staff spinning so fast it was a blur. Mine rose to meet his in the familiar dance. As the wooden poles clacked against each other, I settled into a rhythm. How many times had I done this with Dandelion over the years? More than I could ever hope to count. If Ash thought to find me as weak with the staff as with the sword, he was in for a surprise.

Soon, I had the satisfaction of watching a bead of sweat

trickle down the side of his face. *Now* he was working. I circled and spun, my feet kicking up puffs of dirt as I surged backward and forward, my staff whirling about my head, rising to meet his.

I even managed to land a blow to his shoulder, though it glanced off as he danced away. But clearly it hurt his pride, as he renewed the attack with such ferocity that I realised he'd been holding back before. Soon after, his staff cracked against my knuckles and mine went flying.

He held the point of his weapon against my throat. We stared at each other, both breathing hard.

Slow clapping came from behind me. I hadn't even realised we had an audience, so intent had I been on the battle. It was Mezzi and a woman I hadn't seen before, both dressed in what I was coming to think of as the assassins' uniform of basic black. The woman's hair was as red as Willow's, but she kept it in a sleek high bun. Probably to keep it out of the way. She had the hard look of someone who considered practicalities like that.

"She almost had you there," she said, but there was no approval for me in her tone, only censure that Ash had allowed himself to be tested by his new apprentice.

Ash said nothing but dropped his staff to strip off his shirt. There was a mark on his shoulder where I'd hit him with the staff that looked like it would turn into a nasty bruise. The sculpted planes of his chest glistened with sweat. He looked like Mr January from a firefighters' calendar—only without the smile.

"At least she's not completely useless," he said to the

woman in a tone that made clear how very far from satisfied he was with my abilities.

"How's her magic?"

They both turned to look at me, and I folded my arms. "Pretty much non-existent."

She smirked. "Surely you're just being modest. You managed to find us, after all."

"She's only half fae, Nuah," Ash said.

"Really? Which Realm?"

"Spring," I said shortly.

"Then perhaps you can fix this."

She lifted her hand, and a shower of pine needles—as brown and withered as if they'd been lying on the ground for six months—rained down on my head from the tree above. Her magic had a faint cinnamon smell.

The branch withered before my eyes as she pulled the vitality from it, but I did nothing. Willow could have breathed life back into the tree, but I knew full well that I didn't have that kind of power. Impatiently, I moved out of the way, but the shower of dead needles followed me. "You must be Winter."

"Guess again. Autumn."

An ominous creak was my only warning. I looked up in time to see the branch, now thoroughly drained of life, split away from the tree, and I leapt aside as it crashed to the ground. I gritted my teeth, though I longed to snatch up my staff again and belt her around the head.

"Try not to break Ash's new toy before he's even had a chance to play with it," Mezzi said.

I loved the way they spoke about me as if I wasn't even

a person. I'd had to put up with some casual racism in the mortal world, but human slurs that targeted the colour of my skin were nothing compared to a certain kind of fae's disdain for those without magic.

Nuah looked at him, her eyes wide in fake innocence. "I was only testing her. If she's Spring, shouldn't she have *some* control of plants?"

"Have you tried her with knives?" Mezzi asked Ash.

"Not yet," I said before he could answer. I was sick of them discussing me as if I wasn't standing right in front of them. "How about a challenge?"

"Against me?" His eyebrows rose in surprise.

The woman scoffed. "You think you stand a chance against a full Viper?"

"Don't be so hasty, Nuah. It's not as though she's challenging *Evandir*, is it? We all know knives are my weakness." Mezzi offered me a knife. Its blade looked deadly sharp. No practise weapon, this one. "I could do with the practice. What do I get when I win?"

"Who says you're going to win?" For a brief moment, I considered attacking the three of them with my new weapon, before sanity prevailed and I followed him to face the targets that Evandir had been throwing at with such skill before.

"Best of three?" He let fly his knife as he spoke, and the blade thunked into the heart of the figure painted on the target.

"Sure." I aimed for the head and left my knife quivering in the target's eye.

Mezzi strolled over to the target and removed both knives.

"A little further away?" he asked as he handed mine back to me.

I nodded and followed him until we were double the distance from the target. Much further and we'd be better off with bows than knives, but I still landed a respectable throw—a little closer to the ear than the eye, but still good.

Mezzi's knife hit the red dot that represented the target's heart again, so close to his previous throw that the blade probably slotted right into the same hole it had made the first time. And knives weren't supposed to be his strong suit?

This time, when he handed my knife back, I took an extra moment to draw a deep breath and centre myself. *This time*, the knife would hit that eye exactly. I'd spent years honing my knife skills, though admittedly, I hadn't been as diligent in practising in recent years as I could have been. Since we'd been living in the mortal world, it had seemed a better use of my time to practise guitar than knife-throwing.

I drew the knife back, the blade balanced between the tips of my fingers, and the world narrowed to that painted eye. But just as my arm began to move, something hit me in the back of the head.

My throw went wild. The knife didn't even hit the target, but landed in the dirt off to the side, throwing up a puff of dust as it skidded to a stop. I whirled around, my hand going to my head, as a rock clattered to the ground.

My head stung like a bitch. I wouldn't have been surprised to discover blood, but my fingers came away clean.

"What was that?"

Nuah smirked at me. "A little test of your concentration."

Behind me, Mezzi's knife thudded into the target. Another perfect strike, right into the heart.

I narrowed my eyes at Nuah. "You threw a *rock* at me?"

Lazily, she lobbed a pebble at me, and I sidestepped angrily. This one was much smaller than the first one. I was going to have a king-sized headache from that little stunt. She was lucky I didn't still have that knife in my hand.

"Assassins work in difficult conditions. You have to be able to hold your focus despite distractions. Clearly, you'll need to work on that."

"Or you were just afraid I was going to show up your friend."

She glanced at the target, where Mezzi's knife still stood proudly embedded in the heart. "Oh, I don't think there was much danger of that." She smiled at Ash. "I hope she's better with the bow. You're not regretting your decision, are you?"

He balled up his shirt and used it to wipe his face. "She's only half fae. You can't expect miracles."

"Fancy a bout? It's been weeks since I've ground your face into the dirt."

Mezzi laughed. "Don't rile him up, Nuah, or it might be your pretty face that gets dirtied."

Ash showed her that savage grin, the one that looked

more like a snarl. "Another time, perhaps. We need to get cleaned up."

He jerked his head at me, in a clear sign that I should follow him, and strode off. Seething, I trailed after him. I was not a dog to be ordered to heel.

My fingers crept again to the sore spot on my scalp as I followed him back through the trees. Was that a lump forming? The skin wasn't broken, but it burned like fire. Distraction, my arse. She had enjoyed that.

That was one Viper I wouldn't mourn when I brought them all down.

16

Back at Ash's house, he led the way straight to the empty bedroom. "This will be your room."

Really? "I thought all the apprentices would stay together."

There wasn't even a lock on the door. Evandir's comments about bonking his apprentice made me even more uncomfortable, now. Not that Ash seemed the type for a little apprentice-bonking. That would be too much fun for someone who seemed so dour. Even so, I wasn't sure how I felt about living in his pocket. Having him constantly hovering at my shoulder would limit my opportunities.

"Adepts and their apprentices live, train, and work together. We'll be spending a lot of time together." He looked as happy about that as I felt. "Bathroom's that way. You need to get cleaned up and dressed for dinner."

I gestured at my dusty, sweat-stained T-shirt and jeans. "This is all I have."

He flung open the wardrobe door in an impatient gesture. Someone had been busy while we'd been at the training grounds—presumably the silent servants. An array of black clothing hung there, though it had been empty when I'd checked this room earlier. Some were made of soft and stretchy material, obviously intended for training clothes. That would have been more comfortable than tackling Ash in my jeans and T-shirt. Others were more tailored, meant for everyday wear. Shirts, pants, a jacket, two pairs of boots. I opened one of the drawers and found socks and underwear, too.

It all looked about my size, which was kind of creepy, as if someone had been sizing me up, mentally taking my measurements. Was it Ash? Had he been staring at my boobs, thinking, *Yep, 36C.*

On another shelf in the wardrobe, writing materials were stored—blank notebooks and pens. I was pleased to see they were modern human pens, not the quills beloved of the more old-fashioned fae. But that suggested there was some studying in my future.

And then I noticed a row of books on what had been an empty bookshelf when I'd checked this room earlier. My textbooks, presumably, with titles like *The Poisoner's Handbook*, and several texts on anatomy. I noticed Foramund's *Treatise on Herbal Remedies* among them, looking in much better shape than the one that I'd accidentally stabbed back in the main building.

Thoughts of stabbing brought back my poor showing on the training grounds against Mezzi, and I rubbed at the sore place on the back of my head where Nuah had hit me with the rock. Bitch had enjoyed that.

"Is that troubling you?" Ash asked immediately. He didn't miss much. "Let me see."

"It's fine," I said, but he pushed my hand out of the way and probed the area with unexpectedly gentle fingers.

I stood there, fuming. If he hadn't cared enough to stand up for me while she'd been lobbing trees and rocks at me, I wasn't inclined to accept his solicitude now.

"There's no lump," he said once he was satisfied. "You should be fine."

"No thanks to your friend," I said. "You might have stopped her after she tried to drop a pine branch on my head."

"You needn't sound so resentful." His tone was cool. "You'd be in a worse position if I had. It would have made you look weak, and you can't afford to show weakness here. You'll find mineral salts in the bathroom," he added. "Under the sink. Add some to the bath water so you won't be so stiff tomorrow. You're very out of shape."

I bristled. Out of shape? *Me*? "I can run for an hour without stopping."

"Congratulations. But you are nowhere near Viper standard. That's why we work with sword and staff so much, even if we never plan to use them. This is a physically demanding job, and nothing less than perfection will do." He cast a critical eye over my body. "You have a long way to go."

"I'll be fine as long as you get your friends to stop throwing things at me."

"Let it go, Sage. The Vipers are a wolf pack hungering for fresh meat. If I play sheep dog and protect you, they will see you as prey."

"So I'm a lamb to the slaughter?" Great.

"Only if you choose to be. I can make you a wolf, but you have to trust my methods."

"I'd rather be a dragon than a wolf," I muttered. Then I could burn the lot of them.

"We're expected in the dining room at eight," he continued, ignoring me. "It's traditional for new apprentices to be introduced to the Nest. You don't have a lot of time."

He swept out of the room, and a moment later, his bedroom door closed firmly.

I sighed, pulling a black shirt and matching pants from the wardrobe. There was nothing fancy enough for a formal dinner, so I guessed dressing up wasn't expected.

The strange turn my life had taken wasn't lost on me. Who would have thought, twenty-four hours ago, that I'd be wondering what to wear to a meeting of the Night Vipers? That I'd be their newest apprentice? It was crazy, but it was an unparalleled opportunity. Had any outsider, in the whole history of the Realms, had such access to their organisation? I was perfectly placed to take them down from the inside—as long as I survived the experience.

I shut the bathroom door behind me and started running hot water into the tub. Maybe others *had* had such an opportunity before me, but they'd been caught and killed. A shiver ran over my body despite the warmth of the room.

I couldn't afford to think about such things or I'd lose my nerve, and then I really would be in trouble. I found the mineral salts in a jar under the sink and added a generous scoopful to the water. It clouded over as they fizzed and dissolved. The only way forward was through— through all the obstacles that playing the part of an eager apprentice assassin was bound to throw in my way. My life depended on my acting skills. Hopefully, a few days would be enough. As soon as they gave me the ability to open their damned gate, they wouldn't see me for dust.

I sank into the tub, hissing as the hot water scalded my skin, and lay back. What would Willow think if she could see me? What would Raven?

Well, not that I'd be letting Raven see me naked, of course. That man didn't need any encouragement. But he was probably well and truly worried about me by this time. As Willow would be, too.

I breathed deeply of the steamy air and tried to squash a twinge of guilt. I was doing the right thing; I was sure of it. I just wished I'd had the chance to get them a message before I'd been trapped here.

The bath was deep, the old-fashioned freestanding type with bronze clawed feet. The floor and walls were tiled in black, and the lighting was dim, leaving shadows lurking in the corners of the small room. I closed my eyes and gave myself over to the sensation of the hot water working the kinks out of my abused muscles. It had been a while since I'd had such a thorough workout—I'd been slacking off since Allegra had left. She'd been my regular sparring partner.

I was certainly not *out of shape*. Heat that had nothing to do with the water temperature swept through me. How dare Ash look down his nose at me? *Nowhere near Viper standard* indeed. My body was a well-oiled machine. Just because his was damn near perfect, with those rock-hard abs and sculpted chest. He knew how to use those muscles, too. His sword technique was excellent, and he'd already bested me a couple of times unarmed.

Not that I'd be taken by surprise again. And I knew some dirty tricks that might surprise even that ice-cold assassin. But it didn't matter how perfect his body was; there was something missing inside him, a cold hollow where a heart should be. Or a soul, perhaps.

I'd take him down with the rest of them, without a second thought.

I thought longingly of the bed in the small second bedroom as we entered the dining room. It had been a while since I'd lived on a completely nocturnal schedule, and my body clock was insisting on sleep. I just had to make it through "dinner" at breakfast time, and then I could collapse.

Early morning sun set the tall stained-glass windows afire, making the room look even more like something out of a monastery, though the pictures in the glass were fanciful flower designs rather than biblical scenes.

I looked closer at one particularly colourful one, of huge blood-red blooms and curling vines. A rabbit's head peeked around one of the flowers. No, wait. The rabbit was … inside the flower?

Oh, gross. The vines were twined around the rabbit's struggling body, delivering the victim to the waiting flower. Other flowers, which I'd thought were buds, were actually already closed around writhing bodies, presumably devouring them.

"Nice décor," I said to Ash.

Without answering, he took a seat at one of the long tables and gestured for me to sit next to him. I looked around with interest. Apart from the colourful windows, the room was austere: stone walls, stone floors, all in the same cold grey. Four long tables stretched the length of the room, and I guessed the bench seats could probably seat thirty people at each table—maybe more, if they didn't mind getting up close and personal with their neighbours.

At one end of the room was a smaller table set perpendicular to the others. There was no one at this table yet, though the others were filling as black-clad figures kept entering through the same wide doors we'd come through.

A man took his seat opposite us and nodded to Ash, then studied me with naked curiosity. I stared back, holding his gaze until he looked away. Was he an assassin, too? He didn't have the blank-eyed stare of a servant, so I had to assume so.

More people kept coming in until the tables were a little more than half-full. Servants began bringing in food, but no one ate, as if they were all waiting for a signal.

Grace, perhaps? Who did Vipers pray to anyway? Surely not the Lady. She was a goddess of life, not death.

There weren't as many people here as I'd expected, considering the size of the sith. Some of them could be out on jobs, I guessed. Or dead. I looked down, hiding a fierce smile as I remembered those who now slept beneath the earth of Willow's garden. I'd killed Vipers before. I glanced at the still figure at my side. *And I'd be happy to do it again.*

A small door behind the head table opened and more black-clad figures filed in, Evandir and Nuah among them. Bringing up the rear was Celebrach, and as soon as he entered the room, conversation stopped and everyone at the long tables got to their feet.

Celebrach strolled to the middle seat at the head table, which had a higher back than the others and huge claws carved into the ebony arms. His companions spread out along the high table, taking the other seats, though the one to Celebrach's right was left empty. Was whoever usually sat there dead? Out on a job?

"Who are these people?" I whispered to Ash. If they were important, maybe I should target them first. If I could take a couple of them out before I escaped the Vipers' sith, it could throw our enemies into disarray.

"The Adepts," he said briefly.

At a gesture from Celebrach, the Adepts took their seats, and everyone else sat, too, though he remained standing. Like everyone else, he wore black, though his coat looked like velvet instead of the more practical cloth the rest of us wore. Rings of silver and gold glinted on his fingers, but otherwise, his appearance was plain enough.

The most striking thing about his ensemble was the dagger that hung at his side.

It was the twisted dagger that usually resided on the stand in his office. It had no sheath, hanging from a silver loop on his belt. It was probably hard to find a sheath to fit such an oddly shaped blade. I shivered, remembering the deathly chill of its kiss on my skin.

"A new apprentice has run Ishitil's Gauntlet and joined our number," Celebrach said. He didn't have to raise his voice at all; the acoustics in the room were excellent, the sound reverberating off the stone walls. "Ashovar will have charge of her training."

Whispers started at that, and everyone looked at us. There was speculation on some faces and amusement on others.

"Before we begin our meal, let her name be entered in our rolls."

Ash stood, nudging me to stand, too. A servant brought out a large and extremely old-looking book bound in black leather, laying it reverently on the table in front of Celebrach as we approached.

We stopped in front of the high table, like two kids called before the principal. I eyed the warped dagger uneasily. I hoped there would be no more ceremonial cutting involved. I got a chill through my veins just thinking about the last time.

But Celebrach's only weapon on this occasion appeared to be a quill. He dipped it into a pot of ink that another servant offered and wrote my name halfway down a page that was yellowed with age, at the bottom of a list of other names. *Sage Forester*. His handwriting was large, and he ended with a flourish. All the other names on the page had been entered in the same writing. I wondered how long it had been since the last apprentice had been added, but there were no dates.

More whispering rose nearby, but I didn't see anyone's mouth move. The seated Adepts all watched solemnly, even Nuah, though she looked a little bored and her gaze strayed to Ash, who still loomed at my side.

Celebrach handed him the quill next, and the whisper came again, even closer. It sounded as though someone was standing right behind me, leaning close to whisper in my ear.

The hairs rose on the back of my neck. It was clear enough to make out what was being whispered. The same word over and over again. The long hiss of the s, followed by the vowel sound rolling around the mouth.

"Sssssage."

I bit my lip as Ash signed in the column for *Adept*. Was it my imagination, or was that the faintest stirring of air on my bare neck, like someone's breath? But there was no one behind me.

What was the matter with me? I wasn't the type to imagine spooky shit. Sure, magic was real, and the truth really was stranger than fiction sometimes, but I didn't believe in ghosts and I didn't jump at shadows. I glanced up at the stained-glass windows, hoping to see if there was a wind outside—perhaps that was the whisper I heard. But the creepy killer plants blocked any view of the outside world, and I averted my gaze from the suffering of the doomed rabbits.

Ash handed me the quill, and I dipped it in the ink, hoping it wouldn't drip all over the page. Although it would be fun to see Celebrach's face if I ruined his precious roll, I wasn't here to annoy the Vipers. I was here to take them down, and right now, that goal was best served by keeping a low profile.

I solemnly signed my name—or rather, the name that Ash had given me—next to his. *Sage Forester*. And there was only a little blot at the beginning of the f.

"A toast to our newest recruit," Celebrach said as I replaced the quill in its stand.

A silent servant with a drinks tray appeared at Ash's side. Ash took a glass and handed one to me. A rich, fruity smell rose from the glass, unexpectedly sweet and summery in this gloomy place.

"Sage Forester," Celebrach continued. "May you add to the fame and fortune of this Nest."

"Sage Forester," the other Vipers echoed in unison, raising their glasses to me.

I lifted mine and drank in return, since no response seemed to be expected.

They wouldn't know what hit them. I would burn this nest of vipers to the ground and grind their charred bodies beneath my heel. They would wish they'd never heard the name Sage Forester.

17

———

After dinner, we stepped outside into the bright sunshine. It was ten o'clock in the morning and my body clock was completely screwed. Having been awake for over twenty-four hours, I craved sleep, yet here it was, bright daylight. Fortunately for me, sleep seemed to be the next thing on the agenda.

We didn't speak as we headed back to Ash's little house. A pigeon leapt up from the bushes beside the path with a whir of wings as we passed, and I was so tired I barely reacted. A body can only be on high alert for so long, and mine was done. Ash could murder me in my sleep and I wouldn't even stir.

I went straight to my room and lay down—and then, of course, my mind started buzzing with all I'd seen and learned. There were so many new faces, new dangers, and new buildings. I was gradually constructing a map of the whole complex in my mind, ready to lay before the king. Already, I had more information on the elusive assassins than anyone outside their number had ever had before. Even Raven would be impressed.

I rolled over, burying my face in the cool pillow. Raven might be impressed, but he'd never show it. He was far more likely to make a joke of it. Or act as if he hadn't even noticed I was gone. Anything was possible with him.

He was hard to read, but I was willing to bet he was worried by now, even if he wouldn't show it. Willow would be frantic. I got a sick feeling in my stomach thinking about it, and rolled onto my back again, staring up at the ceiling in exasperation. I should be sleeping, not fretting about my friends.

What had they done when I didn't come home? I hoped Raven hadn't said anything to the king—that would be embarrassing. The king had bigger things to worry about than what some random half-fae was up to. Like dealing with his recalcitrant family.

At least Lily was someone else's problem for now. Poor Willow probably didn't even have time to worry about me. She'd be too busy managing the princess.

I felt better for a moment, until I thought of Zinnia. Zinnia would be worried. She fussed over Willow and me like a mother hen. I bit my lip, hating that I'd caused her more pain.

Now that I'd been officially added to their number, was I assassin enough for the gate to let me out of the sith? I had more than enough information for the king. If I could get home now, Zinnia's fears could be set to rest.

I lay there for a moment, considering the problem. Celebrach had bled me with his creepy dagger; he'd entered my name in the rolls and welcomed me to the happy little Viper gang. Surely that should be enough? Or was there something more? It wasn't as though I could ask Ash, but all this ceremony seemed as though it should do the trick.

The ceiling blurred as my eyelids sagged shut. With a goal decided on, my mind was settling, and exhaustion was creeping in. I pulled out my phone. It was useless here for most things, but I could still set an alarm. I gave myself five hours. If I woke at three, everyone else should still be asleep, giving me a chance to sneak around and check whether the gate would let me out. Now that I was an apprentice Viper instead of an intruder, the wards shouldn't alert Celebrach to what I was doing. And then it would be goodbye, Vipers; hello, vengeance.

Satisfied, I fell into a deep sleep.

When the alarm went off, I thought I must have set it wrong—it felt as though I'd only been asleep for moments. But no, it was three o'clock in the afternoon.

Groaning, I rubbed my eyes. What wouldn't I give for a cup of coffee right now? Maybe even two. Despite the austerity of the house, the bed was ridiculously comfortable, and I could have slept the clock around.

Not that Ash would let me. He probably had plans to boot me out of bed the instant the sun set. Hopefully, I'd be long gone by then.

I sat up and ran a hand through my short hair. Too tired to change, I'd fallen asleep in my clothes, so I only had to pull my boots back on. I stood up, blinking to clear the sleep from my eyes, then tiptoed to the door.

It made no noise as I eased it open. The hall was dim; Ash must have drawn all the blinds. I stood and listened to the quiet for a moment. The only sound was the ticking of the clock on the lounge room wall. Ash's bedroom door was ajar, and I crossed to it on silent feet.

The assassin lay sprawled face down, one muscled arm flung across his pillow. The sheet only covered him below the waist, showing he slept at least topless, if not naked.

His hard expression had softened in sleep, making him look more ... I don't know ... approachable? Human? No, not that. He was fae, as the impossible beauty of that chiselled jaw and sharp cheekbones reminded me. And more than that, a fae who went around killing others. It didn't get much colder than that.

I sneaked down the hallway to the front door, wondering what assassins dreamed about. More killing? Or did they have the same kind of nonsensical dreams as the rest of us?

The door creaked as I cracked it open, spilling sunlight across the hardwood floor. I froze, holding my breath, but there was no sound from the bedroom. Just in case, I slipped out into the fresh air and closed it behind me with agonising slowness. I swear suns could have grown old and died in the time it took me to ease that door shut, but it worked—it didn't creak again. There was only the slightest of clicks as the latch engaged, and then I was free.

Breathing a sigh of relief, I strode down the path—and nearly had a heart attack when the door was wrenched open again with the mother of all creaks behind me. I spun around.

Ash stood in the doorway, blinking a little in the sun, wearing a pair of shorts and nothing else. "Where are you going?"

The sunlight caught the hairs on his chest and turned them golden. His skin was dusted with gold, too, as if he spent a lot of time working on his tan. His legs were thick with muscle. No wonder the bastard had been able to run me down.

I jerked my eyes back to his face, aware that my inspection of his body had taken a little too long, and felt my own skin heating.

"Just ... just going for a walk." Dammit, why did he have to be such a light sleeper? "I couldn't sleep."

He frowned, though I couldn't tell whether it was a frown of disbelief or just his habitual expression of vague annoyance with the world. "Come back inside and I'll mix you a sleeping potion."

I snorted. "Excuse me if I don't fancy drinking a potion made for me by an assassin."

The frown grew more serious, leaving me in no doubt that he was pissed off. He held the door open wider and stepped aside in an unmistakeable gesture. "Inside. Now."

"Sorry," I said ungraciously as I squeezed past him. The fresh, clean smell of ironbark clung to him like a forest damp with dew, and his bare skin was still warm from bed where my arm brushed against him. I could have sworn he'd been fast asleep. That damn creaking door. "I didn't mean to wake you."

"We are linked. I will always know where you are." He

shut the door behind us, closing us inside in sudden darkness.

"We are? How?"

"The ceremony with the Blade."

He pushed past me into the lounge room, and I followed, uneasy. The last thing I wanted was some kind of Viper homing device on me. Having an assassin always know where I was could prove fatal.

"What do you mean?"

He poured himself a drink from the vast array of bottles on the sideboard, then moved to stand in front of the fireplace. The fire was nearly out, and the room was chilly. Maybe he should go put some more clothes on. I found his near nakedness disturbing. Day two of my apprenticeship and he was already so casual in front of me? If he thought I would be one of those *apprentices with benefits*, he was in for a major disappointment.

"When the Blade drank from you, you became part of the Nest." He gave me an impatient glance, as if I should already know this. Why? Did I look like a mind reader? "We are all connected."

I stared at him, horrified. "You mean *everyone* knows where I am?"

"No. Only the Master of the Blade and the Adept you have been bound to."

I remembered the magic that had flared around him after Celebrach had cut me, when the twisted dagger had been laid against Ash's skin. Had that been when this magical link had been forged? I didn't like the sound of being "bound" to him. That implied a lot more of a commitment than I was up for.

"Who's the Master of the Blade? Celebrach?" I was pretty sure of the answer, but I had to check.

"*Lord* Celebrach," Ash said, reproof clear in his voice.

What else did this magical link do? And did it work both ways? "Do I get to know where you are?"

"No."

"Why not? That doesn't seem fair."

"Because I am the Adept and you are the apprentice."

Well, that sucked. "If you expect me to call you *Adept Ashovar*, you're in for a disappointment."

He took a long swallow, then fixed me with a hard look. "I don't expect you to call me Adept anything. What I *expect* is the tiniest smidgen of gratitude for saving your life."

The silence lengthened. "Sorry," I said finally. "I *am* grateful, of course. I'll try not to be too much of an imposition."

A muscle jumped in his cheek. He turned back to the dying fire, so I couldn't see his face. "I never wanted an apprentice, but I've just committed years of my life to training you. I don't think you understand exactly how much of an imposition you are going to be."

I blanched at *years*. No, that would never happen. And then I had another thought. "You ... you can't change your mind, can you?" He sounded as though he was regretting the decision to let me live. Could he take it back?

"Make no mistake, Sage, your life is in my hands." He glanced at me, his grey eyes cool. "As mine is in yours."

Say what? I did a doubletake, half-expecting to see a joking grin, but of course he was as hard-faced as ever.

"What do you mean, your life is in my hands?"

"As your instructor, I'm responsible for your behaviour. If you betray us or break any of our laws, both our lives will be forfeit."

Oh, shit. It was a struggle to hold his gaze. "That hardly seems fair."

Inside, my brain was yammering protests at me. What kind of bullshit policy was that? But I couldn't be responsible for his life. I wouldn't. He was still an assassin, even if he'd saved my life. Normal rules of gratitude couldn't apply here. He was the enemy, and I must never forget it.

"Fairness is for weaklings. Here, loyalty is valued above everything. We are Vipers first, and everything else is second to that. No other loyalties."

He tossed back his drink, a look of such bleakness on his face it made me wonder what loyalties he'd given up to become a Viper. And why he'd done it, if it made him look like that. What was the appeal of joining the assassins?

"You will work hard, and you will accept whatever punishments or orders your betters choose to give you. Some of them, you may consider *unfair*. You will accept them anyway." He stared down at his glass, as if surprised to find it empty. "And if you can't sleep, you may begin your studies. Chapter one of Foramund. Memorise and recite to me tonight."

He turned his back again, making it clear that I was dismissed. I left him alone with the dying fire and his collection of bottles, and returned to my room.

_____

18

Since sneaking past Ash wasn't an option, I lay down again, too tired to undress, and was soon asleep.

My dreams were feverish things, full of assassins and shadows that moved and spoke. Celebrach's twisted dagger was in them, too, though it belonged to me and no longer seemed creepy. The ruby on its hilt was a thing of beauty, and the strange blade was no longer distorted but artful. When my hand closed around the hilt, I felt only peace and a warm sense of security. With this blade at my side, I couldn't help but defeat my enemies. Even Evandir and Nuah bowed before me, their faces full of admiration. And Ash ...

Bloody hell. I woke up, horrified at what I'd just been doing with my cold instructor. Except, in the dream, he hadn't been cold at all. My heart still raced, and when I touched my mouth, I discovered my hand was shaking. His kiss had felt so real I swore I still felt the pressure of his lips on mine.

I sat up, unnerved. It must have been because I'd seen him half-naked. Why *wouldn't* I have dreamed of him after that? Only a dead woman could fail to appreciate the beauty of a body like his. My subconscious clearly had lower standards than I did—little details like morality or even personality didn't matter to it, only his pure physical desirability.

Well, I was awake now, and that was just not on. I threw off my blanket, then stopped, surprised. I'd fallen asleep sprawled on top of my blankets, in the middle of telling myself I'd get up in just a minute and get ready for bed properly. I hadn't even taken off my boots. But now they were on the floor, set neatly side by side, and someone had spread a thick woollen blanket over me while I slept.

That someone must have been Ash, bizarre as that seemed. It was such a nurturing thing to do—and *nurturing* was the very last adjective I would have picked to describe the cold-eyed assassin.

I shrugged it off and pulled my boots back on. I had more to worry about than trying to understand the inner workings of my instructor's mind.

It was full dark outside, so it must be time for apprentice training to commence. My body still ached from last night's hammering. Maybe he'd go a little easier on me tonight.

He came in from outside as I left my bedroom and grunted when he saw me. "You're awake." He made it sound as if I'd been asleep for days. "Are you ready to demonstrate your studies?"

It took me a minute to realise what he meant. I'd almost forgotten he'd told me to read a chapter of Foramund. "I fell asleep after all."

And you covered me with a blanket.

He seemed displeased with that answer. "A Viper doesn't sleep until all his chores are completed."

"Or hers."

He treated me to that icy glare, and it occurred to me belatedly that maybe I shouldn't start the night by antagonising him. Especially if he was going to be my sparring partner again.

"Sorry," I said.

"Two chapters by tomorrow. Eat breakfast; we have other things to do first."

A tray of fruits and nuts and a small bowl of honey were waiting on the dining table next to half a loaf of dark, grainy bread. I assumed he must have eaten already, as there was only one plate. I sighed and sat down to eat, thinking rather longingly of Zinnia's eggs and bacon and other breakfast treats, all so perfectly cooked. Maybe the Vipers hated the world because they were forced to live off fruit and nuts.

We began the evening at the training grounds, where I practised my archery and managed to impress Ash at last. Well, *impress* was probably too strong a word. But his lips didn't thin in the disappointed way they'd done yesterday, so I was calling that a win. I doubted he could manage actual pleasure or approval.

Today's workout was boxing, which I had no experience with, and he got in some good hits, though I got the sense he was going easy on me. He should have been able to knock me out straight away, but he avoided my head, for which I was grateful. It was a good workout, I'd give it that; by the time we finished, I was drenched in sweat and my arms were trembling with effort.

Perhaps a dozen other Vipers were training as well, some with knives or swords or in hand-to-hand combat. I didn't recognise any of them, and none of them spoke. The silence was eerie, punctuated only by the clash of practice swords and the occasional grunt. There was none of that light-hearted banter I was used to from training with Allegra or even at the gym.

I eyed my sparring partner thoughtfully. Was it Ash's presence that made them all so quiet? I caught the occasional glance thrown his way, and everyone gave us a wide berth.

I took a shower in the communal bathrooms afterwards. Thank God they had modern plumbing here. A fae-style bath simply wouldn't have cut it. I set the shower to full cold when I got in and dunked my sweating head gratefully into the icy blast. A full five minutes passed before I felt cool enough to turn the heat up.

I'd assumed that that would be the extent of the physical activity for the evening, but Ash had a surprise for me when I reappeared dressed in clean black clothes. He met me in the foyer of the training building where the wooden practice weapons lined the walls.

"You have a challenge tonight." He led the way down

the corridor, and this time, he stopped at the iron-bound door I'd noticed the night he'd locked me up in here. He took a key from his pocket and unlocked the door, summoning faelight as he did so. The light bloomed and spread across the ceiling, revealing a room lined with weapons that were far more lethal than the wooden ones outside.

The sharp blades of swords glinted from racks on one wall. A whole arsenal of knives and throwing stars bristled on another. The far wall held staves, cudgels, maces, and all manner of other weaponry, some of which I had never seen before. I looked around in amazement. There were no guns, of course, but there were still enough weapons here to outfit a small army. Or a large force of assassins.

"Choose your weapon."

Surprised, I glanced at him. "You're letting me have a real weapon? What kind of challenge is this?"

"You will be expected to make your way through the woods and retrieve a box from the shrine in the centre."

A shrine to the Lady? I was surprised the Vipers even had one. Maybe they used it for target practice. "That doesn't sound so hard. What do I need the weapon for?"

"There will be some obstacles."

"Okay. Obstacles like bushes that I have to cut my way through?" I eyed a pair of machetes thoughtfully. "Or something I need to climb over?"

"Two hunters will be in the woods."

"Hunting what?" When he raised an eyebrow, I groaned. "Hunting *me*?"

This challenge was sounding more unappealing by the minute.

He didn't reply, only bared his teeth in that fierce grimace that passed for a smile with him. I turned back to the walls of weapons. Which one would help me the most if I was being hunted? Or if someone were lying in wait for me?

I eyed the row of staves longingly. The staff was one of my best weapons, and I felt pretty confident that no hunter would get the best of me if I had one. But there was the fact that this was all to take place in the woods to consider. How closely did the trees grow together? How thick was the underbrush? I might not have room to swing a staff properly.

"Can I have more than one weapon?"

He shook his head. "Only one. Choose wisely."

Wow, thanks, Sensei. Some help he was. Still, it wasn't as if these hunters were actually going to try to kill me, was it?

I hesitated in front of the racks of knives, but in the end, I picked a short bow and a quiver full of arrows. They'd be no use in hand-to-hand fighting, but if it came to hand-to-hand combat with two hunters at once, I was pretty much screwed. Better to keep a little distance.

I hefted the bow in my hand, getting a feel for its weight and balance. "You're really going to let me shoot other Vipers?" What if I killed someone? I mean, *I* wouldn't be shedding any tears, but you'd think Lord Celebrach wouldn't be too impressed.

"If an untrained apprentice manages to kill a full Viper,

then that person had no business being a Viper in the first place." Again, he flashed that unsettling grin. "I doubt our hunters will be in any danger from you."

We'd see about that. I felt a perverse desire to kill both of them, just to prove that I could. And maybe I would. Two less Vipers in the world wasn't exactly a bad thing. And if I wouldn't get into trouble for killing them, so much the better.

Out in the woods, I felt less sure of myself.

Ash led me just inside the tree line and stopped. "The shrine is north of us and slightly east, in the centre of the woods. It's small," he warned. "Don't expect a large building. It's easy to overlook."

I shifted the bow to my other hand and wiped a sweaty palm on my pants. "So I just have to get this box and meet you back here?"

"That's all."

I took a deep breath. "Wish me luck."

"Vipers don't rely on luck," he said reprovingly.

"Killjoy," I muttered as I set off into the forest.

"If you're not back here by sunrise you are deemed to have failed," he called after me.

Man, he was just a little ray of sunshine, wasn't he? I didn't look back.

There was a hint of a trail at first, but that quickly petered out. Not for the first time, I regretted that the Vipers didn't run on a diurnal schedule. My night vision was good, but not a lot of moonlight made it past the thick canopy of branches overhead. I'd spent hours in the midnight woods growing up, but the trees on Lord Thistle's estate had grown further apart than these and, of course, I hadn't been afraid to summon faelight. I'd be a fool to do that here; it would make me a sitting duck for whoever was watching for me.

So far, I'd seen no sign of the hunters, though I was on high alert, scanning the shadows and moving as silently as I could. That probably wasn't as silently as a trained assassin, which wasn't a comforting thought. But I pressed on, an arrow loosely nocked in my bow, ready for anything. It was a small bow—and just as well, considering how tangled the undergrowth was in places. Hard as I tried, it was impossible to be completely quiet as I shoved my way through bushes and tangles of branches.

How big were these woods, anyway? The view from the upper stories of the main building had suggested they only covered a handful of acres, but perhaps that had been misleading. It had been past midnight when I'd entered, and now it was closer to two, judging by the position of the moon—I'd left my watch in the change room—and I had the sinking feeling that I still had a long way to go to reach the shrine.

I couldn't even be sure that I hadn't gotten turned around. I could be heading back the way I'd come or in the completely opposite direction from the one I should be travelling in. If only one of Raven's birds were here to show me the way, as they'd done that time that he and Allegra were lost in the Wilds. But the chances of any birds from the outside world making it past the sith's wards in one piece were slim to none. Clearly, the only reason that I'd survived my trespassing was because of Ishitil and his stupid recruitment practices.

I paused at the foot of a large pine. It was so big there was a small clear space all around it where its branches had blocked the light, choking out any saplings that had tried to grow beneath it. Pines were easy to climb, and maybe an aerial view would help. I put the arrow back into my quiver, slung the bow awkwardly over one shoulder, and began to climb.

I had a bad moment when the bow got tangled in an overhanging branch and I was pulled off balance. My foot slipped, and I had visions of plummeting to the forest floor, my challenge over and my dreams of bringing the Vipers down as dead as my splattered corpse. I took a moment, clinging to the sticky trunk and breathing heavily to calm myself before I finished the climb. When I'd gone as high as I dared, I settled myself on a branch and parted the needles before my face, looking out across the treetops.

It was a depressing view. No buildings broke the trees in any direction. Ash had said the shrine was only small, but I'd still hoped for some sign. There was a break in the trees not far from me that suggested a creek or path of some sort. My money was on a creek, since the Vipers were unlikely to make it easy for their apprentices by building paths in the middle of the forest.

As far as I could tell in the dark, the creek cut all the way across the forest, neatly bisecting it. Was that one of the obstacles that Ash had mentioned? But how hard could it be to wade across a creek? I wouldn't even care if I had to swim it, though keeping my bowstring dry would be a problem. But I could probably throw the bow across first.

I sat there a long time, perhaps ten or fifteen minutes, trying to come up with some smart way to short-circuit this whole challenge. What if I left the forest the way I'd come and circled around to re-enter from the other side? The hunters wouldn't be expecting that.

If I were one of the hunters, I'd save myself a lot of trouble and just set up an ambush at the shrine. These guys were pros—presumably at least one of them would do that, meaning that there was no point in trying to be too tricky. I just had to find the shrine and then assess the lay of the land.

I began my descent, thinking grumpy thoughts about assassins and their stupid challenges. What was the point of it, anyway? To see how quietly I could move in the woods? It wasn't as if that many of an assassin's targets would be hanging out in the woods, after all. Fae loved their woodland settings, but most of them lived in actual houses.

Was it just an excuse to shoot me full of arrows and get rid of me? That was probably too paranoid. After all, Ash could have killed me instead of taking me as an apprentice. Why bother with the charade of the apprenticeship if they only meant to kill me a couple of days later? Yet I'd been feeling a prickle of alarm ever since he'd mentioned the hunters. Their weapons would likely be just as real as mine. Would they use them against me? I bet Nuah, for one, would leap at the chance. Surely they were only meant to make my life difficult, not end it.

And what of their magic? If a Spring fae was hunting me, I was completely screwed. They'd be able to turn the whole forest against me—I could be lashed by branches, dragged underground by roots or strangled by vines. Nuah's trick with the dead pine branch would be child's play in comparison.

If I'd had some damn Spring magic of my own, I could have used such tricks against *them*. I had adored my mother, but my father had proved himself to be a complete bastard. And his genetic materials were as big a waste of space as he was himself. But there was no point dwelling on it now—I'd had years to get used to finding other ways around my limitations. Time to focus on what I was doing, or risk a significantly shorter future.

I stopped when I was nearly down to the ground again. I could see back the way I'd come a little distance—and, speak of the devil, there was Nuah, moving silent as a ghost through the trees towards me.

19

———

My fingers clenched on the bow and I had to force them to relax. She hadn't seen me descending. She was looking ahead, scanning the path that I had followed through the bushes, but she wasn't looking up.

This was my chance. I could shoot her and she would never know what had hit her.

Slowly, I moved the bow to my left hand and reached over my shoulder for an arrow. I didn't want the movement to attract her attention, but there was enough foliage between us that I was fairly sure she wouldn't notice. When I had the arrow nocked, I sighted along it, the arrowhead never wavering.

I aimed at her heart; I could drop her dead right now. And yet ... I didn't. I had shot those two assassins in Willow's sith without a moment's hesitation, but that had been self-defence. They had invaded our home, intent on killing us, and I knew it was kill or be killed. In the heat of the moment, I'd had no qualms about taking their lives.

Even in Celebrach's study when I'd tried to shoot both him and Ash, I'd had no trouble pulling the trigger. I'd thought my choices were shoot or die. Those kinds of options tended to clarify my thinking marvellously.

But now ... Don't get me wrong, I didn't like Nuah one bit, and was perfectly prepared to believe that the world would be a better place without her in it. But picking her off in cold blood from the safety of my perch, with her unaware that I was even there, and when I wasn't even sure that she meant me serious harm ... It was surprisingly hard to let that arrow go.

Don't be such a bloody idiot, I told myself. She had Autumn magic, and she'd already proved her willingness to use it against me. She was carrying a bow, and who knew what other weaponry was concealed beneath her clothes. That bow wasn't for decoration; she'd come into the woods hunting, and her prey was me. I'd be a fool to let this chance to even up the odds against me go to waste. But this was only a challenge—surely the hunters weren't actually allowed to kill me? But they were still assassins.

I let the arrow fly.

She was so close it should have found its mark in her heart, but it struck her in the fleshy part of the shoulder. She fell, crashing back into the bushes out of sight.

Heart thumping, I grabbed another arrow and nocked it, but she didn't reappear. Damn. What now? Had she heard the twang of the bowstring being released, or had my hesitation thrown my aim off?

I waited, but there was no sound from the bushes where she'd fallen, no rustling, no shivering of leaves. Was it a trap? My teeth worried at my lip as I hesitated.

I rammed the arrow back into its quiver and scurried down the tree as fast as I could, keeping the bulk of the trunk between me and her. I moved so quickly I couldn't help making noise, but no arrows or throwing stars or knives greeted me, no blasts of withering Autumn magic, and I reached the ground unscathed.

I should hurry over there and finish her off, but my stomach rebelled at the thought. Yes, I had killed before, but I was no hardened killer. The thought of taking out a wounded woman at close quarters revolted me. Besides, I told myself as I hurried away, she was only wounded, not dead, and that meant she was still dangerous. Perhaps she was keeping so still in the hopes that I would do just that, ready to attack as soon as I appeared.

Well, I wasn't falling for that. I headed in the direction of the creek I'd seen, moving faster than before. The knowledge that I had an assassin right behind me, even if she was wounded, urged me on. My shoulder blades prickled with unease.

But even if she was still in the game, she'd have to take some time to get the arrow out and bind up the wound before she could resume the chase. I'd make sure I was far away before then.

When I reached the creek, I found it wider and deeper than I'd hoped. Too wide—here, at least—to jump it, and somehow, now that I was standing on the bank, swimming didn't seem so attractive anymore. The black water glittered in the moonlight, but I couldn't see into its depths, which made me more than a little reluctant to take the plunge. This was a sith, a piece of the Realms broken off. There wouldn't be any crocodiles, but there could be things much worse. My arrows would be little protection against one of the drowning fae, who liked to lurk in bodies of water much like this and drag unwary animals or travellers to a watery grave.

There was nothing to do but head along the creek, hoping to find a bridge or a place that was narrow enough to jump.

That turned out to be a lot harder than I had hoped, as the bank was steep and treacherous. More than once, I slipped as I was clambering over logs and forcing my way through the bushes clustered along the edge of the creek with their roots eagerly seeking the water. After a while, I moved farther back into the trees, keeping the creek on my left hand as I walked. I was still heading roughly east, if I hadn't lost my bearings completely. Ash had said the shrine was a little east of where I had started.

I was well and truly beaten up by the time the creek narrowed, a mass of bruises and scratches from forcing my way through the vegetation. I'd fallen a couple of times, losing my footing in the dark, but it couldn't be helped. I sucked on a particularly nasty scratch on the back of my hand while I considered my options.

I would need a bit of a running start, but I was confident I could make the distance. The problem was that there was no clear landing space on the far side, where the bank was even steeper than it was on this side, eroded away to a sheer, unforgiving drop into the water. The trees on the far side crowded right up against the place where the bank dropped away, jostling each other for room, their branches hanging out over the water.

That gave me an idea. Rather than trying for the bank itself, I could jump out and catch a branch.

No sooner said than done. I made my bow as secure as I could over my shoulder, took a few steps back, and powered forward.

The night air rushed across my skin as I flew across the creek, momentarily weightless, hands outstretched. I caught the branch with a jolt and used my momentum to swing my body up and get my legs wrapped around the limb as well. I hung there a moment, my bow dangling from my shoulder, almost skimming the black surface. Hanging there, I had a sudden vision of a hand reaching out of the water, grabbing hold of the bow, and pulling me down. Two of my arrows fell from my quiver before I could stop them.

Heart racing, I hauled myself up onto the branch, grateful for all those hours in the gym building core and upper body strength, then wriggled along until I reached the safety of the trunk. From there, it was a moment's work until my feet were safely planted once again on the forest floor.

I peered back across the creek, but nothing was stirring on the other side. If Nuah was following me, there was no sign. I turned and plunged into the dark forest. It would be just my luck if there was a bridge beyond the curve of the creek, but hopefully the water would slow her down, too, assuming she was still on my trail. With any luck, she was bleeding out in the bushes instead.

Guilt shivered across my skin, and I squared my shoulders. *Remember Nevith*, I reminded myself. Guilt had no place here, nor did compassion. I had to be as hard and cold as Ash himself if I was to bring the Vipers down.

Time passed oddly in the forest. I moved slowly, trying to keep noise to a minimum, so that it felt as if time was crawling, too. But because I couldn't see the moon's journey across the sky, I had no real idea of how much time was passing. It could have been one hour until dawn or it could have been four. I was really regretting forgetting my watch.

All I was sure of was that time was, indeed, passing, and anxiety's claws curled into my stomach. If I wasn't back to meet Ash by sunrise, I would fail the challenge. He hadn't said what the penalty for failure would be, but I didn't think it would be a matter of writing lines. The Vipers were a little more ruthless than that, as they had shown by sending two hunters after me equipped with real weapons. How many apprentices died on these little challenges of theirs? I had a suspicion that Nuah would have sunk an arrow into me without hesitation if she'd spotted me first, whatever the rules of the challenge said.

By the time I came up against another obstacle, it felt as though hours had passed. A thicket of bushes, bristling with thorns the length of my fingers, blocked my way forward. It looked just like the Aversion that Yriell had surrounding her cottage, but these thorns were real. I scratched myself on a couple before I realised the depth of the barrier facing me and figured I couldn't just force my way through.

I pulled back, examining the darkness before me. The bushes grew low to the ground, too low for me to attempt wriggling underneath the barrier. Since I couldn't fly, going over was out, too, which only left going around. But I had a bad feeling that that wouldn't be an option, either.

Nevertheless, I set off to my right, still circling east and looking for a way through. I thought longingly of the machetes that I'd left on the walls of the armoury. What wouldn't I give for one of those now? Still, I wouldn't have made it this far without the bow and arrow.

It took me twenty minutes to confirm that yes, a thorn hedge—because I was almost certain that was what it was —completely encircled something. What were the chances that it was just a random clump of thorn bushes sitting in the middle of this damned forest? Slim to none, if I was any judge of the deviousness of assassins. What better way to protect their shrine and bamboozle struggling apprentices than to build a vicious, impassable hedge around the goal? There was no doubt in my mind that these thorns protected the shrine I was seeking.

Which meant there was good news and bad news. The good news was I had found my destination—but the bad news was that there didn't seem to be any way to get through to it. Finding myself once again at the same tree where I'd begun my circumnavigation, I hunkered down to think.

Of course, the other bad news was that the second hunter was most likely somewhere close by, perhaps had even spotted me already. I got that itchy feeling between my shoulder blades again, the one that insisted that someone was right behind me, weapon raised to strike. I fought it down. I needed to focus. Time was ticking away, and I still had to get back to Ash with the prize once I'd managed to find my way through the hedge.

The thorns had ripped their way right through my sleeve, and my skin pulsed with pain where they'd dug into my flesh. Touching my arm, I found it warm all around the site of the pain. That wasn't good. The thorns must have some kind of poison on them. Immediately, I gave up any idea of just gritting my teeth and forcing my way through the hedge.

There had to be an entry somewhere. Obviously, the Vipers had some way to get through to their shrine, but if it involved the use of magic, I was screwed. Willow would have been through that hedge in a flash, the thorns bowing at her feet, but I was no Willow. My weak Spring magic amounted to little more than a green thumb.

Maybe I could use the same trick as before and utilise the trees to help me. If I could find a tree whose branches overhung the hedge, I could just shimmy along the branch and drop down inside the barrier. I began to move again, pacing along the outside of the thorny barrier, looking for an appropriate tree. There weren't as many pines in this part of the forest, and none of the ones I saw grew close enough to the hedge to help me.

Twenty minutes later, it became clear that the Vipers had already thought of that. No branches overhung the thorny bushes, or at least not far enough that anyone could use them to access the space they protected inside.

I'd scrambled up a tree—some kind of maple, I thought—and now sat on the branch, squinting into the darkness. I could see the tiny shrine where I wanted to go. Ash had been right: it was very small, no more than an offering bowl on a pedestal protected from the elements by a little roof and a waist-high wall. But I couldn't find a way to get there. I also couldn't see the second hunter, but there were trees inside the hedge, as well as a couple of boulders that would be big enough to conceal a person. What did I do now?

If only I had one of those boulders out here, and a hill to roll it down. I'd smash my way through those stupid thorns. Even a box of matches would do the trick. I bet they'd burn easily enough. But Ash had made sure that I couldn't prepare for this challenge by springing it on me when I'd just gotten out of the showers and all I had on me were the clothes on my back.

I gazed grumpily down at the hedge. It was so thick that it was clearly not a natural formation. Leaves from the trees lay on top of it here and there, caught on the thorns. My arm still throbbed where those thorns had ripped my skin. If the poison was anything serious, I could be in real trouble, but so far I felt okay. Just sore.

One part of the hedge, not far from where I sat staring gloomily down at it, had no stray leaves caught on its flat top. I frowned, my interest caught. As far as I could tell in the dark, there were leaves and pine needles and the odd bit of twig from the nearby trees scattered all over the rest of the hedge, just not in this part. Why was that? Could it be because that part of the hedge wasn't real?

Trying not to get my hopes up, I swung back down to the ground. It could just be the randomness of the wind in this part of the forest. Or maybe there were bare patches like these further on and I just couldn't see them from my perch in the tree in the dark. But anticipation bubbled in my chest as I slipped as quietly as I could through the tree trunks.

At close range, this section of hedge bristled with thorns, as real looking as any of the rest of it. Tentatively, I reached out. Hard, twiggy stems met my fingers.

Damn. My excitement fading, I moved along, carefully testing each section of the hedge. Perhaps I wasn't quite in the right place; it was hard to tell from ground level.

Finally, I reached out, and my hand found empty space though my eyes insisted there was hedge in front of me. Yes! Though the thorny bushes looked just as real here as anywhere else, it was all a Glamour. Flushed with excitement, I was about to step through when a sudden thought struck me.

If this was the only way in, the second hunter was almost certain to be waiting to ambush me as I came through. Hastily, I stepped to the side, wondering if they had already seen me. Did the Glamour protect me from view? Would I only become visible once I moved through it? I needed some kind of distraction.

I looked around for a decent-sized rock. It was an old trick, and I wasn't sure if a Viper would fall for it, but I had to try something. Otherwise, I might as well just walk in there and announce myself in a blaze of light.

Hang on. A blaze of light. *That* was a good idea!

I moved back to the hedge, hefting my rock in my hand, and took up a position just to the side of the Glamoured section. I took a deep breath and sent a silent prayer to the Lady. I wasn't sure I believed in her anymore, but I was right outside her shrine, so it seemed only diplomatic. And I needed all the luck I could get.

Then I hurled the rock as hard as I could over the thorns. At the same time, I summoned a burst of faelight and pitched that after it. Then, I dashed through the opening and pelted for the nearest tree.

A throwing star whizzed past my head as I threw myself behind its meagre cover.

20

———

Squinting against the glare, I risked a peek out from behind my tree. The star had come from some bushes on the other side of the shrine. I might have picked that spot myself if I was going to lie in wait for someone coming through the Glamour. Whoever was concealed there had a fine view of the entry and a clear shot. It was a wonder they'd missed me, even with the sudden burst from my faelights.

I sent the bobbing lights spinning towards the bushes, hoping to catch a glimpse of whoever lurked there in the dark. Instead, they snuffed my lights out.

The second that darkness swallowed the small enclosure, I was on the move, taking advantage of what I hoped was a momentary lapse in my hunter's attention while he killed the lights. I stepped out from behind the tree and sent an arrow at the bushes, then bolted for the shrine, firing arrows as I ran.

If you've ever tried firing arrows while running, you'll

know it's not great for accuracy. Fortunately, the bushes made a nice big target. I just wanted to keep my hunter's head down—actually hitting him was only a bonus.

Stars came whizzing after me. One thunked into my quiver as I hurled myself to the ground behind the dubious shelter of the shrine.

So now I had another weapon.

In the moonlight, the star's edges gleamed duller than the rest of it, and I sniffed suspiciously at them, handling it with care. Something was smeared there—poison, without a doubt. Honestly, these people were all insane. What was the point of taking on apprentices if you spent all their training actively trying to kill them? Or had someone gone off-script? None of the Vipers had been exactly welcoming.

What wouldn't I give for a gun right now? There'd been no sound from the bushes, so I assumed none of my arrows had found their target. That was a real shame.

My blood was up, and I was ready to take out my temper on someone. I'd show him what he got for throwing poisoned stars at me.

"What will you do now, halfbreed? I've got you pinned down."

Even if I hadn't recognised the voice, the word *halfbreed*, thrown at me as if it were the deadliest insult in the world, gave away the identity of my hunter.

"Probably take a nap," I said in a deliberately careless tone. "You're not providing much of a challenge, Evandir."

"Really? From here, it looks as though you're in rather a tight situation." The words were mocking, but I caught a hint of anger in the tone. Fae did so hate to be belittled.

Something moved in the corner of my vision, and I whipped my head around. There was nothing there, just shadows. For a moment, I wondered if I was seeing things again, the way I had in Celebrach's office. Yet, as I stared, a deeper darkness began to creep toward me, rolling slowly across the ground like a black mist.

What the hell was this? It sure didn't seem like a figment of my imagination. Some kind of Night magic? It smelled of smoke, but it wasn't.

I hurled another ball of faelight at the creeping darkness, but it had no effect, bouncing back as if it had hit a wall. Definitely magic. The smoke must be the signature scent of Evandir's magic.

I risked a peek over the lip of the shrine before Evandir could extinguish my light. The offering bowl was empty. Where was this box I was supposed to retrieve?

"Oh, by the way, I should have mentioned." That mocking voice came again, but it had moved. No longer coming from behind the bushes, it appeared to be inside the rolling blackness. Try as I might, I couldn't see a figure within it, and unease tightened my chest. Was he really moving toward me or was he throwing his voice somehow? "That box you're looking for? I took it. If you want it, you'll have to come and get it."

The spreading blackness was giving me the willies. Was this what Raven had called shadow-weaving? But that had sounded like a much more discreet thing, as if the weaver would be invisible. These moving shadows might be dramatic, but they sure weren't discreet.

"Do you always have to cheat to beat the apprentices?"

I was pleased that my voice sounded much calmer than I felt. "Not much of a Viper, are you?"

"Do you think I care for the good opinion of a halfbreed?"

In a moment, the smoky darkness would swallow the shrine, then me. I only had three arrows left; I had to make them count.

I stood up, drawing and firing in one fluid movement. I aimed for the sound of his voice and was rewarded with a grunt. Immediately, I sent my final two arrows flying after the first, but he must have moved.

Ducking down behind the shrine again, I gingerly picked up the throwing star and waited for the darkness to envelop me. The world faded around me, and I shut my eyes. It was less disconcerting that way, and it helped me to concentrate on what my other senses were telling me.

I moved slowly around the shrine, trailing my hand along its low stone wall. When I judged I was on the opposite side from where I had begun, I stopped and listened for any sound of movement. My heart beat a rapid tattoo in my chest. I had never expected this challenge to be a walk in the park. but it was turning out far more dangerous than I'd expected. If I made it out of this forest alive, it would be a bloody miracle.

I thought I heard the sound of breathing, but then it came again from a different direction. My head turned from side to side, seeking it out, but suddenly, it seemed to be all around me. I froze in place and raised the throwing star. If only he would speak again; he must be close. I didn't have any experience with throwing stars, but surely with this poison smeared all over it, all I had to do was nick him. I just needed to know where to throw the damn thing.

He slammed into me without warning and bore me to the ground. His strength was undiminished—my arrow must only have grazed him. The star slipped from my fingers and disappeared into the darkness.

I struggled, but Evandir's weight lay heavy on my back, and all the breath had been driven from my body when he'd landed on top of me. My struggles were weak enough to amuse him.

"I've seen dying rabbits twitch more than that. Is that the best you can do, halfbreed?" He took a painful grip on my hair, hauling my head back.

Terrified that he was about to slit my throat, I found new energy from somewhere and wriggled and bucked enough to half throw him off, though he didn't lose his grip. My hands scrabbled across the grass—which was bloody stupid if you thought about it, considering there was a poisoned throwing star lying somewhere nearby and I was just as likely to slice my finger open on it as use it to end his life. But I was way beyond sensible thinking, acting only on instinct.

"Any final words?"

"Yeah." My desperate hand closed on a rock. "Fuck you."

I slammed the rock into his head, and he cried out. Suddenly, I could see again—he must have lost his grip on whatever Night magic he'd been using. But my reprieve was only momentary. I scrambled back, clutching my rock, but he had a knife. A long, thin hunting knife that would do the job just as well as any scary twisted dagger. And he was coming at me with murder in his eyes.

I kicked out, but he only grabbed my ankle and hauled me across the grass on my back. He was strong—way stronger than me, as most fae were. His teeth gleamed white in the moonlight in a vicious smile. I was out of options and he knew it.

He was straddling me, my arms pinned beneath his knees. I slammed my own knees into his back as hard as I could, and he slapped me across the face with his free hand.

His smile widened. "Why don't you do that again and see what it gets you?"

I felt the prick of the knife at my throat. "What have I got to lose? You're going to kill me anyway."

"You're right about that. But maybe I'll have some fun first. Let's see what makes you so special. Why is Ashovar bothering with a creature like you? Can you really be that good in bed?"

A figure loomed behind him. Something slammed into him, and he toppled forward, crushing me again. His breath was in my ear, so he wasn't dead, but he wasn't moving either. Out cold.

I shoved at his body in distaste, trying to wriggle out from underneath him. Someone hauled him off, casting him aside contemptuously.

I blinked up at the figure standing over me. Ash.

I should have known. He made a habit of looming over me, after all. He reached out a hand, and I let him help me up. "Are you hurt?"

Surely that wasn't concern in his voice? Maybe I *was* hurt. Maybe I was dead and this was all some dream of the afterlife. I couldn't imagine the real Ash caring what happened to me. But if so, it was a pretty shitty afterlife. I wanted my money back.

I rubbed my neck, wiping away a few drops of blood from where Evandir's knife had pricked my skin. "What are you doing here? I thought I was supposed to meet you outside the forest."

He shoved Evandir with his foot, rolling the unconscious fae onto his back. "When Nuah came staggering out, I decided to come in and see what was happening. It seemed as though the exercise had gotten a little out of hand."

"You could say that. Evandir was trying to kill me."

He gazed down at his fellow Viper, fury burning in his eyes. "Yes, I saw."

I eyed him speculatively. Why so angry? Surely he didn't care what happened to his unwanted apprentice? I would have thought he'd be throwing a party if he managed to get rid of me so easily.

"Were you supposed to intervene like that? Not that I'm complaining, mind you," I added hastily as he raised an eyebrow. "You saved my life."

"Your life wasn't meant to need saving. If he can break the rules, so can I."

"Then we're all good? I passed the challenge?"

"I don't know. Do you have the box?"

Seriously? He was still going to demand I find the

damn box after Evandir had gone crazy and tried to kill me? "Evandir said he took it."

Ash folded his arms. "Then get it back."

Fuming, I searched the bushes where Evandir had been hiding, but there was nothing there besides twigs that snagged in my hair and a few beetles that scurried away as I stomped around. This was stupid. Who cared about the damn box?

Ash waited patiently by the shrine.

"Not long until dawn," he said in a conversational tone, making me realise the sky was lighter. His frown was so much clearer, now.

"How big is this box of yours?" I asked, frustrated.

"I've already given you more help than I should have."

"Then a little bit more won't make much difference."

He sighed, then held up his hand, thumb and forefinger a little distance apart. About the size of a small jewellery box, then. Well, if I'd known *that*, I wouldn't have spent so much time trampling the damn bushes. I'd been expecting something a decent size.

I knelt beside Evandir, who was still out cold. "I thought I was becoming an assassin, not a pickpocket," I said as I rolled him over and checked the back pockets of his dark pants. Sure enough, one boasted a suspiciously square bulge. I pulled it out, triumphant, and flicked it open. "It's empty? All this for an empty box? What was the point?"

"You don't need to know the reasons for the orders." He turned that dark scowl on me. "You only have to follow them."

21

"I think you must prepare yourself," the healer says, and Ash's face crumples in grief and denial.

I know the woman is a healer, though I've never seen her before. I'm floating somewhere up near the ceiling, watching this little tableau. In the same way that I know the woman is a healer, I realise I'm in a dream, but it seems far more lifelike than my dreams usually are. The room is clean and the white sheets on the bed are fresh. A strong smell of eucalyptus scents the air, not quite managing to cover an underlying stench of vomit.

Ash's hair is longer, braided down his back, but I'd know him anywhere, though I've never seen that hard face so filled with emotion. "No," he says, and his hands close into fists at his side. "You must be able to save her. A week ago, she was fine. How can she be dying?"

The healer's face is full of sorrow, too, though hers is a calmer, quieter kind than the agony in Ash's expression.

She shakes her head. "I've never seen anything like it before. It's like iron poisoning in the way it has attacked every part of her body."

They both stare down at the girl on the bed, her face as pale as the sheets she lies on. Soft brown hair is tangled with sweat, snaking across the white pillow, and she whimpers in her sleep, a small, animal sound of pain.

Ash sits on the bed and catches her hand in his. "It can't be iron poisoning. She's never left the Realms in her life."

"I know," the healer responds. "If it was iron poisoning, I would have been able to save her. This is something unknown to me, and she hasn't responded to any of my treatments."

Ash leaps up, and for a moment I think he means to attack the healer, such is the violence of his movement. Instead, he hurls the sheet back with a snap of his wrist and gathers the dying girl into his arms.

"What are you doing?" the healer cries as he heads for the door, the girl cradled against his chest.

His eyes are bright with unshed tears, but a new purpose has entered his expression. "If you can't help, I'll take her to someone who can."

The healer stares after him, perplexed, as he strides from the room.

Now I'm in Ash's head, *becoming* him in that strange way you can slip into someone else's skin in dreams. Grief and fury wage a terrible war within him/me. My love is clasped in my arms, and I clutch her warmth to me as if it's the only thing keeping me alive. She feels so light, almost insubstantial already. She's drifting away from me, and I can't bear to look down into that beloved face. Instead, I bury my face in her hair, choking back a sob. I will save her. I *will*. There is a mighty healer among the ghosts of my father's unholy blade. I just have to persuade him to use his power for good for once.

I'm thrown out of Ash's thoughts, and now I'm in another place. With a jolt of surprise, I realise I recognise it. It's Celebrach's study, booklined and shadowy, lit only by the fire drowsing in the hearth and a small faelight that hovers above his desk. The man himself is seated there, writing a letter, and the scratching of the quill across the paper is the only sound in the room.

The door is flung open, shouldered aside by Ash as he enters bearing the girl. She looks even worse than she did before. Her skin has taken on a greyish hue, and the night dress she wears clings to her form, sodden with sweat. There's a wet patch on Ash's shoulder where her head rests.

Celebrach puts the quill back in its stand and picks up his letter, blowing on it to dry the ink. He doesn't seem surprised at this unceremonious interruption. In fact, he doesn't show any emotion at all, merely laying the letter to one side and clasping his hands in front of him on top of the desk.

Ash staggers toward him, and for a minute I think he's going to dump the girl on the desk, but he falls into one of the armchairs in front of it instead, the girl cradled in his lap. His limbs are trembling, though whether from the effort of carrying her or the storm of emotions that rages within him, I can no longer tell. I'm only an observer of this scene, once again watching from outside.

"Help me, Father," Ash says.

Celebrach is his father? Shocked, I look more closely at Celebrach's impassive face. Their eyes are different. Celebrach's are a piercing blue, unlike Ash's cold grey ones. But now that I'm looking for it, there is a resemblance in the shape of their faces and the straight line of their noses. Celebrach's hair is darker than Ash's mid-brown, but they share the same full lips.

"Who is this?" He gazes at the girl without interest.

"Her name is Hattah. She sickened a few days ago. The healers can do nothing. But I know you can save her."

Celebrach leans back in his chair, regarding Ash with impatience. "Her name means nothing. What is she to you that you care so much about her fate?"

Ash lifts his chin as if in defiance. "She is my intended."

"Your intended? Did you think to discuss your plans with your father before you made promises to some girl?"

"She's not *some girl*. I love her, and my life isn't yours to dictate."

"Oh, you love her?" His voice drips with scorn. "What does love have to do with anything? You are my son, destined for a great place among the Vipers. I should never have let your mother have the raising of you. It's made you weak."

"Father, she doesn't have much time." He looks up, his Adam's apple bobbing as he swallows hard. I can tell the next words don't come easily. "Please, will you help her?"

Celebrach reaches behind him for the twisted dagger that always sits on its stand there. Leaning back in his chair, he holds the blade in one hand, tapping it against his other palm while he considers Ash's request.

Finally, he says, "No."

"No?" Ash practically snarls the word at the other man. "*Look* at her, Father. She's dying—and I know you can save her. How can you be so heartless?"

That surprises a laugh out of Celebrach. "Heartlessness is what I *do*, Ashovar. Why should I save this nobody when her life is standing between me and what I want?"

"What do you mean, what you want? She's done nothing to you. She's an innocent!"

Idly, Celebrach spears the letter he'd been writing on the point of his dagger. "Yes, an innocent who will distract you from your true calling. An innocent who will tie you to some mundane life, when your place is here, at my side."

"I'll never be a Viper." There is a world of loathing in Ash's tone. I search his face, surprised, but find nothing but truth there. For the first time, I notice that he's not wearing assassins' black. He looks a different person in a sky-blue shirt and brown pants. Fresher. More wholesome.

"Are you sure about that? Never is a long time."

It seems an odd thing for a fae to say. They are the specialists in eternity, used to thinking about time in centuries.

The girl chooses that moment to moan again, a sound of such pain I flinch. Whatever is wrong with her, she's clearly in agony.

Ash strokes her face, then looks up, a new determination in his eyes. "I'll do anything. I'm begging you, Father. Name your price."

Celebrach sits up straight, his eyes gleaming with interest. I almost expect him to rub his hands like an old-timey villain. "You know what my price is. You must join the Vipers."

"She will never marry a Viper." Ash has the look of a man who knows he is cornered, a look of hollow defeat.

"Then that's the decision you'll have to make. Give her up and let her live without you, or keep her and watch her die." Celebrach shrugs, as if he doesn't much care which option Ash chooses. "You'd better not take too long deciding. She looks as though she won't last much longer."

The girl is making a funny whistling sound now as she breathes, her chest rising and falling in shallow, desperate breaths.

Ash looks up with despair in his eyes. "You leave me no choice."

"Nonsense," Celebrach says briskly. "You have a choice; you just don't like the options." He locks gazes with his son for a moment. "I take it you will be joining the Vipers?"

"Yes." There are storms in those grey eyes. I've seen that look before, and I'm glad that, for once, I'm not the target of that glare.

But Celebrach seems unconcerned. "Excellent." He stands up and walks around the desk, the twisted dagger in his hand. "Hold out her arm."

22

---

week passed, during which Ash drove me harder than ever at training each night, so that I went to bed every morning a mass of bruises and aching muscles. I worked hard, remembering what he'd said about wolves and lambs.

In that whole week, he never once cracked a smile. It was hard to reconcile the cold reality with the man I'd seen in my dream. That man had known overpowering love and great grief. Perhaps also great happiness, though I never found out, since I had woken up before the dream ended.

I was kind of embarrassed by my subconscious self, to be honest. From where had I conjured that man full of feeling and empathy? Certainly not from anything I'd seen in the waking world. Oh, sure, he'd covered me with a blanket once, and I guess he'd saved me from Evandir, but I wasn't sure if that was even about me. It would probably hurt his professional pride to have someone take out his new apprentice so early in the piece. It reflected badly on him, I supposed. People would think that if he'd trained me better, I wouldn't have needed rescuing.

Had I suddenly developed psychic powers, to be having such oddly specific dreams about Ash? That would be a joke, wouldn't it—to long for power all my life, then when I finally developed some, have it turn out to be the ability to have completely random dreams about people's pasts.

Not that there was anything to suggest there was any truth to the dream at all. Trying to blame it on non-existent magic was just an attempt to make myself feel better about my soppy subconscious.

Well, my dream self might be prepared to imagine that Ash had a softer side, but my conscious mind knew what a hard bastard he was, blankets or no blankets.

Nothing was said about that night in the forest, not by Ash—he'd shut me down when I tried to ask him about it —and not by Nuah, who'd disappeared for a couple of days and then reappeared acting as if nothing had happened. I might have thought I had dreamed all that, too, except for the glimpse I caught of the bandages on her shoulder and the fact that her training regime changed to something slightly less punishing. Evandir was much the same as ever. He had already disliked me, so it was hard to see any difference in his sneers and insults, though I took care never to be alone with him.

Not that I really had to worry about that. Ash stuck to my side like glue, playing the sheepdog in spite of his words. When we weren't training, he was quizzing me on the books I had studied, making me draw endless pictures of plants and memorising their uses.

"Are you sure I'm studying to become an assassin and not a botanist?" I'd grumbled to him once.

He had merely waved at me impatiently to continue.

"Half of them look the same to me anyway," I said. "Look at this one: ethenerell. It looks just like starbright, which is nothing special. It grew next to the creek where I used to play as a kid. How am I supposed to tell them apart?"

"If you read the whole entry, you will discover that starbright is one of ethenerell's common names," he said reprovingly. "And also that Spring is the only Realm in which it grows, and even there it is rare. The juice of its pod, if mixed into food or drink, can induce a death-like sleep."

"Sounds handy." Oddly specific, too. Did he mean it did nothing on its own, but only when it was mixed with food or drink? How did anyone ever figure that out? I studied the drawing of the familiar tiny flower with renewed interest.

"Occasionally. It's more of an oddity, since the death sleep only lasts a few minutes. There aren't many practical applications."

"I've never heard starbright had any uses at all. Does Spring know about this?"

He shrugged. "If they do, they certainly aren't spreading the information around."

If it wasn't long lists of plants, he had me memorising histories of the Vipers, complete with names and dates.

And believe me, when people live as long as the fae do, that was a shitload of dates. Even when my head was buried in those books, he was usually somewhere close by, reading or just staring gloomily into the fire. No doubt he was regretting his charitable impulse to take me on, now, and thinking that seven years with his apprentice felt like a hell of a long time.

That was bothering me, too. If only he wasn't underfoot all the time, I could have tested to see whether the gate would let me out now. If I could make it to Willow's sith, it wouldn't matter that Ash knew where I was, he wouldn't be able to follow me there. I was fretting more about my friends with each passing day. Willow would be beside herself, and Raven would be thinking this was all his fault for letting me get involved. They probably thought I was dead. Anxiety tightened my throat and burrowed into my chest every time I thought of home. I wasn't normally a patient person, and this waiting was killing me.

One night, after we finished our training bout, Ash took me into the forest again. This time, he led me away to the west, along a track I hadn't seen on my previous visit.

"Where are we going?" I asked his back as he strode ahead of me. A small faelight bobbed in front of him, lighting his way, but his bulk blocked most of it, leaving me to stumble in the dark behind him. Resentfully, I sent up my own faelight, glaring at the back of his head.

"To the pits."

Well, that was no answer at all. The pits? This whole place was the pits. His habit of technically answering a question without actually giving the information requested was really beginning to get on my nerves. I'd never met anyone who kept his cards as close to his chest as this guy.

How was I supposed to learn anything if he treated information like precious drops of blood, never to be spent except in the most serious of causes? I was his apprentice; he was supposed to be bloody teaching me.

"You know, it probably wouldn't kill you to explain things a little more thoroughly now and then." Resentment seeped into my voice.

"I presume it's the human blood in you that makes you so impatient," he said in a dismissive tone.

"No, I just hate being kept in the dark."

"Then you've chosen the wrong profession. A Viper obeys orders without question." He glanced over his shoulder, his frown clear even in the dim glow of my faelight. I was so exhausted from the constant training I didn't have the strength to make a brighter one. "And without needing to know the reasons behind the orders."

"So you think you're doing me a favour, then, getting me used to the Viper way. You know, even if you hadn't told me, I would have guessed that you've never trained an apprentice before."

"Really." His tone discouraged going any further down this path, but what did I have to lose? I wasn't *actually* going to be his apprentice for the next seven years.

"Yes, really. People tend to do better when they feel like they're part of a team. People *learn* better when the why's are explained, not just the what's."

"And you speak from your vast experience of training Vipers, do you?" He held a protruding branch aside for me, then looked back questioningly when I didn't move.

I faced him, hands on hips. "I have just as much experience at it as you do—which is exactly none. What I *do* have is an understanding of people. That, and the fact that I actually care about anyone other than myself."

"You think that I'm selfish? That I don't care for anyone but myself?" His eyes were black in the fitful light of my flickering faelight, but for a minute, I thought there was something soft in them, despite his harsh tone. Something vulnerable that recalled that dream Ash. "Then you should watch and learn, apprentice. Vipers cannot afford the so-called *finer* feelings. Other people will only twist them and use them against you."

I had the feeling we were no longer talking about his lack of communication, but I was still mad. "So I should stalk through life like a robot with no feelings at all, like you?"

He stared at me so long I started to feel uncomfortable, but I'd be damned if I'd look away first.

"It would hurt less that way," he said at last, then spun on his heel and continued along the path.

Chewing my lip, I followed, feeling unaccountably guilty. He'd saved my life—twice, now—and I'd accused him of being selfish. *He's an assassin*, I reminded myself sternly as we emerged from the trees into a large clearing. *Who cares if you hurt his bloody feelings?*

Three brick circles, about waist-high, filled the centre of the clearing. They could have been wells, except they were much too big. Beyond them, the grass sloped down to a stream, wider than the creek I'd crossed during my challenge but not wide enough to be called a river. At the edge of the water sat a small building, made of the same brick as the circles. Something about it struck me as odd, and it took me a moment to realise what it was—the building had no windows.

A head popped up above the nearest circle. Evandir. Closer up, the wall proved to encircle a wide pit, whose dirt floor was covered in snakes lying in tangled clumps.

I took an involuntary step back, so horrified by the number of serpent bodies down there that, for a moment, I didn't realise that Evandir had brought two of them with him, draped casually around his neck and arms. I shuddered as he drew a wooden ladder up behind him and dropped it on the grass.

"What are you doing here?" Ash asked, frowning.

I made sure to keep him between me and Evandir. Snakes *really* weren't my thing.

"It's feeding time," the other fae replied.

"Where are the servants? It's not your job to feed the vipers."

"I like to visit my babies sometimes. These two need milking, and Idon has had trouble catching them the last few days. Hasn't he, sweetheart? You've been playing hard to get." He stroked the head of one of the snakes. Its tongue flicked out to test the air, ignoring his cooing. The other snake was wound around his right arm like a particularly disturbing tattoo, its head at his wrist.

"Keep your distance," Ash said sharply as Evandir approached. "She has no immunity."

Evandir fake-lunged at me, laughing when Ash shoved him hard in the chest. The snake by Evandir's ear struck toward Ash, but he had already stepped back out of reach.

"Tut, tut," Evandir said. "You're disturbing the vipers."

"I'll disturb more than the vipers if you aren't careful."

"So chivalrous. See what high esteem your instructor holds you in already, girl? I hope you're expressing the appropriate amount of gratitude." He ground his hips at me suggestively.

"Everything is about sex with you," Ash growled, stalking off toward the windowless building.

I followed, keeping a wary distance from Evandir's snake-clad arms since he was heading that way, too. Inside, the building reminded me oddly of a science lab, with long benches along the walls and shelving above them full of glass tumblers. It was well-lit with bright yellow faelights and surprisingly warm.

Ash went to another room and returned with a large barrel. He attached a hose and began to fill it with water from the white porcelain sink, while Evandir took down a small glass jar and covered it with what looked like paper-thin fabric.

Then he thrust the jar at one of the snakes, who bit it. With his fingers behind its head, Evandir held it in place so that it couldn't withdraw its fangs from the jar's cover. "That's it, my darling," he said approvingly, putting the jar down on the bench to free his other hand. "Give us all your lovely venom."

"What kind of snakes are they?" I asked Ash, unable to look away from the creature, whose jaw was horribly distended. It looked like it was trying to swallow the jar whole. With his free hand, Evandir massaged the sides of the snake's head, coaxing more venom from its sacs.

"Night vipers," Ash said casually, fiddling with the hose as the water splashed into the barrel.

Okay, now I could look away. I stared at him in shock. The night the assassins attacked our sith, the Hawk had said the Night Viper assassins were named after a deadly snake, which supposedly didn't exist anymore. So much for that theory.

"I thought they were extinct?"

"It certainly suits us to let people think that. But they *have* disappeared from the wild. These ones in the sith are the only survivors."

Evandir continued baby-talking to the snake as its venom trickled down the inside of the jar. It was beyond creepy. He was acting as if he was cuddling a cute little kitten or puppy. I mean, the creature was pretty in a snaky sort of way, with vivid bands of green and yellow across its body, but I couldn't see the appeal. I couldn't imagine casually handling something that could kill me.

"And you breed them?" Not as pets, whatever Evandir's attachment; that much was obvious. This whole set-up, with the pits and this milking and storage area, suggested the snakes were serious business. "Exactly how deadly are they?"

"Death occurs within three to six minutes after a bite. There is no antidote."

Very handy if you were an assassin. No wonder there were boxes of syringes on the shelves. This place could easily deal more death than the weapons room. This would be good information to give to the king—if I ever managed to get out of here.

Evandir released the snake from the jar and resettled it around his neck. There was only a tiny amount of fluid in the bottom of the jar, perhaps a teaspoon's worth. It hardly seemed enough to cause such damage. But then, I'd been living in Australia for a few years. They had plenty of snakes and spiders that could kill you with one bite. Maybe it wasn't such a stretch of the imagination.

Evandir fussed around, taking a second jar and covering it with the same light covering as the first one, then coaxing the second snake into striking at it. I watched in a kind of horrified fascination, the only sound in the room the rushing of the water, which frothed halfway up the barrel, now.

Ash shut off the hose and took the first jar of venom from the bench. Evandir ignored him, focusing on the snake he was milking. With an eye dropper he took from a drawer, Ash sucked up some of the venom, then very carefully added a single drop to the water barrel.

"You know there's plenty of that already mixed in the next room," Evandir said, watching him stir the water with a gigantic wooden spoon.

"I prefer to make my own," Ash replied. "That way I can be sure of exactly how much is in it."

When it was stirred to his satisfaction, he ladled some

out, filling a large glass bottle. Then he poured some from the bottle into a glass, which he offered to me. "Drink."

"You're joking, right?" I stared at him, aghast, but he only pushed the glass toward me with an impatient sigh.

"Our Ashovar never jokes," Evandir said with a grin. "Always so serious, right, Ash?"

"Drink it," Ash said. "It won't kill you."

"But you just said—"

"I said a bite would kill, not a single drop diluted in this much water."

I eyed the glass with deep misgivings. "I get the feeling it's not exactly a health tonic, though."

He sighed again. "You may feel a little unwell, but it will be worth it in the long run. All apprentices drink some of this every day. We'll gradually increase the amount of venom in the water until you will be able to survive a bite."

Well, at least he was being more forthcoming with information—perhaps he'd actually listened to what I'd said earlier. But I still wasn't keen. "Why can't I just stay away from the snakes?"

"It's a Viper tradition," Ash said. "And an insurance policy, since all apprentices are expected to learn to handle the vipers."

"Besides," Evandir said, "you never know when there may be an accident."

The second snake withdrew its fangs from the covered jar as he spoke. Without warning, he threw it at me.

I shrieked, but Ash whipped out his knife. The snake was pinned to the floor at my feet, impaled through the head, before I could do more than stumble back. And Ash hadn't spilled even a drop of the water in the glass.

He and Evandir glared at each other for a long moment while I shuddered in reaction. If that snake had bitten me, I'd be dead. Shakily, I reached for the glass and downed it in one gulp.

"You play a dangerous game," Ash said finally, his voice low and menacing.

Evandir laughed and kissed the snake that was still wound around his neck like the world's most menacing scarf. For someone who acted so fond of the snakes, he didn't seem at all bothered by the dead viper on the floor. "Just trying to help. You were having trouble convincing your apprentice of the wisdom of the idea—and look, she's drunk it all up like a good girl. Though I doubt your father will be pleased about you offing the vipers. It's practically sacrilege."

Ash's father? Who was that, and what did he have to do with anything?

The memory of that dream confrontation between him and Celebrach nudged me for attention, but that was crazy. That had just been a dream. Celebrach couldn't really be his father.

"There are plenty more vipers," Ash growled. "You could have killed her."

"Nonsense. He'd just been milked—he probably didn't have any venom left."

Probably wasn't good enough for me, or Ash either, judging by the fury in his eyes.

"Why do you care?" Evandir added airily. "You didn't

want an apprentice anyway. Or have you changed your mind? Taken my advice about bedding her? I must admit, I'm looking forward to my own apprentice's return. The nights are so cold."

Ash stoppered the bottle of envenomed water with more force than was strictly necessary, then led me back outside into the night without another word, his back ramrod straight and his shoulders stiff with anger.

23

Ash marched me back to our cottage, where he sent me to my room with a gruff injunction to study my botany. The Vipers sure went in for a lot of study of poisonous plants and their uses. I hadn't thought it strange before, but now I wondered why they bothered if they had the venom of the fabled night vipers to use. Maybe that was only for special occasions. Was it an honour to be killed with snake venom rather than by a plain old knife or iron poisoning? Or were they afraid that people would realise that the vipers weren't extinct after all if they used their venom too frequently?

Dawn was breaking when I looked up from my work. In a couple more hours, it would be time for dinner. I stretched, rubbing my stiff neck and feeling the shriek of abused muscles everywhere in my body. The cottage was quiet.

Was Ash still in the lounge room? I hadn't heard any

movement from him in hours. I got up and ghosted down the hallway, avoiding that one board that always creaked when I stepped on it.

I stopped in the doorway to the lounge room. Ash was asleep in a chair by the fire, his head lolling against the back of the chair. An empty glass was tipped on its side on the carpet by his dangling hand. I stared at the strong line of his throat, now so exposed and vulnerable. His lashes lay long against his cheeks, and his face had a softness to it in sleep that reminded me of that dream Ash, tugging unexpectedly at my heart.

What a crock of shit. Dream Ash was a figment of my imagination.

Instead of mooning over how soft and sweet the sleeping assassin looked, I should be taking this rare lapse in his watchfulness as the opportunity it was. I tiptoed down the hall and eased the front door open with agonising slowness, mindful of how easily the slightest sound could wake him. He was a man who lived life like a coiled spring, ready to explode into movement at any moment.

I left the door ajar, unable to face losing my chance because of a closing creak. Moving slowly, acutely aware of how I placed every step, I eased away from the cottage like a shadow on the wind. Once I judged I was far enough away, I stepped up the pace, eager to reach my objective, though I couldn't help glancing behind every so often to check that he wasn't on my tail. I had learned great respect for the uncanny sneakiness of my reluctant instructor.

It was all so easy. The early morning sun shone down on me, giving the sith a golden glow that lifted my spirits. I arrived at the gate within a few minutes, not having seen anyone on the way. My body was taut with excitement, my heart beating a rapid tattoo against my ribcage. I reached out and took the massive handle of the gate in a firm grip.

And then ... nothing. It refused to move, no matter how much I strained and tugged at it.

I was still trapped.

A rush of panic weakened me, and I sagged against the gate. Denial roared for release, my heart pounding as if I'd run all the way here. I'd been so sure that *this* time it would open for me.

Now what? Was I truly trapped here for the whole seven years of my apprenticeship? I couldn't do it. I couldn't possibly keep up the façade that long.

I would die here, surrounded by my enemies, and Willow would never find out what had happened to me. My eyes burned with tears as I leaned my head against the cold wood. *No.*

I'd never felt so alone, not even the night my father had left me to live with strangers. At least then I'd had Willow.

I didn't know how long I stood there. It was a wonder no one saw me. Perhaps they were all gathering in the dining hall. At last, I straightened up and tried the handle one more time, just in case. It didn't open, of course, and I took a deep breath.

Well, onward and upward, then. What else could I do? Surely they wouldn't keep me inside the sith for the whole seven years? One day, my chance would come, and when it did, I'd seize it with both hands. In the meantime, I'd learn everything I could, both about being an assassin and about the organisation itself: their people, their procedures, their future plans. Everything.

When I finally got back to report on what I'd learned, we'd have everything we needed to take them down.

Ash was awake when I returned. If he'd moved from his seat by the fire, it could only have been to refill his glass. The curtains were drawn, shutting out the beautiful morning outside, the room's only illumination the red flames dancing in the hearth.

He didn't look at me as I flopped into the chair beside him and sneaked a sideways glance at his dour expression. Seven years with this guy? No way.

"You know, for a Winter fae, you spend a lot of time in front of the fire. I thought you people didn't feel the cold."

"It relaxes me," he said. "Watching the flames is a kind of meditation."

Interesting. I'd never expected him to admit anything so human, or that sounded even remotely like a weakness. "Playing the guitar does that for me," I said. "I just kind of zone out and stop thinking about anything else."

"Sometimes the cessation of thought is a relief," he agreed. I just bet it was, in a job like this—although that implied he must feel some twinge of conscience over what he did for a living. "I used to play the guitar myself."

"Really?" I glanced at the long, elegant fingers curled loosely around his glass. I'd always thought they looked like the hands of a musician. An unexpected feeling of kinship woke in me. "Why did you stop?"

He shrugged, and a silence fell between us. He watched the fire, and I surreptitiously watched him, wondering what kind of man he really was under the harsh exterior he presented to the world.

"Are you done?" he asked eventually.

"Done with what?"

"Trying to leave the sith. I know where you went."

I stared at him, my heartbeat kicking up a notch. Damn. That stupid link between us. He'd said he could sense where I was at all times, but he'd been *asleep*, for God's sake. At least, I'd thought so.

Well, no point denying it. "When will I be able to open the gate of the sith?"

"For someone who seemed so eager to join the Vipers, you're very keen to leave our hospitality."

"I feel like a prisoner."

"And so you are. I know you didn't come here to become an assassin—"

"Of course I—"

"Don't bother protesting. I know you're lying, and I don't care. It doesn't matter." He shifted in his chair, that grey gaze boring into me. I felt stripped naked, as if he could read all my secrets. "It doesn't matter why you came. The point is, you're here now, and you still don't seem to grasp how very *permanent* your situation is. Being a Viper is not a job you can resign from, Sage."

I didn't know what to say. Such plain speaking was so unlike him. It felt dangerous, though he seemed happy enough to keep my secrets. For now, at least. How long could I count on his discretion?

Was he really as all-seeing as he sounded, or was he making some educated guesses? I tried to talk myself down from the edge of panic.

"I can understand you wanting to leave," he added.

I glanced at him, startled, but he was still staring into the flames, their light reflected in his eyes. As usual, his face gave nothing of what he was thinking away.

"Evandir seems determined to end your stay here prematurely."

That almost sounded as if he cared what happened to me. I studied that handsome, distant face more closely. All this must be the alcohol talking, surely. How much had he had to drink? Maybe I could get some more answers out of him.

"The gate?" I prompted.

"Forget the gate. It's not important. You should be worrying about your safety. I can't be with you every moment."

He'd been doing a pretty good job so far. The constant surveillance was maddening. "You seriously think Evandir would kill me?" I asked. "Isn't that, like, against the Viper code or something?"

He let his head fall back against the chair with a sigh. "There you go with that fairness rubbish again."

"But you said Vipers had to be loyal!"

"To the Lord Serpent and the interests of the Vipers as a whole, not necessarily to each other. This Nest is full of ambitious people who are highly skilled in making death look accidental, and for some reason, Evandir has taken against you."

"What does he gain from killing me? I'm just an apprentice. I'm no threat to him."

"Evandir sees everyone as a threat to him. It's no secret that he aspires to be Lord Serpent one day. He craves the power of Ni'ishasana."

"What's Ni'ishasana?" Was it some strange fae magic I'd never heard of before?

"The Thief of Souls. The dagger Lord Celebrach uses to bind us all together."

"I thought you said it only bound Adepts and their apprentices. You said you always knew where I was, but no one else would."

"It binds Adepts to their apprentices and links all of the Vipers to the Lord Serpent. It turns servants into walking shells of people with no life, no soul." He sounded almost bitter. He must resent the fact that someone had such power over him.

And no wonder all the servants were so eerily quiet. They were bloody zombies.

"That's awful. Why would anyone want that?"

He snorted. "You have a lot to learn about people if you need to ask. Some men can only feel big by making others small. But that's not all the dagger bestows on its wielder. It grants such a range of powers that its wielder is virtually invincible. Evandir longs for that kind of power."

Well, didn't we all? Finally, something I had in common with that piece of garbage.

Ash brushed his hair from his face in an impatient movement. "But you're right; I doubt he sees you as a threat. He probably attacks you merely to annoy me. He hates me. Thinks my father favours me above the others, and he's afraid that means I'll be the next wielder of Ni'ishasana."

"Your father?"

"Lord Celebrach," he said wearily, and my pulse jumped.

I'd dreamed that Celebrach was Ash's father. Had I heard it somewhere before and not consciously registered it? Evandir had mentioned Ash's father earlier, when Ash had killed the viper, but he hadn't specified who it was, and I couldn't recall anyone else talking about it. How had I known? Had it really been only a dream? But what kind of magic could send me true dreams? I could still recall every detail, instead of it all fading into smoke the way dreams usually did, but I'd never heard of magic that could do that.

I stretched my legs out towards the fire, feeling the warmth on the soles of my feet. Ash had always been so closemouthed. If he was in a talking mood, I'd take advantage of it. "Why do you care if Evandir kills me anyway? You didn't want an apprentice."

He gave me a glance laden with impatience mixed with alcohol. "Do you think I didn't have the stomach to kill you myself and I'm just hoping someone else does it for me? Such a good opinion you must have of me."

An awkward silence fell, since that *was* pretty much what I had been thinking. "No, of course not," I said finally.

"But you don't like having me here. Why did you take me on?"

He shrugged. "You're an innocent."

"Isn't everyone you kill?" Thinking of Nevith, my voice came out a little accusatory. I had strong feelings about this. "What's different about me?"

"Innocent?" He snorted. "No. Most of them are players in the intrigues of the Lords. Politics is a dangerous game, and people play at their own risk."

"*Most* of them, you say. But not all. That sounds like an excuse to salve your conscience."

He barked a short, bitter laugh. "You think I still have a conscience? That's a luxury I had to dispense with."

"You're full of shit," I said, taking a chance. "You've got a conscience. You've saved me from Evandir twice."

His eyes looked different, more human—which seemed an odd thing to think of a fae. But normally, he kept his feelings under such tight control that it was like he had no personality at all. Like he was just a killing machine, a robot that Lord Celebrach could wind up and send out to kill. Now, there was pain in his eyes, flickering along with the reflection of the dancing flames. "You don't want to rely on me to save you. I tried to save someone once before, and it didn't end well."

"Who?" In my memory, the girl from my dream sagged in his arms again. Was it her? If that was a true dream ... I hated not knowing. Hated having to wonder if someone's magic had invaded my dreams. Better to imagine he was talking about someone else. My heart beat a little faster as I waited for his reply.

"No one. A friend. You remind me a little of her."

A friend. That girl had seemed like more than a friend. I relaxed a little. Was this friend, whoever it was, the reason he'd wrestled with the decision of whether to kill me or take me as an apprentice? Because I reminded him of someone he'd lost? He hadn't wanted an apprentice—he'd even vowed never to take one, apparently, and yet here I was. I should buy that friend of his a beer.

Something about his expression, however, suggested that she was no longer around to drink it. What did *it didn't end well* mean, exactly? I felt uneasy all over again. Whatever it was, he clearly blamed himself. Maybe he thought that saving me would make up for his previous failure—though, judging by the look on his face, he wouldn't be forgiving himself any time soon.

"What was her name?" I almost didn't want to know.

"Hattah."

I swallowed hard. So it was true—some strange magic had been invading my dreams. Hattah had been the dream girl's name, the one he'd begged his father to save. And his father was Celebrach. Bloody hell.

This was too much to be a coincidence. No one had ever mentioned any Hattah to me before. I was certain of that. And I was no seer, to dream true dreams. So whose magic was at work here? Or was it something to do with the bond that the twisted blade had forged between us? At least *that* would be better than thinking someone was purposely sending me dreams—though things had to be pretty bad when an evil magical dagger seemed like the best option.

That dream had ended on such a hopeful note, with Celebrach about to save her, I'd thought—but where was she? "What happened to her?"

He drained his glass, and I thought he wasn't going to answer me. But then his eyes met mine, a kind of reckless challenge in them. "I killed her."

24

---

was still thinking about that conversation three days later. Ash had reverted to his usual silent self, though sometimes I caught him watching me with an intensity that unnerved me. There'd been no more revelations about Viper politics, though that one chat had given me plenty to think about.

Probably because I was thinking about it so much, I'd dreamed of the dagger every night. They were dreams of longing, dreams of violence and blood. I killed Celebrach in every imaginable way in those dreams just to get my hands on Ni'ishasana, its name like a half-remembered snatch of music that teased at the edge of my consciousness. That rippling blade was a thing of beauty and terrible power, something to be desired and fought for with all my might.

Sometimes when I woke up, I felt physically ill at the memories of what my dream self had done to get her hands on that dagger. Surely this was more dream magic?

Where had this obsession with the dagger come from otherwise? Awake, the oily sheen of its blade repelled me, but in my dreams, it was a different story. I'd done some messed-up shit in my time, but this just wasn't me.

Why couldn't I dream about having to sit an exam naked like a normal person? Or flying. Growing up, I'd had lots of dreams where I'd soared above the world. Wings like Raven's or the Hawk's were literally the stuff of dreams to me. I'd always wanted to be a winged fae. The fact that I wasn't had been almost as disappointing to ten-year-old me as my lack of magic.

It got to the point where I was afraid to go to sleep, but the workouts I was getting on the training grounds every night meant I could barely keep my eyes open once my head hit that pillow, whatever my fears. Plus, Ash had begun memory training, where he would give me a detailed picture to study for a minute, then take it away and have me describe everything in it to him.

Sometimes, he varied it by taking me to a room in the main building, letting me study the layout for a moment, then having me draw the room to scale, with the size and placement of everything in it noted. These exercises were even more tiring than the physical activity, as I tied my brain up in knots trying to remember every-thing. So I had no chance of staying awake, even though I wanted to.

One day, Ash sent me with a message to Lord Celebrach.

"While you're there, I want you to practise your memory skills on his office. When you get back, I'll expect a full report, including every detail of Lord Celebrach's attire and everything on his desk."

He never called his father anything but *Lord Celebrach*. Such an excess of politeness might have just been because he loathed the man, but perhaps it was also an attempt to minimise the other assassins' feelings that he was being favoured by the Lord Serpent. Not that they were likely to forget his parentage, but there was no need to throw it in their faces every day.

"You won't know if I'm right," I objected. "I could say anything."

"You like arguing, don't you?"

"I don't! I'm just saying ..." I trailed off under his *I told you so* stare, realising I'd just argued again.

"While a quick mind is an asset to a Viper, too much independence is not," he said reprovingly. "You need to learn not to question everything. Focus on your task. Trust me to know if you get it wrong."

Fine. I headed off through the moonlit woods towards the main building. Even this much freedom was a rare thing—I was kind of surprised he was letting me wander around on my own, given his fears about Evandir. Maybe Evandir was out on a job. Ash knew those kinds of things but never shared them with me.

I made the most of my excursion, counting the number of trees, memorising their placements along the path. When I finally got out of here, I would be able to draw the most accurate maps imaginable of the sith, making it easy for the king's forces to bring down the Vipers. Ash was fond of saying that the brain was a muscle that needed training, just like other muscles. He should be thrilled that I'd be putting his training to such good use.

I passed only a silent servant as I strode through the quiet corridors of the main building. Now that I knew the truth about the servants, a shudder of horror rippled down my spine every time I saw one. No memories, no self, no *soul*. This was even worse than straight-out killing people, and even more reason to wipe the Vipers from the face of the earth.

And all because of that horrible dagger. I knocked on Celebrach's door, but there was no answer. He wouldn't take well to being disturbed if he was deep in the middle of something.

Well, he should have answered, then. I straightened my shoulders, determined not to be cowed by the man. Whatever his powers, knocking on his door was hardly a crime. But I still breathed a sigh of relief when I opened the door to discover the room was empty. I could leave my note and go.

Except I had to memorise the stupid room, didn't I? Sighing, I laid the note on his desk where he couldn't fail to find it when he returned, then swept my gaze slowly across the desk. Blotter, inkstand, quill. Two pencils and a notepad. Nine books, piled on top of each other in a haphazard tower. The one on the bottom was the smallest, adding to the instability of the tower.

Would Ash expect me to memorise the titles of each one? The top one was dark blue, leather-bound, and didn't have a title or any markings on the outside. I flipped it open and found a ledger of some kind, with names and amounts of money recorded in a neat hand.

I slammed it shut again when I realised it was a record of hits ordered and paid for, of clients and targets. Shuddering, I turned my attention to the other things on the desk. A jar full of pebbles—what was that all about?—and a pile of papers nearly half the height of the book tower.

Tempted to read them, my gaze skittered across the one on top. It was a letter in an ornate flowing hand that was difficult to read. But there was nothing exciting about the letter—it seemed to be full of gossip about people I didn't know.

Maybe this was some kind of Viper code, and that was something else I'd have to learn, but I decided not to risk rifling through the rest of the stack. I really shouldn't linger here—who knew when Celebrach would return? I might be able to explain that Ash had instructed me to memorise his room, but not if I was found reading his mail. Ash would have a cow if he thought that was what I was doing.

I finished with the desk and looked up. Immediately, my gaze was snagged by the dagger on its stand. Why hadn't I noticed that as soon as I walked in? It was pretty hard to miss in pride of place on its shelf.

I swallowed as my violent dreams returned to me in a rush. Me holding the dagger. Wielding it. Driving it through Celebrach's ribs into the vulnerable heart beneath. And then the rush of power filling me, like a million orgasms all at once, only better.

I breathed out shakily, the sound loud in the still room.

How had I ever thought the dagger ugly? It really was a beautiful weapon, its blade gleaming in silver ripples, like water disturbed by the wind. Without thought or hesitation, I reached for it.

And the world goes black, shadow filling my vision. Coldness floods me, spreading from my fingers up my arm and into my chest. I can feel it racing through my veins, spreading its tendrils through my body. Suddenly, I'm on fire.

Ash is here, supporting the dying girl. Hattah. Celebrach rounds the desk, the dagger in his hand.

"Hold out her arm," he says.

Ash curves his body protectively over hers. Suspicion and loathing war in his gaze as he stares at the warped blade. "Why?"

"I will need her blood for this."

The tension drains from Ash's body. I can read his thoughts in his eyes. She will be saved, and his world along with her. His relief is overwhelming, though sadness lurks there, too. He knows she won't have him once he joins the Vipers. Her world is one of light and love, a simple world of family and music and small, everyday things. Someone else will take his place eventually, will win her kisses and her heart. But at least she will live.

If that's all he can do for her, it will be enough. His love is a pure thing, bigger than his desires. He can't have her, but that's not as important to him as knowing that, somewhere in the world, she will go on living her life because of his sacrifice.

Celebrach pauses. "Actually, perhaps we should take care of you first. Wouldn't want you to change your mind."

Ash looks up, his expression hardening. "She doesn't have much time left."

"Then you'd better not waste any of it. Give me your hand."

Ash takes a deep breath, then offers his hand to his father, who takes it in a smooth handshake position before flipping it over, exposing the vulnerable underside of his wrist. He draws the dagger over it, slicing through the veins. Ash watches, his mouth set in a grim line, as blood drips to the carpet and a blue light flares around the dagger.

Suddenly, there is no more blood, as if the dagger has drunk it all down. With typical dream certainty, I know this is true, even though the dagger is not alive.

Ash takes a sudden shocked breath. "What is that?"

"What is what?"

"Something ... in my head. A voice?" His own is filled with horror.

Shadows swirl in the corners of the room, forming vaguely humanoid shapes then disappearing like smoke again. I don't think Ash sees them—his eyes are on his father's face, outrage and impotent fury in his expression.

"Come now, Ashovar. You know enough about the Vipers to know the answer to that already."

"That's the bond?" He looks at the dagger with loathing. "That's Ni'ishasana? I didn't expect it to feel so *obvious*."

His father's face is smug as he smiles. I want to punch

it, but I'm insubstantial as mist, as the shadows that still boil behind the desk, forming bodies and faces before disintegrating and reforming. "The sensation will fade. You'll barely notice it's there unless it's activated."

"Unless you have orders for me," Ash says. Unmistakeable loathing fills his voice.

"That's right," Celebrach says, though the smugness is gone, and he looks irritated instead. Though why he should, when he's got what he so clearly wanted, is beyond me.

"Time to honour your side of the bargain," Ash says, looking down at the woman in his arms.

Ash gently takes Hattah's wrist and extends her arm out straight, his eyes never leaving her face—so he's not looking when Celebrach slams the dagger into her heart.

Ash cries out in horror, raw agony in his voice, and tries to pull the dagger out. But his father hasn't let go, and Celebrach is strong. Hampered by the girl's body in his arms, Ash is easily overpowered.

"*What have you done?*"

"Relax. This is the only way."

"But I thought you would *heal* her! This is ... this is—" Again, he struggles to remove the dagger, his face white with shock. "I don't want her to be a *slave*."

"But what else did you expect? Ni'ishasana's power is great, but it can't work miracles. She's too far gone for anything else."

Blue light floods the room, centred on the dagger. I squint against the glare. The girl has stopped breathing, her chest still. She is clearly dead.

The blue light flares, then fades away. When I can see again, the girl's eyes are open. She stares up at Celebrach with a blank expression, not seeming to notice Ash at all. He is outright crying, now, his cheeks streaked with the silver tracks of tears.

Celebrach motions to her, and she sits up, untangling herself from Ash's arms. "You said you wanted her alive," he says to his son, gesturing at the girl as if to show off his handiwork.

"Not like *this*. Bring her back!"

"You know I can't."

The girl stands up, silent, and steps away, unmoved by Ash's tears. Her nightgown is slashed where the knife entered her breast, but there isn't a single drop of blood.

"You did this on purpose." Ash stands, too, and in one violent movement draws his own dagger and launches himself at his father.

Celebrach gestures with a casual flip of his hand, and Ash flies across the room to crash against a bookcase. There is unmistakeable pleasure on the Lord Serpent's face as he watches his son stagger to his feet.

"You're mine, now, Ashovar. Mine to command. Come here."

Ash crosses the room, his steps as jerky as if he were a marionette. His expression shows furious concentration, as if he's fighting every movement, but he still ends up standing once more in front of his father. His knife hangs uselessly at his side. There is fear in his eyes, mixed with the fury and grief. What else can his father force him to do?

"You will never attempt to harm me again, is that understood?"

He nods, unwillingness in the jerky movement of his head. His eyes blaze with fury, and Celebrach turns away, his defenceless back showing more than words could how little he now has to fear from his son.

Ash's eyes stray to the girl, still standing there, mindlessly waiting for her next order. Waiting for her life of slavery to begin. I suddenly understand that this is how the zombie servants are created. This is how Ni'ishasana, Thief of Souls, drains them of their essence, leaving an empty shell behind.

I realise what he's going to do almost before he does. It seems inevitable, given how much he loves her. Loved her. Because she's gone, that beautiful carefree girl, and it would have been kinder to let her die than leave her like this, a mindless servant.

The knife rises again behind Celebrach's back, but the Lord is no longer his target.

Tears running down his face, Ash buries his non-magical dagger in the girl's breast, catching her falling body in his arms, heedless of the blood. And this time, there are *oceans* of blood.

"What do you think you're doing?" a voice demanded roughly, back in the here and now, and suddenly, I was back in my own body, dizzy and disoriented.

I was still in Celebrach's study, and I snatched my hand away from the dagger and turned to confront the speaker, hiding my hands behind my back as if I'd come to steal it. Lord Celebrach himself faced me, his frown of displeasure leaving me in no doubt of his opinion of apprentices who wandered around fondling daggers that didn't belong to them.

"My lord, I'm sorry." Ash and the dying girl were gone, as if they'd never existed. Great. So now I had true dreams while I was sleeping *and* visions when I was awake. Visions that felt so real that I *knew* they had once been right here in this room, and everything I'd just seen had really happened.

My heart was breaking for Ash's pain, and I had no doubt this time that I'd seen the truth. Darkness still crawled at the edges of my vision, which unsettled me. What kind of freaky magic was this that could send me visions when I was wide awake? Things were going to get damn awkward if I could lose myself like that without any warning. All I'd done was touch the stupid dagger. Had that been what triggered it?

I almost looked back at Ni'ishasana, but that seemed unwise with an angry fae right in front of me, so I stopped myself in time. "Ash sent me to deliver a message, my lord, and when you weren't here, I came in to leave it on your desk." I moved so he could see the message waiting there.

"And did he also tell you to treat the place as if it was your own and touch whatever you pleased?"

"He told me to ... to memorise your room. For a memory exercise." I was having trouble focusing on the reality around me, despite the warning signals that Celebrach's frown was giving off. My head was still lost in the vision.

Ash had told me that he'd killed the girl he'd tried to

save, but now that I'd seen the vision, I understood why he'd done so. It had been a mercy killing, not a murder.

And in that case, I had to completely rethink my initial impression of Ash. When he said he'd taken me as an apprentice because I was an innocent, he'd really meant it. He wasn't the man I'd thought he was at all. He hadn't wanted to be an assassin; he'd been trapped, like me. Maybe his years as an assassin had turned him into the cold man I knew. But then I thought of his face by firelight last night, and the things he'd told me, and I felt certain that that cold face was nothing but a façade.

Someone rapped on the door, and I jumped.

"Come," Celebrach said without taking his eyes off me.

The door opened, followed by a sudden indrawn breath. "What is *she* doing here?"

We both turned to look at the speaker. In the doorway stood Atinna, the girl Rowan had so infamously picked up in the bar—the assassin who'd tried to kill Allegra. She was staring at me in outrage.

25

———

"Atinna," Celebrach said. "You're back."

She had the blond hair and delicate appearance I remembered, but there was nothing delicate about the look she was giving me. There was death in that stare.

I drew in a shaky breath. I'd forgotten all about her. What a shitshow. In the corner of my vision, the shadows moved, advancing on me, and I shifted uneasily from one foot to the other. Why the hell was I seeing these things? I needed all my concentration here.

"Have you met your fellow apprentice?" Celebrach asked her.

Holy shit. *She* was Evandir's missing apprentice?

"Apprentice?" Atinna frowned in confusion. "But she's … she's the Spring heir's best friend. Why would you accept someone like her? She's here to spy on us."

They both stared at me, and I almost wished the stupid shadows would swallow me up. At least that way they'd be

253

doing something useful. The fury on Celebrach's face didn't bode well for my continued health.

"Are you sure?"

"Of course I'm sure." Atinna sounded miffed at being questioned. "I studied them all a few weeks ago, when you sent me to remove Allegra Brooks. Her name is Sage Domani."

Celebrach's head whipped around so fast it was a wonder he didn't give himself whiplash. "Fallon Domani's daughter?"

"Yes."

For once, I couldn't think of a single thing to say in my own defence. There was no point lying; Celebrach wouldn't take my word over Atinna's, and the facts were easy enough to check anyway. I swallowed hard. Here I was, without a weapon—and I still couldn't open the damn gate of this blasted sith. There was no escape this time.

Celebrach's eyes lost their focus for a moment, and I felt a tug somewhere inside me. Was he about to force me to kill myself, or worse? But my panic subsided when nothing else happened. "We will wait for Ashovar and Evandir," he said to Atinna.

That tug must have been the echo of his summons of Ash.

Impatiently, Celebrach gestured Atinna into the room and shut the door behind her. I backed up, hoping to snatch Ni'ishasana from its stand, but Celebrach's magic wrapped me in invisible chains before I could move my hand, and he force-marched me around the desk to stand by the bookshelves. He seated himself behind the desk and folded his hands on top of it, and then we waited.

The room was so silent I could hear Atinna breathing. She eyed me with naked hostility, her arms folded across her chest, as the seconds ticked by. It felt like eternity, but it was probably only five minutes before there was a sharp rap on the door and Ash entered, followed by Evandir.

His gaze landed on me first, a wariness in his eyes, before he turned to his father. "You summoned me, lord?"

"Yes." Celebrach sat back in his chair, apparently relaxed, though he watched Ash carefully as he spoke. "Apparently, your apprentice is the daughter of Fallon Domani, the necromancer, as well as best friend and confidante of the heir of Spring."

Ash's expression didn't change, though I caught a flicker of surprise on Evandir's face before he smoothed it away.

"Yes," Ash said calmly. "I'm aware."

"You told me her name was Sage Forester."

Celebrach was smiling, but icy rage was in his words. As they faced each other, I was struck by the family resemblance. Their profiles were almost identical. A shiver of déjà vu ran through my veins. I'd compared them in the dream, too, and reached the same conclusions: they had the same nose and face shape. It was unnerving to be playing it out again in real life.

"I'm sure you have an excellent reason for keeping this information to yourself."

"I do," Ash said.

I marvelled at his calm, but it helped me relax a little.

I'd been certain I was about to die when Atinna revealed my true identity, but Ash acted as if nothing was amiss. I was curious about his reason myself. Why had he tried to conceal the truth from Celebrach?

"I didn't think you would give her a chance if you knew who she really was," he said.

Evandir had moved to stand beside his apprentice, and a sneer curled his lip. He'd certainly never been interested in giving me a chance, though I couldn't understand what I'd done to piss him off so comprehensively.

Ash ignored him, holding Celebrach's gaze as he spoke. "But she has already proven herself a worthy candidate to become a Viper. It would be a shame if we lost such a capable apprentice because of some nervousness about her background."

"Nervousness? Are you mad?" Atinna burst out. "I've seen her with the new Lady of Illusion, with the Hawk himself. She has the king's ear."

"Atinna, be silent," Evandir said curtly, as if he were telling his dog to stop barking.

She jerked as if he'd poked her, and I wondered if he'd put some power into that command through their bond. She closed her mouth with a sullen bow of the head, and I was suddenly immensely grateful that it was Ash I had followed into the sith that night and not one of the other assassins.

He was still staring coolly at his father, as if my whole future—and perhaps his, too—wasn't at risk. If Celebrach didn't believe him ...

Why was Ash doing this? He'd said I reminded him of

Hattah—was this all some kind of cosmic payback? As if saving me would make up for not being able to save her? Obviously, his conscience was alive and kicking, whatever he claimed. But to risk everything for a stranger? He was crazy.

"But that's a good thing, Atinna," he continued. "Never before have we had someone placed so close to the king."

"Why, has someone ordered his assassination?" Evandir asked, with obvious interest. A chill lanced through me. Would they use me to get to Rothbold? "I thought those lily-livered Lords were all too frightened of the curse of the Brenfells."

Celebrach waved him to silence. "There are other advantages in such access to Whitehaven." He turned his gaze on his son, and it was still icy. "But that doesn't explain why you kept this piece of information from me. Such insubordination will have to be punished. Did you think me senile, that I couldn't see the advantages the Lady has dropped in our lap? Or do your thoughts wander in another direction entirely? The daughter of Fallon Domani—are you contemplating treason?"

"Of course not, my lord," Ash said mildly, ignoring his father's threatening tone. "But I know you are zealous in your protection of the Nest's security. I hoped to have Sage prove herself first, to set your mind at ease."

How long had he thought Atinna would stay away? With everything that had happened, I'd forgotten about her and the threat she represented. But he didn't have that excuse. Surely, he must have realised she would squeal like a pig the minute she saw me. Or didn't he know that she'd been sent to kill Allegra a few weeks ago and could identify me?

"Well, I won't be too hard on you, as it turns out I have
the perfect assignment for that." Celebrach smiled, and my
heart nearly stopped at the venom in that smile. Clearly,
whatever he was about to say was bad news for us. "We
have a new contract, and I believe Sage is acquainted with
the target. If she truly can be trusted"—and here he shot
me a look of such loathing I was convinced he wanted me
dead—"her past loyalties will not affect her performance."

"You're sending Sage on a mission already?" Now, Ash
looked unsettled. "But she's barely started her apprenticeship."

"You will be the mission leader, of course. But Sage
must make the hit. I will send Evandir and Atinna to
observe. They will know what to do if she proves herself
false."

I caught myself biting my lip and forced myself to stillness. A terrible dread weighed on my heart. Who was the
target? All I could think of was Willow. *Don't be ridiculous*, I
told myself. *Why would anyone want to take out Willow?* But
still my heart thundered in my chest. Maybe it was Allegra.
That would be just as bad. And the new Lady of Illusion
had certainly managed to make a few enemies.

"And the target?" Ash asked.

"Lord Nox of Night."

26

Raven's father. My initial relief at not hearing either of my friends' names quickly turned to horror. The meeting broke up, but I was barely paying attention. All I could think of was warning Raven. His father was a target—they had to do something to protect him. I had to get a message to him.

But how? I was trapped here in the sith.

Ash had been quiet as we walked back to our cottage after the meeting, refusing to answer any questions. When we entered the firelit living room, he went straight to the sideboard and poured himself a drink from one of the decanters there.

"You drink too much," I said, watching him swallow half the glass in one gulp.

"And you talk too much. I should silence you, the way Evandir silences his apprentice."

"I'm not buying this tough act anymore, so you may as

well give it up." He shot me a glare, but I forged on. "Why did you lie to your father to protect me? Why didn't you tell him my real name the night I came here? You knew who I was, and you deliberately gave him a false name."

"If I wanted to save your life, it seemed like the only option." He emptied the glass, but it didn't appear to help his mood. "Lord Celebrach is a careful man. The Vipers have flourished as long as they have because of his caution. Your real name would have been a death sentence."

"Because of my connection with Willow? With the king? But he seems pleased about that."

He threw me a withering look. "Because of your *father*, Sage."

I stared at him, non-plussed. "My father? What's *he* got to do with anything? I haven't even seen him in years."

Nor did I want to. A chill shuddered over my bare arms and trickled down my spine at the thought of the last time I'd seen him—the knife, the blood, the blazing madness in his eyes. Willow, ensnared in vines, a sacrificial lamb to his dark ambitions.

Ash didn't know what he was talking about. His dad and mine had so much in common, they'd probably be best buddies if they met.

"Lord Celebrach knows what your father wants. Fallon Domani's been searching for that dagger, or something like it, for years. And Lord Celebrach sees conspiracies everywhere he looks. He would never have believed you weren't here under your father's instructions."

He gazed into the fire, his grey eyes shadowed, face solemn. A muscle jumped in his jaw as he clamped down on some emotion. The room was still, and we were alone in our firelit bubble. I moved closer, watching the strong pulse beat in his neck. I wanted to reach out and touch that patch of skin, feel his heartbeat at my fingertips.

He glanced up as I approached, his gaze lancing through me. I almost forgot to breathe.

"How did you know I wasn't? Why did you care?" Why had he gone so far out of his way to save the life of a perfect stranger? Because I somehow reminded him of his dead love?

Surely that wasn't the only reason. After what I'd seen in that vision, I was convinced there was more to Ash than the hard assassin surface. He'd never wanted to be one, after all. Maybe there was still a decent man lurking underneath, struggling to get out. All of a sudden, it seemed hugely important to find that man.

He shook his head and turned back to the fire, and the spell was broken.

"Tell me about this new mission, then," I said, struggling to make sense of it all. Now, more than ever, I needed an ally among the Vipers. "When do we move against Lord Nox?"

"Still keen to get out of the sith, Sage? I hope, for both our sakes, you remember what I told you: you're a Viper for life. Evandir and Atinna aren't just coming along to watch us, you realise. Lord Celebrach is wary, now—my little bit of rebellion has caught him by surprise. At the first hint of disobedience or betrayal, their job will be to take us both out."

I shrugged as if unconcerned, though inside my heart was pounding. "They—and you—have nothing to worry about. I'm just eager to see some action outside the training grounds."

"And it doesn't bother you in the slightest that we'll be killing your boyfriend's father?"

"Raven's not my boyfriend!"

"Maybe not yet." His grey eyes watched me closely. "But you've been seeing a lot of each other lately, and *his* intentions, at least, are clear."

Really? Nothing about Raven was clear to *me*. And how the hell did Ash know this, anyway? Atinna was supposed to be the one who'd been watching me and my friends.

"Have you got nothing better to do than spy on my personal life?"

He slammed his glass down on the mantelpiece, sudden fury in his eyes.

"At the moment, I seem to be fully occupied with keeping you alive. Sage, Sage." He grabbed my upper arms and dragged me closer, forcing me to look at him. The room fell away, and all I could see was those eyes and the frustration boiling in them. "Have you no sense of self-preservation at all? This is serious!"

It was as if all the emotions that he usually held back had all come storming out at once, and the room didn't feel big enough to contain him.

"You're hurting me," I said coldly.

He let go on a sudden indrawn breath, as if my words had scalded him, then looked down at his hands for a long moment.

"That was not my intention. That is *never* my intention." He took a deep breath. When he looked up, that iron control was back in place. "But Evandir will probably seize this opportunity to try taking you out again, regardless of whether or not you follow orders. Lady knows enough can go wrong on a mission even when everyone is on the same side, and he is *not* on our side. It's a perfect chance for him to remove you without any repercussions."

"No repercussions? Are you saying you wouldn't take revenge for me?"

He held my gaze in challenge. "Would revenge bring you back?"

All the fight went out of me in a rush. I sagged forward, exhausted, and let my forehead rest against his broad chest, while emotions swirled within me. Sorrow, disappointment in myself, and shock at a sudden, unwelcome insight into my own motivations.

"Sage?" He gathered me gently against him. "Are you well?"

Was I? *Would revenge bring you back?* Revenge never brought anyone back. It wasn't as though I hadn't already known this. Revenge wasn't about doing anything for the dead; it was about soothing the grief of those left behind, giving them something to do in the face of their loss.

I'd said I'd wanted *justice* for Nevith, not revenge. Justice would have ended at the front door of this sith.

Justice would have taken me straight back to Raven and the king to report what I'd discovered.

But I'd let my anger and grief drive me, casting aside all common sense. What was I doing here? Nevith was dead and there was no changing that, no matter how many assassins I killed. I was such a fool. Revenge wouldn't bring him back. All the drive for revenge had done was trap me here, where I would very likely get myself killed. And I was no cold-blooded killer. My friends would be worried sick, and it was all for nothing. I hadn't even been able to kill Nuah in the woods that night, though I'd had a perfect shot. I'd done nothing but delude myself since I got here.

Now I was trapped here, where an assassin I should despise was the one trying to keep me alive in spite of my best efforts to get myself killed. His arms around me were strong and unexpectedly comforting—so much so that I was quietly horrified at myself.

What was I thinking? How could I feel attracted to a man like this, a man who killed for a living?

But it's not his fault, I reminded myself. *He didn't want to be a Viper any more than you did.* I rested my burning face against the black cloth stretched over his muscled chest and felt his heart, beating sure and strong beneath my cheek. It was strangely soothing.

Then his fingers were under my chin, tipping my face up to his. His grey gaze caught mine and held it.

He was impossibly beautiful, but it wasn't his beauty that called to me. I'd been surrounded by fae beauty all my life.

It was his pain that reeled me in—that deep sadness

lurking at his core. It called to the child in me who had lost her mother, whose father had abandoned her among strangers. I wanted to *fix* it for him, show him that it was possible to move through the pain and find life waiting on the other side.

I was intensely aware of the heat of his body, only a breath away, and of the softness of his skin against mine where his fingers still cradled my chin. His lips parted as I gazed at them, and a flush of heat swept across my face. I'd kissed those lips in my dreams, tasted his mouth and done so much more. His gaze was on my mouth now, too, and my blood roared in my ears.

What was wrong with me? He was the enemy. But I couldn't care about the people he'd killed, with the firelight playing on his face, his eyes pulling me closer. I could drown in those haunted eyes.

I leaned towards him, drawn inexorably into a moment that felt unavoidable. When had I first felt the pull? When he'd saved me from Evandir's viper? Or when I'd seen the avenging fury on his face as he pulled Evandir off me in the midnight woods?

Our lips were about to touch, and my heart pounded in an erratic rhythm. He filled all my senses—the fresh forest scent of him, the warmth of his body. His breath was soft on my face, and I was melting into him when shadows leapt to life in the corners of the room.

I drew back with a gasp. Here, too? The darkness boiled, forming the shape of a woman, her dark hair coiling free around her head like serpents. The shadows had grown bold.

"What's wrong?" Ash's hand fell away as he stepped back, leaving me bereft.

"Nothing."

The shadow woman moved closer. *"See what you could have if you joined with us?"* she whispered. *"He wants you, too. All he needs is a little push."*

Resolutely, I turned my gaze from her, back to his face. But it was too late. The moment had dissipated like smoke, and his mask was back in place.

"Sit down," he said. "I'll get you a drink."

I didn't need a drink; I needed *him*, but I didn't quite have the guts to come out with that. I peeked in the corner, but the shadow woman was gone again. Maybe I'd imagined the whole thing. Maybe I was crazy.

No, I was definitely crazy. No maybe about it. Crazy to think a relationship between us could ever work. The yearning I thought I'd seen in his eyes was gone, and he was all business as he mixed a drink, bringing it back to me in my fireside chair.

Had I imagined the whole thing? He *had* been going to kiss me, hadn't he? I'd been with enough guys to be able to read the signs, but I was suddenly unsure of myself. I'd never known anyone like Ash before.

I took a long gulp of my drink, welcoming the burn of alcohol down my throat. Then I gazed down into my glass, watching the swirl of amber liquid around the edges. Time to drag this conversation back to where it should be.

I'd screwed up big-time coming here, seeking a revenge that wasn't in me to take. But being here gave me an opportunity to save Lord Nox, so at least some good would come out of it.

And maybe I could save someone else, a little voice whispered. If that someone wanted to be saved. Maybe that could be a way out for us all. *Focus, Sage.*

I cleared my throat. "Do you think Lord Nox is being targeted as revenge on Raven? For messing with the Vipers?"

"Targeted by whom? By us?" He snorted. "We're not in the business of personal revenge. It doesn't pay. And your Raven isn't the first person who's reneged on a deal. We don't take it personally. People have second thoughts all the time. The Vipers only deal in deaths that are bought and paid for by others."

"Then who has paid for this one?" It wasn't that I couldn't imagine Lord Nox having enemies. He'd been one of the king's staunchest supporters, even when such support was unpopular, so he probably had dozens. Maybe I was being paranoid, but I couldn't help finding the timing of this hit suspicious. Lord Celebrach could hardly have designed a better test for me.

Ash shrugged. "Lord Celebrach rarely shares that information."

"But he records it somewhere, right?" I'd seen the blue, leather-bound book in Celebrach's study, full of clients' names and the hits they'd ordered, complete with the amounts they'd been willing to pay to have their enemies removed without getting their own hands dirty.

Ash's glass stopped halfway to his mouth, and he frowned. "Don't get any ideas. But why does it matter who ordered the hit? The Vipers have been paid, and it falls to us to deliver. That's all you need to concern yourself with."

My turn to shrug. I'd concern myself with whatever I wanted to, but no need to burden him with that.

"So how do we do this?" My mind was racing; surely there'd be an opportunity somehow to get word to Raven. I could hardly take out his father while trapped in this sith. At some point, they'd have to let me out.

"Surveillance first." One leg was crossed over the other as Ash tapped his empty glass against his knee in thought. "We need to establish his routines; numbers of guards; defences, magical and otherwise."

This must be why they warned clients a hit might take up to a month. Planning took time. My heart sang. So many opportunities in a month! "Great. When do we start?"

"*We* don't. You will remain here while I look after this part."

"But Lord Celebrach said I had to do it."

"The kill, yes. But you're too new for surveillance. You'd likely give us away before we even had a chance to get close. I won't risk you until I have to." He leaned closer and took my hand, his expression softening. "I know it will be hard for you to kill him. It takes a while before you learn to stop seeing targets as people. I would do it for you if I could, but Lord Celebrach has been quite clear that it must be your hand that delivers the killing blow. But I will handle everything else. I'll make it as easy for you as I can."

I nodded, touched by his concern. What a strange

world I was living in, when an offer of help with an assassination could bring a tear to my eye.

He stood up, signalling the conversation was over. "I'll take Evandir with me. You can stay here and work on your studies—Lady knows you need it. You should have years of study behind you before your first kill. We'll just have to pray that a few weeks will be enough."

27

When Ash had been gone a week, loneliness drove me out of the cottage. The only people I'd seen since he'd left had been servants, and they hardly qualified as people. One of them delivered meals to the cottage at regular intervals, but I was tired of eating alone. Even assassins seemed like better company than staring at my textbooks while I ate for one more meal.

Besides, it was a good opportunity to learn more about the Vipers, while Ash wasn't there to listen to everything I said. I entered the austere dining room just before dinner was served and slid into my usual place near the end of the table, telling myself I was doing it for the king. Of course, I didn't miss Ash—half the time, he didn't talk to me even when he *was* there. Why would I be craving his dour company? The fact that we'd almost kissed once meant nothing. He'd caught me in a weak moment. I'd given myself a good talking-to and it wouldn't happen again.

Atinna came in and stalked straight over to me. "You're in my seat."

Great. My second-favourite person here, after her obnoxious instructor. I stared up at her, raising a lazy eyebrow. "Yeah? I don't see your name on it."

I'd been sitting in the same spot ever since I'd arrived. Maybe it *was* her seat—she hadn't been here to claim it—but what did it matter? There was an empty seat right next to me, the one where Ash usually sat. Two more opposite. But no, she had to make a big deal about the one I was sitting in. Petty bitch.

"Everyone has their place." Her gaze was hard and implacable. "The Adepts at the high table, senior assassins at the heads of the long tables, then partners, family, support staff. Apprentices right down the end here. And that's my seat."

Briefly, I entertained a daydream of stabbing her in the face with my fork, then I shrugged. Whatever. I shifted into the seat on my left. "Happy now?"

She sat down, scowling, and served herself from the platters in the middle of the table. I ignored her, looking around the room while I ate my food. Lord Celebrach sat at the high seat among the Adepts. He didn't have his dagger with him tonight. Maybe he only brought it for ceremonial occasions.

Evandir's seat at the high table was empty, of course, and so was the one on Celebrach's right, which had been empty every time I'd eaten here.

"Whose seat is that on Lord Celebrach's right?" I asked

Atinna. May as well pick her brains if I had to put up with her scowling at me over the curry.

The scowl changed to a look of scorn, as if she couldn't believe anyone could be so ignorant. "Ashovar's, of course."

I blinked, as if she might laugh and say she was joking, but the poles would melt before that happened. I took another mouthful, chewing slowly as I considered that.

Ash was *an Adept*. I'd known that all along, but somehow I'd never made the connection before. The Adepts were the ones who sat at the high table in a place of honour with the Lord Serpent. I'd read about them in one of my interminable texts on the history of the Vipers: nine Adepts, the most skilled of all the Vipers, entrusted with the most important kills. They formed a kind of high council to assist the Lord Serpent. When Lord Celebrach died, the next Lord Serpent would be chosen from among their ranks.

And Ash's rightful seat was at his father's right hand. No wonder Evandir hated him. Such a position was a sign of favour—there was no doubt who Celebrach intended to inherit his position. Evandir's own chair was right at the end of the table.

So why had Ash been sitting with me, in the lowly place reserved for apprentices, every time we'd eaten here? Because he didn't want me to be alone? He didn't trust me?

Or because he wanted to protect me? A warm and fuzzy feeling crept over me. Somehow, I knew that was it. The man had a protective streak a mile wide, and it had been focused on me ever since I'd arrived. So much for not playing the sheepdog.

No wonder everyone had stared at us. I'd thought they'd just been interested in the new arrival, but they'd probably all been wondering why an Adept would show such favour to a mere apprentice. Heat surged in my cheeks—they'd likely assumed we were sleeping together.

Speaking of sleeping together ... I glanced sideways at Atinna. "Have you heard from Evandir?"

"Nope." She was sopping up the last of her curry with a piece of bread and didn't bother looking at me.

"But he's gone with Ash, right, to help with surveillance?" I paused, but she ignored me. Either that curry was the tastiest thing she'd ever eaten, or she got off on being rude. I was going for option B. "I just thought there might be some news."

"There'll be news when they get back," she said dismissively.

"Do you like killing people, Atinna?"

She flicked me a sideways glance. "Do you?"

"There are a few people I imagine it would be very satisfying to kill."

She scowled at me, but I gave her an innocent look. It wasn't my fault if she took my comments personally, was it?

"It's not as though you get a choice of who to kill," she said.

I nodded. "Only whoever Lord Celebrach tells us to, because of the whole magic dagger compelling our obedience thing. Doesn't anyone ever have any 'accidents'?"

"I don't think you understand how Ni'ishasana works."

"So tell me."

She shrugged. "There has been the odd *accident*, as you call it, among the Vipers themselves. Power struggles are not unheard of. But it's not possible to actively go against an order from the Lord Serpent. It would be like trying to stop yourself from breathing. It can't be done."

"How is this dagger so powerful?"

"How could it not be?" She finished the last piece of bread, then licked her fingers. "It contains the powers of all its previous wielders, and all those powers may be accessed at will by its current holder."

My eyebrows rose in spite of myself. That was pretty damn impressive. No wonder Celebrach had been able to stop my bullet in mid-air. Some powerful Air mage must have held the dagger once before him. How did you bring down someone with access to powers like that?

"All their powers, even from other Realms?" I asked, just to be sure. Celebrach was a Winter fae like his son.

"All of them."

"And how many people have wielded this dagger?"

"Enough." A brief longing flitted across her face. "Lord Celebrach's powers rival those of the king himself."

I glanced across at the subject of our discussion, who was chatting to the Adept at his side. "If I had a dagger like that, I'd never let it out of my sight. Isn't he afraid someone will steal it?" If the Vipers were as big a bunch of backstabbers as Evandir's behaviour implied, it seemed like a serious risk.

"No. The dagger is loyal."

I glanced curiously at her, but Atinna's expression was as serious as ever. "How can a dagger be loyal? It's a thing."

"You sit surrounded by fae, in a place built of magic, and you ask how a dagger can be loyal? Something of its previous owners' essence clings to it."

"Like, their souls?"

She nodded, and I suppressed a shudder. This was nasty stuff. No one should go messing with people's souls after they were dead.

I stared down at my plate. The shadowy woman I'd seen, the odd whispers I'd heard—were these previous owners of the dagger, or what was left of them? Was Ni'ishasana itself trying to talk to me?

The more I considered it, the more sense it made. I'd started seeing the moving shadows and hearing odd voices as soon as the dagger had tasted my blood. The dreams and visions had begun pretty soon after that, too. But why was the dagger trying to communicate with me? What possible interest could such a powerful entity have in me? Let's face it, I wasn't exactly assassin material. I was surprised the dagger had even noticed me, much less kept trying to attract my attention.

But my attention had been well and truly caught by its little trips down memory lane. Those strange dreams and visions of Ash's past weren't my imagination. I'd already realised some powerful magic must be at work—and it didn't get much more powerful than the Thief of Souls. For some reason, Ni'ishasana wanted me to know the circumstances in which Ash had joined the Vipers—but why? It hardly showed the dagger or its current owner in a good light.

Although perhaps *good* didn't mean quite the same thing to me as it did to an ancient soul-stealing dagger.

"And it binds us all to him, as well?"

"Of course. Vipers are dangerous people, but our loyalty to the Lord Serpent is assured."

Assured by magic. By a kind of magical slavery. She sounded proud, but the idea horrified me. If only there was a way to get that dagger off him. Without it, the Vipers would fall, torn apart by backstabbing and fighting among themselves. Something else to tell the king when I got out of here. The taste of revenge may have soured in my mouth, but shutting down the Vipers' operations was still a worthy goal. A *just* goal. This sick system couldn't be allowed to continue.

Celebrach was the puppet master, lurking at the centre of everything, pulling strings that brought down Realms and maybe even kingdoms. And none of them cared. It was all just about the money to them.

Whose money had paid for Lord Nox's death? That would be something else that the king would be very interested in knowing.

No longer hungry, I left before dessert was served. At least, I was no longer hungry for food, or Atinna's so-charming company. Information, on the other hand, I had an unquenchable appetite for.

With everyone else still at dinner, it was a simple matter to sneak upstairs and let myself into Celebrach's study unseen. My eye went straight to the dagger on its stand. Ni'ishasana, Thief of Souls. Now that I truly understood its power, I was even more repelled by the warped blade.

How many fae souls were trapped inside its rippling surface, lending their undead strength to Celebrach, helping the Vipers flourish? I could hardly conceive of the kind of power he had at his disposal. I would have been happy just to be able to perform the kind of magic anyone from Spring had access to.

"*Sssage.*"

Goosebumps shuddered down my back as my name reached my ears. That voice came from no living throat, human or fae. I glanced once at the dagger, then turned my back on it, determined not to have anything to do with such an evil thing.

"*Sage.*"

The woman with the snake hair was back, emerging from the shadows that lurked in the corners away from the glow of the fire in the hearth. She beckoned me closer, but I was having none of that. As soon as I located that book, I was out of here. I checked the stack of books that still teetered on the edge of the desk.

"*Sage.*" Her hair rippled like seaweed in the current. Or perhaps it blew in an invisible breeze. Maybe she was the Air mage whose powers had stopped my bullet. Even more reason not to have anything to do with her. That bullet would have solved a lot of problems.

She raised her hand, and the shadows formed other shapes. Ash and me, coming together in a passionate embrace. I goggled for a moment, then went back to my search, tugging open the desk drawer with hands that only shook slightly.

"*Join with us. You can have him. You can have anything you want.*"

"Who says I want him?" I squeaked. Man, this was creepy. If those damn shadows came any closer, I would scream.

My hands closed on a book bound in dark blue leather, and I pulled it out, tugging impatiently when the corner caught on the edge of the desk top. I had to get *out* of here. *Join* with them? What the hell did that mean?

It was the handwritten journal I'd seen before, and I flipped to the end, resolutely focusing on the pages and doing my best to ignore what the writhing shadows were doing. I was never coming back into this room alone again. I could feel waves of power emanating from the damn dagger, and it set my teeth on edge.

I ran a trembling finger down the columns on the last page until I found Lord Nox's name. And there, under the "client" column, was the name of the person who had ordered his death.

Sir Ebos, Knight of the Realms.

28

What did I know about Sir Ebos?

He was a dragon fae, one of the rare few who lived outside the Realm of Fire, and thus immensely powerful. His brother was the Lord of Fire and, according to Allegra, there was some bad blood between them, but I hadn't paid much attention to the details. He was one of the King's Chosen, the knights tasked with the king's protection, so he was at the very heart of the web of power that connected the Realms of Faerie.

He ought to have been as trustworthy as the Hawk, his fellow knight. He should have been devoted to the king's safety and interests. Yet here he was, arranging the assassination of one of the king's staunchest allies.

I'd thought something was off about him from the moment Allegra returned from a mission to the Realm of Fire without him, saying he'd been killed by trolls. Trolls should never have been able to kill a dragon. And his odd behaviour on that mission had almost gotten Allegra herself killed. A suspicious person might even have wondered if getting Allegra killed was his whole purpose.

When he'd turned up later, miraculously back from the dead, his oddness had taken on a more sinister turn. Was it really a coincidence that he had arrived in the middle of a confrontation between the king and the Lord of Summer at the exact moment Lord Kellith needed him? His support set off a chain of events that could have gone very badly for the king and his allies. Who was he really working for, the king or his enemies?

If I was the king, I would have found a reason to pack dear Sir Ebos off to some distant fortress until I could be satisfied as to the answers to these questions. Instead, King Rothbold had kept him close, which I guess had the advantage of knowing what he was up to—but the Dragon wasn't a man I would care to have "protecting" me under the circumstances. I hoped Rothbold was only biding his time, gathering evidence, and didn't actually trust him anymore.

Still, if it was evidence he was after, Sir Ebos's name on the Vipers' accounts was pretty damn conclusive. The man was a traitor and needed to be dealt with before he caused any more harm.

By the time Ash returned two days later, I was in a fever of impatience. I had so much to tell the king that I was desperate to get out of this place. And I still had to stop the Vipers assassinating Lord Nox. I could never look Raven in the face again otherwise.

The fact that I was the one meant to be doing the assassinating was a little detail that I still had no idea how to overcome. Baby steps. First, I needed to get Ash on my side.

I finally broached the topic after we'd finished a practice match with short swords that left me drenched in sweat, my right arm trembling with fatigue. Ash certainly hadn't lost any of his edge while he'd been gone, and I'd spent too much time with my books and not enough honing my still-limited skills. Still, letting one of the Vipers come at me with a sword had seemed like a bad move, especially without Ash there to make sure things didn't turn murderous.

"I found out something worrying while you were away."

"More worrying than the way you walked right into that thrust?"

I nodded tightly, forcing myself to unclench my teeth.

"Tell me as we head back for lunch. I still need a report of your studies while I wasn't here."

He was brusque and businesslike, with no sign of our brief moment of connection. I could have been anyone, or no one. It made me annoyed with myself for being so pleased to see him when he'd turned up with the breakfast tray.

"I found out who commissioned the hit on Lord Nox," I said once we were on the path that ran through the trees back to our cottage, and could be sure no one would overhear us.

He closed his eyes for a moment and sighed. When he opened them again, they were hard. "Do *not* tell me how you found that out."

"It was the Dragon. Sir Ebos." He showed no reaction —he was probably inured to betrayal after all these years as a Viper—so I hurried on. "Don't you think that's suspicious? Why would a knight want to kill one of the Lords? I'm worried it's a trap."

Now he did react—just a little flinch, but I caught it. "It's funny you should bring that up. Lord Nox is in Spring. That's an odd coincidence, don't you think? If it's a trap, it's one to get you back."

"What do you mean?"

"You followed me here after I met with Raven, and now Night and Spring are meeting. What is the one thing they have in common? You."

There was a weariness in his voice that tore at my heart. Yes, he'd seen a lot of betrayal, and now he was armouring himself for another one. And the worst part was, he wasn't even wrong. Oh, he was wrong about Night and Spring working to free me from the Vipers—or, at least, I thought he was. Raven might be able to persuade his father to help, but Lord Thistle wouldn't give a crap what happened to me. But he wasn't wrong about the rest. I hadn't exactly come here with peace and love to all Vipers in mind, and the weight of the guilt was crushing me.

"Rubbish. Raven's just a guy I know from Court. I only met him because he helped out a friend."

"That's not true." He stopped on the path and turned to face me. Moonlight through the branches gave his skin an ethereal glow and darkened his eyes to unreadable depths.

"I saw you with him outside The Drunken Irishman. He kissed your hand. Standing close, like this."

He took my hand and drew me closer. My feet obeyed without even querying the orders with my brain. His scent filled my nostrils as he pressed a kiss into my palm, his eyes never leaving mine, then closed my fingers over it with infinite tenderness.

"No more lies, Sage. At least not between us. You came here to spy."

"I didn't." It was a pathetic protest, but in my defence, he was mighty distracting. He was taller than me, but not so tall that those full lips weren't frighteningly close to mine. All I had to do was tip my face up to his. I couldn't seem to look away from his mouth.

"And now your friends are frightened because you've been gone so long," he continued with ruthless focus.

I tore my gaze away from his lips and met his eyes. They had that haunted look about them again, the one that said he was preparing himself to be hurt, because pain was all he ever expected. The one that made me desperate to help him heal.

"They probably hope to seize hostages to trade for your safe return, so they get Sir Ebos to order a hit on Lord Nox, then gather together to wait for us. If they catch one of us, they think Lord Celebrach will give you up."

"They don't know where I am." This time, my protest had more force, trying to wipe that look from his eyes. "They probably think I'm dead. The only plot against the Vipers is in your head."

His hands tightened on my shoulders. "You're lying to me; I can tell. Do you plan to betray us?"

His gaze held me pinned, and I couldn't look away. His intensity was overwhelming; there was nothing else in the world for him in this moment but the answer to his question. But how did I answer it? How did I reconcile two such differing goals? Was there any way to save both Lord Nox and Ash?

"How could I betray you?" I whispered.

As I did, my voice faltered, and a shadow crossed his face. Shame flooded me as I watched him retreat behind the armour that shielded his soul from the realities of his life. The mask of the cold assassin dropped back into place.

I continued, trying to fix it. "Ni'ishasana compels my obedience the same as yours."

But the fabled dagger, for all its chattiness, was remarkably silent on this point. There were no warning signs, though I planned a betrayal every bit as bad as he feared—nothing less than the destruction of his whole organisation. Maybe the dagger didn't notice plans; maybe it was only actions that counted, and I'd be struck down as I tried to save Lord Nox.

"And yet Lord Celebrach doesn't trust you. Do you think apprentices normally go on jobs? This is a test, and if you fail it, both our lives are forfeit."

I pulled out of his grip and resumed walking. The cottage was only a little further on, and for once, I wouldn't be objecting to his habit of trying to pour alcohol down my gullet. I was ashamed and miserable and frightened, and the storm of emotions was almost more than I could bear.

"Well, he doesn't trust you either, does he?" I threw over my shoulder.

His laugh was bitter. "Trust is a foreign emotion to Vipers. Lord Celebrach hasn't got where he is by trusting anyone."

Once inside, I went straight to the sideboard and poured myself a drink. I'd downed it before he'd even shut the front door behind us.

"How can you stand living like this?" I poured myself another, and one for him, too. "Always watching your back. Never trusting anyone or letting anyone get close. You do everything your father asks of you and it makes no bloody difference at all. He still doesn't trust you. He doesn't even seem to *like* you. He's not going to win any Father of the Year awards, is he?"

Ash took a sip of his drink, watching me over the rim of the glass. "I'm not exactly the son he dreamed of, either."

"Then he needs better dreams," I said shortly, surprising a bark of laughter out of him. "Not that I can talk. My father tried to murder my best friend in front of me. *Did* murder some good friends of mine," I added softly, thinking of Dandelion and the other guards who'd fallen to my father's duplicity that day.

"My father destroyed the woman I loved."

Oops. In a face-off between evil dads, his still won hands-down over mine. At least mine didn't steal people's souls when he killed them. "I'm sorry. I didn't mean to remind you."

He sighed. "It's not as though I will ever forget, whether I am reminded or not. But you are the first person I've ever talked to about Hattah. Sometimes, now, I remember her as she was … before."

"That's good, I guess."

He smiled at me; a genuine smile that softened his forbidding appearance and brought a rare warmth to his grey gaze. "It is. It *is* good."

He lifted his glass to me and drank. Mine had somehow got itself emptied again, so I refilled them both.

"Are you sure our fathers aren't twins separated at birth?" I asked. "Mine's a necromancer, and yours is a—" I gestured broadly with my glass, spilling a little sticky alcohol onto my fingers. I stopped to suck it off. "Yours is whatever he is. Lord of the Deadly Dagger. Stealer of Souls and Poacher of Powers. We should drink to their destruction."

I raised my glass, and he clinked his against it solemnly.

"To the destruction of our fathers," he said. "May they and all their works end in ruin."

"I'll drink to that." I drank to it a little too vigorously, because some of the amber fluid slopped out the side of the glass and ran down my face.

He reached out and wiped it with his thumb in an infinitely gentle caress, then carefully took the glass from me. "That's probably enough for you."

I was pleasantly buzzed and emboldened by the alcohol. And perhaps also by the tenderness of that kiss he'd pressed into my palm. I could still feel the tingle of his lips on my skin. I caught at his hand. "So why do you stay, Ash? You hate him, you hate the Vipers—why not leave?"

"Because the choice isn't mine." The bitterness was back in his voice. "The dagger holds me to his will. What I want doesn't come into it."

"But you'd make that choice if you could."

"What's the point of discussing it? It's hopeless."

"Say it wasn't, and you *could* leave. Would you?" I held my breath in anticipation of his answer. So much was riding on it. *Tell me you really don't want to be a Viper.*

He looked down at our clasped hands. "Perhaps. But is a different life really possible? We carry our burdens with us wherever we go. I'm afraid there is no escaping the past."

I wanted to tell him everything, but I was still just sober enough for a little restraint. I wasn't a hundred per cent certain of him yet. But if I could persuade him to join with me against the Vipers, I could save Lord Nox. We could leave this terrible place, and all I would have to do would be to keep us both locked away and unable to answer the dagger's call until King Rothbold could destroy both Celebrach and the hateful blade.

And then we would be free.

He sighed and released my hand. "But this is all fancy. Ni'ishasana holds us all captive, and we have a job to do."

"Lord Nox," I said. "What else did you find out?"

"The Lord of Night is in Spring for an extended visit, and Lord Thistle and Lady Feronique plan a masquerade ball in his honour."

"When?"

"In three days' time."

So soon? I knew exactly what he was saying—a masquerade was a perfect opportunity for assassins who wanted to pass unseen. He had already chosen this as the time for the strike.

"We will use poison," he added. "There will be plenty of opportunities for you to slip it into his drink at the ball, and poison is less ... confronting ... than some of our other options. I want this to be as easy as possible for you."

So I had three days to come up with a plan to save Lord Nox's life. I felt abruptly sober again as the weight of it threatened to crush me. How could I manage it, with both Evandir and Atinna on guard, ranged against me? Would I have to kill them both to have any chance of success?

And what if, in the end, Ash didn't want to leave the Vipers with me? Would I have to kill him, too?

29

I'm sitting at the high table in the long dining room, in the throne-like chair that used to belong to Lord Celebrach.

No longer. It is mine. Ni'ishasana hangs at my side, a comforting weight that reminds me of my power. My fingers tingle with it, as if the magic I now command is too big to be confined in one person's skin, and it wants to break loose. I could level mountains, if I wished. Raise waterspouts. Fly. It is everything I ever dreamed of when I was only a weak halfbreed.

That power connects me to every person in the crowded room. All those faces turned toward me—I own every one. They are my Vipers. I can bend them, break them, send them wherever I wish. Each one will do my bidding or die trying.

Even the ones that hate me.

A special kind of satisfaction fills me as I contemplate Evandir, seated at the end of the high table. He thought

Ash was his big rival and totally discounted me. His mistake.

"Evandir," I say, and he looks up from his meal.

"Yes, Lady Serpent?" His tone is calm and compliant, but he can't quite hide the loathing in his eyes.

My smile widens as I push my chair back from the table. I cross one black-clad leg over the other. "My boots are dirty."

Puzzlement creases his brow. "Shall I call for a servant?"

The other Adepts at the table are watching, and a hush begins to settle over the room as the Vipers at the lower tables become aware that something is afoot.

"I would prefer you to take care of it yourself."

"Now, my lady?"

"Come here."

The sound of his chair scraping back over the floor is loud in the suddenly quiet hall. His face is a mask, but through the magic that links us, I can feel the anger burning like wildfire inside him. He kneels at my feet and pulls a handkerchief from his pocket.

"Not like that," I say. "Use your tongue."

Someone gasps, but I don't take my eyes from his face, enjoying the brief rush of fury that distorts his features before he gets himself under control again. He takes my boot in a firm grip, then leans forward, tongue extended, and licks a speck of dirt from its shining surface.

Heat jolts through my body, tingling from my suddenly erect nipples right down to my core. Who knew that power could feel so good?

"You missed a spot," I say, arousal filling me as I watch his pink tongue dart out to caress my boot again.

"Better?" he asks, sitting back on his heels. His eyes burn with a savage hatred that only inflames my desires further. Humiliating Evandir would be my new favourite sport if I didn't have another, even better one.

"Much." I press the sole of my boot against his chest and shove, sending him sprawling across the floor. I can't wait a moment longer. I stand abruptly and offer my hand to Ash. "Let's go."

He takes it with a grin. He's learned my appetites already and knows what's coming. We've spent long, languorous days twined together, getting to know every curve and hollow of each other's bodies. There is magic in the way we fit together, as if we were made for each other.

He is like an open book to me now, this once enigmatic man, and the haunted shadows are gone from his eyes. When they look at me, they shine as if dazzled by the light from the sun.

I owe it all to Ni'ishasana. My fingers curve around the dagger's warm hilt, caressing the blood-red stone there gratefully as we gain the sanctuary of my chambers. Through the bond the dagger has created, I feel his urgency, his desire rising to meet mine.

"Sage," he whispers against my throat, and my name is like a prayer on his lips.

I shudder with need as his lips burn a trail down my skin to the hollow at the base of my neck. Urgent hands tear my shirt open, heedless of the buttons, and I cling to his shoulders, so dizzy with lust I can barely stand upright.

There are too many clothes between us. I need to feel his skin hot against mine. I haul his shirt out of his pants and run my hands over his broad back, wriggling to get even closer to him. He groans as my nails skate over his skin and wrenches his shirt off, flinging it to the corner of the room.

"I need you," he whispers, the words coming out in a throaty growl.

We tear our clothes off, and I fall back on the massive bed that dominates the room, the silken sheets cool against my fevered skin.

"Yes," I whisper, dragging his face down to mine.

His mouth takes mine, while his hands wander lower, his thumbs brushing against my sensitive nipples. I moan and writhe against him, needing more, needing all of him. He presses against me, but he's still holding back, prolonging the delicious agony.

"Now." I wrap my legs around him, urging him on.

"As my mistress commands."

Slowly, he slides into me, and I can barely breathe as each delicious inch fills me. My hips rise up to meet him, my whole being centred around that exquisite tingling heat where our bodies join.

We move together, and I can barely remember my own name; I'm so lost in him and the incredible sensations he's arousing. His skin under my hands, the clean ironbark scent of his hair filling my nostrils, the weight of his body on mine—these things fill my world. I teeter on the edge of something monumental, about to explode into shards of ecstasy.

"Wait, wait, wait." I think I actually said the words aloud. They echoed in my head as I crawled the last few inches out of the dream and broke through the surface of sleep. I opened my eyes and stared up at the ceiling, breathing hard.

What the hell was *that*?

Oh, the raunchy dream about Ash I could totally understand. The man was hotter than Papa Bear's porridge, and there was no denying my growing interest in him ... but stroking the damn dagger? Making Evandir lick my boots? I shuddered. That was not me. Where had that come from?

"*It can all be yours,*" a voice said, just a whisper on the edge of sound. "*Only join with us.*"

I sat bolt upright, heart hammering. Someone was in my room.

The shadow woman was back, her hair writhing around her head in a gale that only she could feel. Behind her, other shapes shifted in and out of being—a proud fae man with a circlet on his head; another who stood with arms crossed, watching me in silence. The woman's eyes bored into me from the foot of the bed.

"That was you, wasn't it?" I threw back the sheet and sprang out of bed. She'd sent me that sicko dream. "Get out of my head!"

"*Such protests!*" she said. "*Are you sure you're not tempted? We offer you power, Sage. More power than even you have ever dreamed of.*"

I marched over to the window and hauled the blind up. Bright daylight flooded the room, blasting the shadows away. To my great satisfaction, the woman and her companions dissipated into thin air. The dagger was becoming more insistent, seizing every opportunity to hit me with its propaganda.

The part I couldn't figure out was, why the hell did it want me so much? What on earth did I have that it needed? Absolutely nothing, as far as I could tell. And yet it persisted in these dreams and visions of me taking Celebrach's place, seizing his power for myself as if it thought it could tempt me to stage a coup.

I'd be lucky to stage a bake sale at the rate I was going. I was over my head already just trying to stay alive and keep Lord Nox that way, too. Overthrowing the head of the Vipers simply wasn't on the agenda. I'd need King Rothbold and all his resources to make that happen—and if the dagger thought that I'd happily step in as the head of the Vipers after that, it was crazy. My ultimate goal was to destroy the Vipers, not co-opt them as my own merry band of killers.

Sure, some of those mighty powers the dagger could confer were tempting. Not that I needed anyone to lick my boots, but a little respect was long overdue. It was hard growing up surrounded by magic-users when it almost exhausted your own powers just to summon a faelight. But I'd seen what the search for unbridled power could do to people. My own beloved father had abandoned me, then turned into an unrecognisable monster in his quest for forbidden necromancy.

For the first time, I wondered if he had started out with a craving like mine. Was a lust for power in my blood? Was

I doomed to repeat the mistakes of my father? Was *that* why the dagger had targeted me?

I never did find out if he found what he was looking for, but he certainly lost himself in the process. Ni'ishasana might think it was being so clever, showing me visions of all I could have if I fell in with its schemes, but it didn't realise that it was also showing me all that I stood to lose.

I was strong enough to resist it. I had to be.

I knew dark magic when I saw it, and stealing people's souls and turning them into zombie slaves was the very definition of dark magic. The kind of person who thought that was a good thing—the kind of person who actually *caressed* the damn dagger that did it like some satanic pet —was *not* the kind of person I was or ever wanted to be, however tempting other aspects of power might be.

I had the feeling it didn't know Ash as well as it thought it did, either. At least, there was no universe in which I could imagine him gazing at me with that bedazzled expression in his eyes when I held such power over him. He hated his servitude to his father, hated that the dagger forced him to submit. He wasn't going to feel any happier about it just because the hand holding his reins had changed. If I was his boss, he would never look at me as though I was his sun and moon.

But, of course, I didn't want him to, did I?

30

———

*A*sh had been gone all evening, leaving me with instructions to catch up on my reading. I was too nervous to really take the words in, and spent more time pacing the small lounge room and staring into the fire than actually reading. It was close to midnight when he sauntered in and handed me a small black package.

"What's this?" I asked, putting down the book with relief. It was another history of the Vipers. They say that history is written by the victors, but this author had really gone to town with the self-congratulations.

"Your outfit for the masquerade," he said, and my heart began to beat faster.

It was no more than a handful of slinky black satin studded with crystal butterflies, so light and slithery it hardly weighed anything at all. There was a mask, too—jewel-encrusted and beribboned, with black feathers sweeping out from the sides—and a pair of low-heeled shoes.

"Should I get changed?"

When he'd disappeared earlier in the evening, I'd hoped that the plans had changed. Now the moment was here, and I was woefully unprepared. I had only the barest glimmerings of a plan, and there'd been no chance to warn Raven or anyone else about what was coming. All I had on my side was a little insider familiarity with Spring and the hope that, when the time came, I could talk Ash around to my side.

He nodded, so I went to my room and slipped into the dress. It clung to my body like a second skin, though the skirt had a slit up the side that allowed me to move freely. Where was I supposed to hide a weapon?

The answer to that, apparently, was on my thigh. When I came back into the lounge room, Ash produced a small knife in a sheath and knelt to strap it around the top of my leg. His fingers lingered on my skin, and I shivered a little at his touch.

When he stood up, he offered me a tiny glass vial half-full of some colourless liquid.

"There's a little pocket just inside the neckline," he said, so I took the vial and hid it away inside its purpose-built pocket in my cleavage. The Vipers thought of everything.

He still wore his regular black clothes, so he probably intended to work a Glamour on himself instead of actually changing. It was only me who couldn't manage her own transformations and had to traipse around the countryside in evening dress with a mask dangling from her fingers.

I bet the shadow woman with the snaky hair could

have glammed me up with a snap of her insubstantial fingers. It was a shame that the monumental power she offered came with such a hefty price tag.

Ash led the way outside, where Evandir and Atinna were waiting. Evandir nodded at Ash, but both he and Atinna ignored me. That suited me just fine. We hadn't gone far before Ash took us under a stone archway. I'd passed through it many times during my stay with the Vipers, but before, it had always led down a narrow, cobbled passageway between buildings.

Now, however, mist swirled around us as we passed beneath the arch, and trees reared up on either side of us instead of buildings. We had entered the Wilds.

I had only travelled the Greenways of the Wilds a handful of times before, and always with someone else. I *probably* had enough power to navigate them on my own, but I'd never had any reason to put that theory to the test. They were tricky, requiring a great deal of concentration lest the walker lose focus on their goal and end up halfway across the Realms from where they'd intended to go. Or worse, became lost forever on the shifting paths.

Willow and Allegra had both hammered into me the need to stay on the path—Allegra in particular, given her rather horrifying experience the one time she'd left it. She'd ended up fighting massive, doglike monsters called dharrigals, but that had been nothing compared to what might have happened if Raven hadn't found her and brought her back to the path.

Thoughts of Raven tightened my throat as I followed Ash's back along the Greenway. My embryonic plan to save his father had holes in it big enough to drive a truck through. Maybe I should push Atinna and Evandir off the path and let the monsters of the Wilds take care of part of my problem—but they were both behind me, Ash having decided to sandwich the apprentices between the two Adepts. Evandir was bringing up the rear. There was no way I'd be able to do anything to him once he saw me push Atinna into the underbrush.

If I even could. I glanced over my shoulder and met her steely glare. No, there'd be no catching her by surprise. Over her shoulder, I caught sight of the trees closing in behind Evandir as he passed, the path disappearing as if it had never been. I turned back to face front, my shoulders tense. Maybe Atinna would be the one doing the pushing.

A branch snapped somewhere off to our right, and something big rustled the bushes as it moved through the undergrowth. None of the others seemed concerned, so I swallowed my unease and kept walking.

I liked forests, and had spent a lot of time roaming the woods of Spring as a child, but they'd been a damn sight more welcoming than the tangled trees of the Wilds. Here, they crowded together, leaning over the path as if they were intent on blocking every last scrap of light. This was the forest from every fairy tale where witches and monsters lurked, ready to spring on the unwary.

So it was a relief when a simple wooden arch appeared across the pathway, twined with flowers and vines—even though it meant we had arrived at our destination and I had to put my holey plan into action. Mist drifted around us as we stepped through the arch, and the familiar floral scent of Spring hit me. There was always something blooming here. Wild roses, if my nose was any judge.

A wave of homesickness caught me by surprise as I breathed in their scent. This was the first time I'd been back to Spring since Willow's parents had thrown me out. It seemed a long time ago, though it was only a little over five years. So much had happened since then.

What a homecoming. I'd certainly never pictured my return to Spring like this—skulking in, a knife strapped to my thigh and poison in my cleavage. And at least two companions who wanted to kill me. Talk about an interesting evening. If Lord Nox and I were both still alive at the end of it, I'd count it as a win.

We moved quietly through the woods, Ash still in the lead. We'd arrived outside the estate proper, of course, since Lord Thistle would hardly make it easy for enemies to open gates straight into his domain. A soft trickle of water nearby put us somewhere near the creek that ran just beyond Lord Thistle's borders. I'd spent hours here in my youth, catching tadpoles and splashing about pretending to be a water nymph with Willow.

The noise of water over rocks grew louder, and a different scent began to crowd out the roses' perfume. Relief washed over me—that was the scent I'd been searching for. Ash led us to a section of the creek that was narrow enough to jump across without getting our boots wet. He leapt across, but I paused for a moment, scanning the darkness under the trees for the source of that scent. There!

I followed him, but my foot "slipped" on the damp

ground, and I dropped to one knee, putting out a hand to stop my fall. In the darkness, no one noticed me snatch a handful of starbright. It grew like a weed along the water's edge, here, and I hadn't forgotten my studies. All my hopes were pinned on this tiny flower.

Ash frowned at me as I got up but said nothing.

Evandir wasn't so restrained. "I hope your apprentice isn't going to embarrass us tonight," he said, giving me a wintry glare. "Is she always this clumsy?"

"Anyone can slip," I said, hiding the flowers in my closed fist.

"Vipers don't."

While no one was looking, I stuffed the starbright into my bra.

"How are we getting in?" Atinna asked as Ash started moving again. He wasn't going in the direction of the road that led to Spring's main gates, which had me intrigued. He obviously had something else in mind.

"Through the fence."

"What about wards?" Atinna asked.

Ash glanced at me. "Wards won't stop a member of the family and her companions."

"If you mean me, I'm not a member of the Spring family. I bet Lord Thistle wasted no time in changing the wards after he threw me out, to make sure I couldn't return."

"If he did, he's changed his mind since," Ash said.

"How do you know?"

He smiled, but it was his feral assassin's smile. I hadn't seen it for a while, and it still gave me shivers. "I don't, for sure, but that's my assessment. You are in the king's favour, now, and Lord Thistle is the kind of man who will use that to his advantage. I'm surprised he hasn't already made overtures of reconciliation to you."

In fact, it was his wife who'd made the first moves towards a reconciliation. For the first time, I wondered if her stiff-necked husband had put her up to it, unwilling to unbend quite so far himself.

"Lord Thistle isn't the forgiving type," I said. "I think you're making a mistake."

"Well, we'll find out if I'm right in a moment."

"And if you're wrong, the whole of Spring will know that the Vipers have invaded."

Ash was surprisingly perceptive, so perhaps he was right, but this was still more reckless than I had expected from him. He'd always struck me as the controlled type— someone who would never make a move without a plan A, B, and C, without knowing every detail and accounting for it. If he'd been human, he would have been the spread- sheet guy who entered every moment of his day into his project management software.

Could I get them to abort this mission? What if there *was* no Plan B?

Evandir huffed a sigh of annoyance. "What other options do you think we have? Security will be tight with a visiting Lord. There will be magic defences and guards checking everyone who comes in the front gate."

I glanced at him in frustration. "But I thought we were going to dress up in masks and mingle with the guests?"

Atinna laughed scornfully. "When we get inside, yes. But masks won't get us in."

We'd still been walking as we argued, and now, we had arrived at a very familiar border. A wild green hedge confronted us, not particularly high—the topmost branches waved just above my head. Not particularly thick, either. This hedge marked the boundaries of Lord Thistle's estate, and I had crawled under it and through it countless times over the years. There were even a couple of gates in it, though my childhood self had always spurned those. They would surely be guarded today.

They all stopped in front of the hedge, waiting.

"It's not going to magically open up for me, you know." I looked around at them. "It's not like your hedge around the shrine back at the Nest."

And if Ash was wrong about the wards, it would actively keep me out. I'd seen people caught by the hedge before, pierced by thorns that appeared from nowhere and held fast until guards, alerted by the activation of the wards, came to investigate. All of a sudden, I hoped that Ash was right. Some of those thorns had been very long.

Evandir levelled a menacing glare at me. "Off you go, then. We haven't got all night. Unless you're having trouble remembering where your loyalties lie?"

"Don't be ridiculous."

I exhaled and rolled my shoulders, considering the barrier before me. Talk about a no-win situation. If I made it through the hedge, that meant Ash was right and the Vipers were free to enter, which left me with the problem of saving Lord Nox from my companions. If Ash was wrong, I was in for a world of pain.

Well, then. There was no way out but forward, I supposed. Scanning the hedge, I found a place where the lowest branches didn't grow quite as close to the ground and dropped to my belly. I wriggled forward, heart in my mouth, expecting to feel the sharp thrust of thorns at any moment. Somewhere far away, a fae flute was playing, so faint it was almost drowned out by the rustling and scrabbling noises I was generating.

I had a bad moment when the strap of my dress got snagged on a branch, but no thorns appeared. I slithered all the way through and stood up, checking that the starbright was still safely hidden in my bra. "Seems like you were right."

Ash's dark head followed a moment later. Somehow, his entry was less ungainly than mine, as if some invisible grease helped him slide gracefully under the hedge. Evandir and Atinna followed in quick succession, while I scowled and focused on picking bits of leaf and twig out of my hair.

When Ash stood up, he still wore black, but now his clothes were fit for a ballroom. His silken shirt looked liquid in the moonlight, pooling across his broad shoulders and billowing in full sleeves. His belt buckle gleamed with diamonds, and his tight pants were tucked into leather boots with such a shine on them I could almost have used them as a mirror. He looked like a pirate, or some sexy Regency buck, except that his eyes glittered from behind a jewelled black mask that no pirate would have been caught dead in.

"You'd better put your mask on," he said.

I nodded and tied the ribbons of the mask behind my head. Atinna and Evandir wore more glamorous outfits now, too. Like Ash's, the faintest hint of Glamour clung to them. Keen observers would know they weren't real, but no one at the ball would care—the majority of the guests would be using their power to devise the most outrageous costumes possible. Masquerade balls were always a hit with the fae, who loved dressing up even more than the average five-year-old.

Atinna was in dark blue velvet as lush as the midnight sky, and her mask shimmered between blue and green as if it were made of rainbow drake skin. Evandir wore black, like Ash, but as he moved into a patch of moonlight, his tight-fitting shirt shimmered in a way that reminded me uncomfortably of snake scales. I felt sure that was deliberate. Other partygoers might think he was going for a dragon look, but I knew better. He was proclaiming his allegiance to the Vipers, and I could only wonder whether he meant it as a challenge to Ash or a threat to me.

The sooner this guy had an unfortunate accident, the better. I almost wished we would be discovered by the guards and, as I followed Ash through the dark woods, I entertained a happy fantasy of watching some burly guard lop off Evandir's offensive head.

The fae flute was louder, and a light drumbeat had joined it. Laughter and the tinkling of glasses floated through the trees as faelights began to appear, bobbing effortlessly as balloons among the branches, casting a golden glow over the scene.

Lord Thistle's estate was a much larger version of Willow's sith. We only had a handful of pavilions, but there were dozens here, scattered among towering oaks and smaller ornamental trees. A little stream meandered among them, occasionally swelling into a pond full of waterlilies, where fountains played. The three biggest pavilions were completely open, their roofs held up by elegant columns, and were used as common spaces, while the smaller pavilions were usually open only on one side to allow the inhabitants some privacy. Lush green grass filled the spaces in between.

Ash skirted around smaller pavilions among the trees. Every step awakened memories in me—some happy, others sad. We passed Willow's private pavilion, and I wondered who lived there now, or if her parents had kept it as she'd left it, hoping to one day welcome their daughter home. There was the pond I'd pushed her into the night we met, deep pink waterlilies floating serenely on its surface. There was the kitchen where I'd spent many a happy hour chatting with Zinnia and Nevith. And there were the stables. How I'd loved those horses. It had almost broken my heart to have to leave Lightning behind, but my banishment had happened so quickly I'd had no choice.

The main pavilion was full of people, spilling out onto the surrounding grass. Some of them were clearly drunk already. One guy with ram's horns was staggering around after a delicate-looking winged girl who would be lucky not to get impaled on them considering the way he was moving, though she laughed every time he reached for her and stumbled.

A few more winged fae were perched on the roof of the pavilion, sharing a bottle of golden wine between them in their own private party. Below them, the pavilion was awhirl with colour. Sparkling jewels, fabulous dresses, weird and wonderful masks. Some hadn't bothered with masks but had given themselves animal heads instead. I saw three foxes, a falcon, and several owls among the dancers.

"Let's split up," Evandir said, watching the swirling crowd. Lord Thistle sat on his throne on the dais above the dancers, but the seat at his side was empty. Perhaps Lady Feronique was dancing with someone else.

Ash nodded, and Evandir and Atinna sauntered out from the trees and made their way into the packed pavilion.

"Remember," Ash said softly, "they're here to watch you. You can't afford any mistakes. Do you still have the vial?"

My hand crept to my breast, where the vial rode in its hidden pocket. "Of course."

"Are you all right?" His brown hair gleamed with golden highlights under the bobbing faelights, and his eyes glittered strangely behind his mask, full of remembered pain. "The first time is hard. I'd do it for you if I could, but ..."

"Evandir and Atinna are watching," I finished for him. "Don't worry, I'll be all right." I squeezed his hand, warmed by his concern. "What will you be doing?"

"I'll help you find the target. The sooner we get out of here, the better. The longer we stay, the more likely it is that someone will recognise you. I'll take the dance floor and you check the trees."

The *target*. Did it help him to depersonalise his victims like that? To pretend they weren't real people with names and lives and loves? It broke my heart to think what Lord Celebrach had done to his once-gentle son.

"*Lord Nox* might be dancing with Lady Feronique," I said, indicating her empty throne.

He nodded. "Be careful." Then, he stepped out of the shelter of the trees and disappeared into the crowd on the dance floor.

I circled around the pavilion, narrowly avoiding a collision with the horned guy when he lurched into my path, but I didn't go far. I had an illogical fear that one of the others might find Lord Nox before I could and decide to take matters into their own hands. I caught sight of Atinna's blue dress as the dancers swirled apart and came back together, but I had no idea where Evandir was, and I'd lost Ash already, though his black-clad form should have stood out among all these bright partygoers, like a crow among lorikeets.

Nervous sweat broke out under my arms and prickled down my cleavage. Where was Lord Nox? A blond man in a white feathered mask bowed before me, asking for a dance, but I pushed past him impatiently. My heart was hammering like a drum as I scanned the glittering crowd.

There! No. As soon as the man turned, I realised it wasn't him. Not that I was that familiar with Lord Nox, having only met him a handful of times. The masks didn't make it any easier, though at least no one looked twice at me. I just hoped he wasn't one of the people currently sporting an animal head. That would really screw things up.

Someone grabbed my arm. They were lucky that dagger was still strapped in its sheath, or they might have gotten a nasty surprise. My nerves were shot.

"Sage! Is that you? What in all the Realms are *you* doing here?"

I'd found the missing Lady of Spring.

31

"You're most welcome, of course," Lady Feronique said, pulling me into a surprising hug. I could count on one hand the number of times she had hugged me growing up; things must be grim indeed in her life if she had changed this much. Or was she just doing her husband's bidding? "But I'm so surprised to see you. Raven has been filling our heads with fears."

I stepped back as soon as I politely could. She might be eager to let bygones be bygones, but I wasn't so quick to forgive. Besides, I was afraid she might feel the knife in its sheath under the flimsy fabric of my dress.

She smiled at me in apparent delight, still holding my hands. Her dress had soft green skirts that shaded to a bodice of rosy pink, like the first blush of spring flowers. Rose buds twined through her hair, which was swept up into a messy bun from which sweet ringlets curled around her face, and the scent of jonquils clung to her. She was the embodiment of Spring.

"I ..." *What the hell should I say? I'm here to assassinate your guest of honour* probably wouldn't go down well. *Heard you were throwing a party, thought I'd drop in* wasn't really going to cut it, either.

As the silence stretched between us, I threw caution to the winds and opted for the truth, or at least as much of it as I thought she could handle. I'd soon find out whether her change of heart was real or if she was just being nice to me on her husband's orders.

I tugged on her hand and pulled her behind one of the pillars that held up the pavilion. Now was the time for her to prove that she really had changed. "Please, don't tell anyone I'm here."

"But Raven has been so worried about you." She glanced reflexively over her shoulder, as if looking for him. "That's all he's talked about since the delegation from Night arrived. Where have you been? Are you in trouble?"

"You could say that." If you were heavily into understatements. "But I can't tell you anything. It could cost me my life. Please, just pretend you didn't see me."

It could cost Lord Nox his life as well. My embryonic plan, such as it was, depended on remaining anonymous. Suddenly, the mask I wore didn't seem like much of a disguise. Had I really expected a few jewels and feathers to hide me from people who'd known me all my life? A faint suspicion entered my mind. Had Ash *meant* for me to be caught? Was I only a diversion while one of the others carried out the real assassination?

"Your life?" Feronique asked. "Do you need help? What's going on?"

Uneasy, I stuffed thoughts of betrayal away. Lady Feronique was staring at me, a growing concern in her eyes, and I didn't have time to consider anything other than my immediate situation.

"I can't tell you, I'm sorry. But I mean no harm."

A new wariness entered her eyes. "What do you mean? Why would you mean us harm?"

I was an idiot. What a stupid thing to say. I didn't have time for this; if Evandir or Atinna saw me talking to her, they would assume the worst. They'd think I was betraying the Vipers and one of them would kill Lord Nox, followed shortly thereafter by me. *Shit, shit, shit.* Why couldn't I learn to think before I opened my mouth?

"Do you trust me?" Desperate to cut this conversation short, I held her gaze, trying to project trustworthiness. And indeed, I *was* trustworthy—I was trying to save everybody's arses here, after all. It was just that my method might look a little dodgy at first glance.

She stared at me for a long, drawn-out moment. The notes of the fae flute swirled around us, twining in and out of the dancers' laughter and the sounds of their feet pounding on the grass. Nerves prickled over my skin. I had that horrible feeling that people were watching me, and I didn't dare look around to see if it was true. Ash, at least, probably was. I quivered with impatience. Any minute, he would decide my part in the mission was compromised and take matters into his own hands.

"My daughter does," Lady Feronique said finally.

"Once before, I didn't trust you. I judged you for the sins of your father, and I was wrong. I won't make that mistake again. I ask again, do you need my help?"

I shook my head. "The only thing I need from you is your silence. I won't stay long. Please, just forget you ever saw me and tell no one that I was here."

Her gaze held mine a moment more, her eyes steady behind the green mask she wore. "And you swear your actions here will bring no harm to Spring?"

"I swear that my intention here is to *prevent* harm to Spring. Whether or not I am successful partly depends on you."

She bit her lip, then nodded once decisively. "Very well. I never saw you."

I let out a long, relieved breath as she skirted around the dancers, back toward her throne. I shifted slightly to give myself a better view of the crowd. No sign of Evandir or Atinna, though I caught sight of a head that might have been Ash's before a crowd of masked revellers got in the way. Perhaps I was still safe.

A waiter passed with a tray of silver goblets frothing with pink bubbles. I let that one go; I had the feeling that Lord Nox would prefer something a little less frivolous, though it was a favourite drink here in Spring. I'd still seen no sign of the visiting dignitary. There were a couple of chairs on the dais to Lord Thistle's right, as empty as Lady Feronique's had been until a moment ago. She was seated next to her husband, now, and I ducked behind a dancer, careful not to catch her eye.

A golden-haired man in a fox mask grabbed my hand

and tried to drag me into the dance. The music tugged at me, urging me to join him. That was my human blood talking—humans were so susceptible to fae melodies that some of them had danced themselves straight into the grave when stolen by careless fairies.

"No, thank you," I shouted over the noise, tugging my hand free. "I'm looking for someone."

"And you have found him, pretty lady," the man replied, spreading his arms wide.

I laughed, shaking my head, and forced my way deeper into the crowd. I had to find Lord Nox.

A few minutes later, having been asked to dance several more times—plus propositioned in more explicit ways and having my arse groped to boot—I emerged from the dancers on the far side of the pavilion. Food was laid out on tables here, a feast in honour of the visitors from Night: a whole dressed pig; a roasted swan with all its feathers stuck back into it so that the poor creature looked just as it had in life; trays and trays of pink sugary creations and luscious displays of fruit. As a result, a large crowd of non-dancers was hanging around. I snagged a bunch of plump green grapes and began to work my way through the crowd.

The grapes exploded in my mouth, juicy and sweet, like little bursts of magic. The food in the Realms was almost as intoxicating as the wine. Nothing in the human world came close—except maybe chocolate. That was one earthly delight that the fae had yet to beat.

When I was about to despair of ever finding the elusive Lord of Night, I spied a gleam of silver from under the trees on the far side of the banquet tables. Lord Nox stood there, clothed in midnight blue with silver stars picked out in shining thread all over the long cloak he wore. Raven stood at his father's side, chatting to a couple of young women I didn't recognise, probably also from Night.

Damn. I faded back behind a tree, my heart pounding. The last thing I needed was to run into Raven. I had no hope of getting close to his father with him standing right there. What was wrong with him? Both of those girls were gazing up at him with stars in their eyes. Couldn't he do the decent thing and ask one of them to dance?

I waited in the shadows for what seemed an eternity until one of the young women evidently tired of waiting to be asked and caught Raven's hand instead, dragging him into the crowd of dancers. The other girl watched them go with a forlorn expression, then turned and spoke to Lord Nox. If she was asking him to dance, it didn't work out for her. He smiled and shook his head, and she wandered off in search of a more amenable partner.

I gulped in a nervous breath. All of a sudden, the moment was here. I slid a hand into my bra and pulled out one of the starbright flowers. It had lost a couple of petals and was looking rather battered, but the little green pod to which the remaining petals were attached was still intact, and that was all that mattered. Holding it casually between my thumb and forefinger, I hurried over to Lord Nox before someone else could get there.

"You don't dance tonight, my lord?"

He glanced down at me with a smile. He had the same black, fathomless eyes as his son, though there was something a little more hawkish in his face. Raven always gave the impression that he was laughing at some private joke —perhaps it was the twinkle in his eyes. There was no such suggestion in Lord Nox's.

"I don't," he replied. "But I'm sure my son would be only too happy to oblige a pretty lady, if you will wait for his return."

He turned back to watch the dancers, taking another sip from his goblet. Just as I had expected, it was half full of a deep red wine, most likely an ancient vintage. Lord Thistle would have pulled out all the stops for this occasion.

I stepped a little closer, my heart pounding, and placed a hand on his arm. "Are you sure I can't tempt you, my lord?" I leaned into him, staggering a little as if drunk, jostling the hand that held the goblet.

He grabbed at me with his other hand, clearly concerned I was about to fall. "Perhaps you had better sit down for a while, my lady."

I laughed, swaying where I stood. The little green pod was empty now—I had squeezed its contents into his drink. Only a drop or two, but that was all it took. "Perhaps you're right. Forgive me for intruding, my lord."

"No forgiveness necessary, my lady. Take care." He raised his goblet to me, then drank again.

I gave him a little wave and slipped back into the crowd, feeling like a traitor. Such a nice man. So much more approachable than Lord Thistle, who would have been more likely to throw his wine into the face of anyone drunkenly falling on him than to drink a toast to them. I pushed my way through the dancers, eager to be gone now that the deed was done. How long would it take for the starbright to take effect? I couldn't remember how long I had. Three minutes? Five? I remembered it was fast acting, but the stress of the moment had driven the details from my head. Best to be far away before anything happened.

I saw the Lord and Lady of Spring on their thrones through an opening among the dancers. Lord Thistle had leaned over to say something to his wife, but her gaze was elsewhere as she listened. She appeared to be watching Lord Nox, and a shiver of doubt ran through me. Had she seen me talking to him? Would she realise what I'd done?

I turned hurriedly in the other direction and bumped into a couple twirling past.

"Careful!" the man cried, shoving me none too gently out of his way.

A man in a black feathered mask looked over, his attention caught by the commotion. "Sage!"

Oh, shit, I was in trouble. It was Raven.

I admit it—I panicked. I turned and dived into the crowd, but a moment later, he caught my arm and spun me around to face him.

"Sage! Where are you going? Lady's tears, I thought you were dead."

And then he swept me into his arms and kissed me long and deep. I was so surprised that my body took over and I fell into the kiss. One strong arm around my back pressed me against him, the other hand tangled in my hair, cupping my head as if it were the most precious thing he'd ever held. His mouth on mine was soft as silk and sweet as all the sugared confections of Faerie. I melted against him, my knees actually trembling.

And then my brain rebooted, and I struggled away from him.

He stared down at me, eyes wild behind his raven mask. "Where have you been? What are you doing here?" He had released me at the first sign that I wasn't as into the kiss as he was, but he hadn't quite let me go—his hands still gripped mine, as if he was afraid that I would disappear into the crowd again if he didn't keep a firm hold on me.

"The Vipers caught me," I said, gazing up at the full lips I'd just kissed, more than a little bemused. That had certainly been an ... enthusiastic greeting. Raven's dance partner stood behind him, her mouth open in surprise. She didn't appear too impressed at being shoved aside without a second thought, but it was clear Raven had forgotten all about her.

He began to drag me through the crowd, leaving her stranded alone among the dancers. "But you escaped?"

"As you see." I looked down at my feet as we navigated a path through the swirling crowd, the music thrumming through my body. I felt giddy, unmoored from reality. His reaction had completely thrown me. I needed to shake him off, but how?

He glanced back at me over his shoulder. "You couldn't get word to me?" There was more than a hint of accusation in the words, and I tried not to bristle at his tone. He must have gone through hell. I could hardly blame him for being upset at finding me apparently free as a bird in the middle of the party to welcome his father to Spring. "When did you get here?"

"Only a moment ago." That much, at least, was true. Should I tell him the rest of it? He was my friend—hell, more than a friend, if that kiss was anything to go by—and he would help me.

There was a break in the dancers ahead, and Raven was steering us toward it. Beyond lay the trees and one of the other public pavilions—a smaller dining hall. Evandir moved out from behind the trees, and suddenly, I pulled back against Raven's grip. No doubt Evandir had seen me with Raven, but I didn't need to deliver Raven to him like a present already wrapped and tied with a bow. Evandir was no friend of mine, and I didn't want him close to the people who were. Who knew what he would do to them, if he thought it would hurt me?

Raven looked back enquiringly, though he didn't release my hand. "What's wrong?"

I glanced back toward the banquet tables where I'd spoken with his father. There were too many people in the way to see if he was still there, and no *time* to explain the whole mess to Raven. And how could I even begin to explain Ash and my complicated feelings for him to a man who had just kissed me like that?

"I thought I heard something," I said, rather lamely. Better to stick with the original plan and get out of here as fast as I could before the whole shaky house of cards came tumbling down on my head.

And then I did hear something—an unholy shriek.

Half the dancers stopped in their tracks, heads swivelling towards the sound.

"Help! He's dead, he's dead! Somebody help!"

Raven stared at me, an odd look on his face. Damn. If I'd waited another moment, that wouldn't have looked so dodgy. Then a name rippled through the crowd. *Lord Nox. Lord Nox has fallen.*

Raven's head came up like a hunting dog who has caught the scent, a stricken look on his face.

"Your father. Go to him," I urged.

He hesitated, though the gasps and cries of horror were building. A little knot of onlookers was growing bigger by the moment, and the Lord of Spring had plunged down off his dais and was forging through the crowd toward it.

Raven changed direction, dragging me back through the crush of people towards his father. The flutes had fallen silent, the drums had ceased to pound. The only pounding now was my own heart thundering in my ears. I had to get out of here.

I jerked my hand savagely, freeing it from Raven's grip. He looked back at me, fear for his father mingled with concern for me.

"Go on." I made shooing motions at him. "I'll get help."

Help. What a joke that was! I didn't know what use he thought I could be among all these powerful fae, but he nodded as if reassured and disappeared.

I stared after him for a moment, guilt gnawing at my insides at the trusting look on his face. Then I turned and ran into the trees, looking for Ash.

32

I headed away from where I'd last seen Evandir. If I was lucky, I'd never see him again. Once Lord Nox fell, he should have left for the rendezvous point. We were all supposed to be meeting back where we'd come through the gate. I just had to catch Ash before he got there.

A tall figure stepped out from the shadow of the trees into the moonlight, and some of the tension in my chest relaxed as I recognised Ash. Wordlessly, he took my hand and pulled me along with him. We hurried away from the crowd, passing others running towards the commotion. Hopefully, we looked like a couple seeking privacy and not criminals fleeing the scene.

When we were nearly back at the hedge where we'd entered, he said, "I didn't think you would go through with it."

I glanced up at his face, still masked, his expression stiff and unreadable. "Were you watching?"

"Oh, yes," he said softly. "I saw everything."

He bit each word off as if it had personally offended him, and an uneasy feeling stole over me. I scooted under the hedge and waited for him.

When he stood up, he was dressed once again in his plain clothes, the masked pirate gone. Without the mask, the chill in his grey gaze was clear. "Do you still contend that you have no feelings for Raven?"

"What do you mean?"

Anger sparked in his eyes. "I saw you kissing him. He was practically eating you alive, and you didn't exactly look unwilling."

Did I have feelings for Raven? The memory of that kiss lingered on my lips, sweeter than strawberries in summer, like the caress of night-dark feathers on my cheek. I liked Raven very much. I was grateful to him for the help he had given both me and Allegra in the past. I would even admit that I found him attractive. But did I care for him as more than a friend?

Before that kiss, I would have said no. Now? There was a spark there, sure, a possibility that something might grow between us, but, hell, if I was completely honest, I could say the same about Ash.

Not when he was being a total butthead like this, of course.

"I can't believe we're having this conversation now. Really? You think *now* is the appropriate time to discuss my relationship with another man, when we're fleeing the scene of an assassination?" I glared at him. "But if we're going to talk about our feelings, let's start with yours. Why do you care who kisses me? Are you jealous?"

I got no reaction, not even a blink.

Time to state the obvious. "But surely that would mean *you* must have feelings for *me*?"

I stared at him, hands on hips, a challenge in my eyes. If he was going to come over all possessive, he should at least admit that there was more between us than an Adept-apprentice relationship. And maybe then we could move on to what I *really* wanted to talk about. Would he agree to leave the Vipers and come away with me? Nervous butter-flies fluttered in my stomach. What would I do if I revealed the truth and he still refused? Would I have to fight him?

"It's my duty to keep you safe," he said after a moment, "and to see that you don't get distracted from your task."

Stubborn bastard. He wouldn't admit anything. Fine.

"So what if I kissed *you* instead?"

I moved closer, so close that my breasts pressed against his hard chest. A little shiver of excitement ran through me as I felt the heat of his body through the flimsy fabric of the dress I wore.

"You seem indiscriminate with your kisses. Will you bestow them on every man in Spring?" His eyes glittered as he stared down at me—but he didn't push me away.

His expression was still stern, so I reached up and trailed my knuckles down his cheek. Could he really be that angry about the kiss with Raven? A cautious hope flared to life in my heart. That was a good sign, right? If he was pissed off about another man kissing me, that must mean he had feelings for me. Would he be open to my plan?

"Ash, you hate being a Viper. Leave them. Come with me—you could have a better life. A *normal* life."

A shutter came down over his face, and I felt his muscles tense, as if he was preparing to reject me. "You think either of us are free to choose a different life?"

I clutched at his shoulders. "Don't push me away. You've done nothing but push people away since Hattah died, and what has that got you? You're miserable. You have no life beyond killing and obeying the father you hate. What kind of life is that? You deserve more."

His face in the moonlight looked as though it had been carved from granite, but I forged on anyway. "You're worried about the dagger and its power over us. But I can get us to a safe place where we won't be able to answer its call. The king will move against your father and then it won't be a problem anymore."

His eyes widened. "You will bring Rothbold against the Vipers? Against my father?"

I licked my lips nervously, and his eyes followed the movement. Possibly telling him I meant to kill dear old Dad wasn't the best way to sell my plan, but I was counting on his hatred for his father to carry the moment.

"When you put it so baldly, I admit it doesn't sound good. But you don't care for any of those people. You hate your father, and you would never have joined the Vipers if he hadn't tricked you into it." I poured all the passion I felt into my voice, holding his gaze so he could read the sincerity in my own. He had to understand how important this was. "I'm offering you a fresh start. All you have to do is come with me now."

"Come *where* with you now?" another voice asked.

Lord Celebrach stepped out of the darkness under the trees, a look of polite enquiry on his face.

Bloody hell. Where had he sprung from? And how much had he heard?

Ash gripped me warningly. "My lord," he said. "She was only making sexual suggestions. She hasn't yet learned her place."

"And yet you don't seem averse to those suggestions," Celebrach observed dryly, pointedly eyeing how close together we were standing. "Is this the degree of professionalism I can expect from my Vipers when they are out on a job?"

Ash let go and stepped away, but not that far. He positioned himself between me and his father, though he made it look casual. "I didn't expect to see you here, my lord. Is there a problem?"

"It's quite clear you didn't expect me," Celebrach said with a sneer. "But there is no problem. This is an important hit, so I thought I would check up on my troops. Where are Evandir and Atinna?"

"We are to meet them back at the gate," Ash said.

"I see."

I began to breathe a little easier. Celebrach wasn't acting like a man who'd overheard my whole pitch to Ash. Maybe he'd really only arrived in time for that last, impassioned *come away with me.*

Or maybe he was playing a deeper game. I still had

my knife in its sheath on my thigh, and Ash was undoubtedly armed to the teeth, but I didn't see what use any of our weapons would be against Celebrach if he decided to move against us. Not with Ni'ishasana hanging at his side. I could feel the power emanating from it from where I stood, its faint whisperings at the edge of my hearing.

"And yet you delay here with your *personal business.*" Storms brewed in Celebrach's eyes. "Since when has personal business come before Viper business?"

"Our Viper business has been successfully concluded, my lord," Ash said.

How the hell did he remain so calm in the face of his father's fury? I could feel it beating at me like a wave of heat when you stood too close to a fire. And Ash's link with the Lord Serpent was stronger than mine, since I was only an apprentice.

Shadows rose around Lord Celebrach, and I glanced at Ash in alarm. Was this the harbinger of an attack? Ash appeared unfazed. Could he not see them?

"So Nox is dead?"

"He is, and at Sage's hand," Ash said, meeting his father's gaze without flinching.

The shadows boiled and took on familiar shapes. I repressed a sigh. No, I was guessing Ash couldn't see them. There was Snake Lady, again, and her two silent friends. This time, they were joined by others, as if the dagger kept putting more and more power into its efforts to entice me. They stood arranged behind Lord Celebrach like ghostly bodyguards, only way more threatening. I was sickened by what they represented and turned my eyes resolutely away from them.

"That is excellent news." Celebrach glanced my way, some of the fury leaving his face.

So, crisis averted? For the moment, it seemed—but now I was left with a new dilemma. How long had passed since we left the Spring pavilion? The starbright I had used would keep Lord Nox in a suspended, death-like state, but not forever. How long did I have? Five minutes? Ten? It all depended on the dosage, but of course I hadn't measured anything accurately. Nor did I know how much of the poisoned wine he'd actually drunk. For all I knew, he was already up and walking around as if nothing had happened. The sooner we were all out of here the better. But how to evade Celebrach and make my escape with Ash now?

"We should move to the rendezvous point," I said. "Evandir and Atinna are probably already waiting there for us."

"Finally, one of you comes to your senses," Celebrach said. He glared at Ash. "We shall speak more of your behaviour when we return to the Nest. I have no objection to you dallying with your apprentice on your own time, Ashovar. But not when you are working. I thought better of you."

I glanced at Ash, but his face remained impassive. His father's censure was hardly likely to cause him any concern.

The shadows moved restlessly, catching my eye again. As we followed Celebrach into the darkness under the trees, the snake-haired woman fell into step beside me. Or as much into step as a being without feet could, I supposed.

"*This is your chance.*" Her voice whispered in my mind. "*He rarely leaves the Nest. We brought him here to you so that he would be vulnerable. Move quickly. His back is unprotected.*"

I swiped sideways at her, trying to banish her, but my arm slid harmlessly through her shadowy form. It only billowed and drifted back together. Ash glanced at me curiously but said nothing.

Was it truly that easy? With Ni'ishasana on my side, could I overcome the bonds that were supposed to hold me loyal to the Lord Serpent? Would a knife in the back prove just as fatal to him now as it would to any normal fae?

Part of me itched to find out. With his death, the Vipers would be thrown into disarray. I wouldn't even need King Rothbold's mighty magic and all his troops to bring down their hateful organisation. Just one single death would do it. My fingers crept towards the slit on my skirt and lingered on the hilt of the dagger in its sheath.

Could I really do it? Could I really murder someone in cold blood like that? Fired up by Nevith's death, there'd been no question in my mind that I could, but I'd found my limits since then. And yet ... would it really be a murder to rid the world of this poisonous man? More like a goddamn public service.

My fingers closed around the hilt of the dagger, but still I hesitated. If I killed him now, I owed it all to his hateful dagger. What would be the consequences for me?

Ni'ishasana expected something in return for its betrayal of its current bearer, something that I was absolutely not prepared to give.

"*Do it*," the shadow woman urged. "*Hurry, before it's too late.*"

I let my hand fall away from the dagger. There had to be another way. Ash and I could shake the others off somehow. We'd create a different gate, leave them all behind, and go straight to Rothbold, or to Willow's sith. Anywhere but the Nest of the Night Vipers. My hand was wet with perspiration, and I wiped it surreptitiously on my dress. I just had to create an opportunity to get clear of Celebrach—now, before we ran out of time.

"*Someone comes*," the shadow woman warned as we crossed a small open space between the trees.

I looked back and saw Evandir and Atinna enter the clearing. Evandir shot me a look that could only be described as triumphant. My heart began to beat faster. I was running out of time and options.

"My lord," Evandir said as they joined us. "This is an unexpected honour."

"It was not intended as such," Celebrach said. "I decided to check on the progress of the mission."

"Then I'm sorry to have to report to you that it was a failure."

My blood pounded in my ears, and I fought to keep a calm expression on my face.

"How so?" Celebrach asked.

Evandir could hardly control his smirk. "Lord Nox has just woken up."

Ash flinched in surprise.

His father turned a look of icy fury on me. "What?"

"Ash's little apprentice has been playing a double game."

"There must be some mistake," Ash said.

I caught my lower lip between my teeth, desperately casting around for some advantage. It was dark—could we run and lose ourselves in the woods? Maybe make it back into Spring through the hedge?

But Celebrach would compel Ash's obedience, and mine, too. Unless I took Ni'ishasana up on its wholly uninviting offer. The shadow people had multiplied into quite a crowd, and they were all watching me expectantly, no doubt thinking they had me over a barrel—and they were probably right. I couldn't see any way out.

"I think our only mistake was in accepting a spy into our midst," Celebrach said evenly.

At his gesture, Evandir and Atinna began to circle around, one to the right and one to the left, trying to get past Ash to me. No one drew a weapon, but then, no one needed to, did they? Their magic was just as lethal as any weapon.

Celebrach looked at his son and continued, "And perhaps believing that *you* would remain loyal. Are you tempted, Ashovar?"

"By what, my lord?" Ash stepped back, keeping both Evandir and Atinna in sight.

"By her inducements to make a *fresh start* somewhere away from the Vipers."

Shit. So he *had* heard that. Now we were really screwed.

I pulled my knife from its sheath—no use pretending anymore. It wouldn't be any use against magic, but I wasn't going to die without some kind of fight.

Evidently, Ash came to the same conclusion. He raised his arms, and a whirling mass of air appeared between his outstretched hands. Knowing that he'd chosen my side warmed the cockles of my terrified heart, despite the fact that it looked like our time together would be horribly short.

Celebrach laughed. "Defiance, Ashovar? That has never ended well for you before."

The Lord Serpent flung his own hand out in a casual gesture, and knives of ice flew through the air towards us. Ash deflected them in Atinna's direction, and she had to resort to an undignified scramble to get out of the way in time.

I was tempted to take advantage of her distraction to hurl my knife at her, but I was saving it until I really needed it. I only wished I had a few more. The vial of poison still tucked in my bra was hardly going to help. I could just see Evandir or Celebrach agreeing to drink it in the middle of our fight.

"Kneel, Ashovar," the Lord Serpent said. "You know I can force you."

"Then force me," Ash snarled. "I'm done obeying your orders willingly."

Anger flashed across Celebrach's face, and he raised his hand again.

Before he could unleash his power, a storm of black wings descended on him.

33

There must have been thirty ravens attacking Celebrach. Maybe even more—it was hard to tell among the flurry of wings. Feathered black bodies were everywhere, sharp beaks striking, and the harsh screams of the birds filled the air.

One of the ravens fluttered to my side. In the blink of an eye, it became a man dressed in black, the same man who'd just kissed me with such passion on the dance floor. *The man whose father you just poisoned,* I reminded myself. *That's the relevant part here, not how good a kisser Raven might be.*

"Mind if I join the party?" Raven asked.

"You should get out of here." Although I had to admit, his arrival was pretty handy. "Don't get mixed up with these people."

"Oh, I think it's a little late for that, don't you? We're already well and truly mixed up." He drew his sword, flinching as another bird hit the ground in a broken mass of feathers. They'd done well at first, attacking with beaks and claws. For a moment there, Celebrach had reacted purely on instinct, lifting his arms to shield his head, as if forgetting the mighty magic at his disposal. His head streamed with blood, but the initial shock would soon pass.

Or perhaps there was more to it than mere shock. The little clearing was thick with shadowy figures, surely far more than could ever have held the dagger, all jostling shoulder to shoulder, as if every soul that Ni'ishasana had ever consumed was here. Were they all working against him? Clouding his mind, perhaps?

Ash seized the opportunity to hurl a rain of ice spears at his father, making the clean, fresh scent of his magic fill the air. One pierced Celebrach's thigh, but the others did more damage to the birds than they did to the Lord Serpent. Then Atinna landed a throwing star in Ash's shoulder, and he had to turn to face the new threat.

The vortex leapt from between his hands and lunged at Atinna in a blast of frigid air and blue magic, whipping her with ice and freezing everything in its path. Frozen leaves smashed to the ground, stripping the trees bare. She got up some kind of shield just in time to avoid becoming a block of ice herself.

Celebrach remembered himself and raised his hands, so Raven leapt forward to help his birds, bringing an impenetrable darkness down on the small clearing. I stumbled to the left, dagger raised, hoping to find Atinna and take her out by more mundane means.

"*I can help you,*" the shadow woman whispered, so close to my ear that I flinched in surprise.

"I don't want your help. I don't want *you.*" Why wouldn't the stupid knife take no for an answer? What did I have to do to convince it that I wasn't interested in its offer? And I definitely didn't want its minions—or ghosts, or whatever the hell they were—distracting me in the middle of a fight, dammit.

It was darker than the inside of a dragon's stomach in the clearing, and I mentally cursed Raven. Maybe *he* could see in pitch black darkness, but the rest of us couldn't. Was his magical darkness really the best use of his Night powers right now? I froze to the spot as it finally occurred to me what a dumb idea it would be to try to stab Atinna when I couldn't see a damn thing. I could take out Ash by mistake. The very thought made me break out all over in a cold fear sweat.

The tail of an icy wind caught me, and I started shivering. This was *not* a safe place to be. Not only could I accidentally kill Ash, but he could wipe me out, too.

I strained my ears, desperate for some idea of where he was. We could take advantage of Raven's darkness to escape. If Raven had any brains, he would have already done that. Plan A might work after all. All I could hear over the howl of the wind was the occasional shriek of a raven. Of course, they were all bloody assassins, used to moving without making any noise.

And then my eyeballs were blasted with a blinding white light. It was as if a bank of floodlights had suddenly been switched on over the clearing. Everything lit up with glaring intensity, and the darkness fled as if it had never been. Even Ni'ishasana's shadow people faded, becoming more like blurs in my vision than semi-solid shapes.

I took in the whole scene in a glance. Atinna was down, with Ash crouched over her, though I couldn't tell if she was dead or merely unconscious. Evandir was nowhere to be seen. Raven had fallen back, one hand upflung to protect himself from the light. He looked as if it pained him. If it had vanquished his magical darkness, it had probably struck at his power.

Celebrach stood over Raven, glowing like a thousand suns, Ni'ishasana raised as if about to strike.

"No!" I screamed.

Celebrach had murder in his eyes. Once that blade came down, Raven would either be dead or a zombie servant.

I hurled my knife into the brightness around Celebrach. What other options did I have? Maybe I'd be lucky and he'd be too distracted by the Day magic he was working to see it coming.

"Sage!" Ash shouted, a look of horror on his face as he whipped a blast of icy, rain-scented air in my direction.

I rolled to the side, only just evading the blast. What the *hell*, Ash?

I heard a grunt behind me, followed by the sound of a body hitting the ground. Evandir lay there, a sheen of ice on his face and frost shimmering in that bright blond hair. His green eyes stared sightlessly up at the sky.

My eyes met Ash's for a fleeting instant, my limbs weak

with relief. Evandir had been right behind me and I hadn't even known. Ash had just saved my life. Again.

"Still obsessed with your little apprentice, I see," Celebrach said, letting his radiance die down until the normal darkness of a Spring night filled the clearing. He spoke without effort, though he had Raven by the throat, holding him off the ground as if he weighed nothing. Raven's feet kicked wildly as he struggled, and his fingers clawed at Celebrach's hand, his sword useless on the ground. It made no difference. Celebrach's magic was too strong.

Shakily, I climbed to my feet. "You can't kill him. You'll have every fae in Spring *and* Night howling for your blood."

"Be silent," he snapped at me, returning his attention to Ash as if I were no more than an annoying toddler begging for a grown-up's attention. "You should have let Evandir kill her. Now you have cost me an Adept. Don't imagine I won't make you pay for that."

Ignored by both of them, I focused on the twisted blade. Celebrach held it carelessly in his free hand, gesturing with it as he talked. Its oily surface caught the moonlight and shone like a fallen star.

"Still, she has a point," Ash said. He let his Winter vortex die and spoke as calmly as if they were chatting in the Lord Serpent's study back at the Nest, instead of facing each other with murder in their hearts. "Spring will be bound by the laws of hospitality to join Night in avenging his death—and we haven't been paid a single coin. It's not the Viper way to take on such risk without adequate compensation."

A raven croaked softly nearby. A dozen of them sat in the branches of a tree at the edge of the clearing, in various stages of disarray. There were missing feathers and drooping heads, and the dark shimmer of blood stained many a wing and breast. At least there were a few survivors. Far too many of their brethren littered the ground around Celebrach in a sad circle of broken bodies and scattered feathers.

"Do not presume to tell me what Vipers do," Celebrach spat. "You, of all people, you disgusting, traitorous filth. You betray us for a powerless halfbreed?"

Celebrach shot me a glance of such pure loathing that I knew straight away that Raven was doomed. He would kill him just to get back at me. Fear swelled in my throat, and I had to take a gasping breath to get control again. What could I do? I couldn't stand here and watch Raven die, but *what could I do*?

"*Save him,*" the shadow woman whispered in my ear.

The clearing was packed with Ni'ishasana's shadows. I could hardly believe no one else could see them—they had grown so solid, and even assumed some colour. With the harsh light of Day gone, they looked almost like real people in the silvery moonlight. One man wore a red velvet jacket that stood out like a beacon amongst all the Viper black. The snake-haired woman by my side had dark skin, darker than mine, and wore a dress of deep purple. I was afraid that if I reached out, my hand would find solid flesh and warm skin.

"*Only join with us,*" she said, "*and you will have the power to save him. But be quick. His time is running out.*"

Raven's face was a frightening red. Did Celebrach mean to choke the life out of him? But the dagger was still in his hand, the gleaming blade ready to do worse than take his life.

That blade drew my eyes, my heart pounding as if I'd just run a marathon. Every panicked fibre of my being was screaming *no*. It would take me and consume me, just as it had with the other shadows. It would tie me forever to the Vipers. The idea even of touching it was abhorrent.

But Raven ... I couldn't stand by and watch him die.

Still, I hesitated.

"*Ashovar will be yours,*" the woman said. "*Take this.*"

I glanced down. She was holding out a dagger. It was the one I'd thrown at Celebrach earlier, only for him to knock it aside.

"Been there, done that," I said, keeping my voice low. How was she even holding it? The idea of taking it from her hand, of touching her, made my skin crawl. "Might as well throw rocks at him."

"*Don't throw it. Get closer.*" She pushed it at me impatiently, and I stared helplessly at it, knowing that if I took it, I was accepting far more than a simple knife. "*We will be with you.*"

She watched me, a predatory gleam in her eyes. Ash said something to Celebrach, but his familiar voice washed over me without my registering a single word. All my attention was on the dagger in her hand and the bargain it represented.

"*Join us,*" she urged.

I couldn't do it. "No."

I bent down and snatched up a handful of dirt. The birds had managed to distract Celebrach earlier. Perhaps I could again. He wasn't that far away—only a few strides separated us. And Raven's sword was lying there on the ground by his feet, just begging to be picked up and put to good use.

"Celebrach!" I shouted, then threw the dirt.

It caught him in the face as he turned toward my voice, just as I'd hoped, and I lunged for Raven's sword, pushing my way through shadowy bodies that felt disturbingly solid. My hand closed on the hilt, and exultation filled me as I drove upward, aiming for Celebrach's heart.

But something caught me instead, freezing me in an odd half-crouching position, all my muscles still tensed for action. I was trapped, the tip of the sword halted in its rise toward its target, my arm not yet fully extended.

My eyes sought Celebrach's and found a triumphant smirk there.

"I think not," he said.

I couldn't turn my head, but I could still move my eyes. Ash was frozen, too, his arms outstretched toward me as if trying fruitlessly to stop me from making a very big mistake.

Because that's what I'd done. In the heat of battle, I'd forgotten Celebrach's power to control the Vipers. All of them, including me.

"You have annoyed me long enough," Celebrach said in a bored voice. "Time for you and your Night friend to die."

Time seemed to slow down as the hand holding

Ni'ishasana began to rise. I watched the sharp tip of it moving in a graceful arc that would end with it buried in Raven's heart. My own heart threatened to stop. I had a bare fraction of a second left.

"*I'll join you!*" I shouted.

Suddenly, I was free.

Before Celebrach could even understand why I was shouting, I had completed my movement. I felt the resistance of his flesh and the scrape of metal against a rib, but I put all my strength behind the thrust. The tip of my sword found his heart, and I drove it in so hard that it came out again through his back.

His body sagged, almost pulling the sword from my grip. I jerked it free as he fell, half horrified, half exulting in what I'd done. Ni'ishasana dropped from his hand into the grass, and Raven staggered free, holding his battered throat.

Celebrach stared up at me, his mouth working as blood pumped from his body. "How?" he croaked.

Then, the light faded from his eyes.

I glanced at my gory blade in a kind of wonder. The Lord Serpent was dead, and I had killed him.

34

"*Pick it up, pick it up.*" The shadow woman stood at my elbow, hunger in her eyes and a thrill of urgency in her voice.

The clearing was full of the shadow people, all converging on me with eager faces. I could barely see Raven and Ash through the press of dark bodies.

A sense of unreality was growing in me, as if none of this was really happening. Half-convinced it was all a dream, I bent down, my fingers stretching toward the blade. It lay in the grass, glowing softly in the moonlight.

"Sage, stop!" Ash shouted. "What are you doing? Don't touch it!"

I was dimly aware of him lunging toward me, and Raven moving to intercept him, but none of that felt as though it mattered. Ni'ishasana filled my vision, and the blood in my veins beat in time with the soft throb of power emanating from it.

"Get away from her!" Raven's voice was a tortured

croak, but he moved like the night wind, snatching his sword up from the grass where I'd dropped it.

Neither he nor Ash paid the slightest attention to Celebrach's blood still dripping from its blade, or even to the man's body on the ground between them.

"Go, Sage." Raven's voice was taut with tension. "I'll deal with this one."

Go? Might as well tell me to turn into a bird and fly away. Ni'ishasana wasn't done with me, and I had no power to fight it anymore.

Helplessly, I reached lower, compelled by the blade's magic. It was fate, unchangeable as the tides. Who was I to set myself against it? I watched my hand reach for the hilt as if it belonged to someone else. I had no power to refuse, no choice but to obey Ni'ishasana's summons. My consent had been given, and there was no way out for me anymore.

Shaking, my fingertips grazed the cool metal, and a moan escaped me. It was like touching the sun. Power roared through me, slamming into my body, tearing me apart and putting me back together unutterably changed.

When I could breathe again, I straightened up, my vision still full of dancing dark spots, and admired the marvel in my hand. Inside me, a whole world had opened up.

I glanced across at Ash, feeling a deep connection. I was aware of him in a way I'd never been before. His luscious lips and cool grey eyes were the most beautiful things I'd ever seen, but now, I knew him on a deeper level. His soul was open to me, laid bare before my power.

Such an expression those eyes held—horror and grief

mixed together. He stood rooted to the spot, the point of Raven's sword at his throat, staring at me as if his heart was breaking.

But I felt strangely disconnected from whatever ailed him. My head was exploding with new information as I looked around the clearing. I could feel Atinna, too. My gaze fell on her, and I knew immediately she wasn't dead. In fact, she was stirring, having only been stunned by a blow from Ash.

She struggled to her feet, her mouth falling open in shock as she took in Celebrach's dead body. Then her eyes locked onto Ni'ishasana in my hand, and I felt the tug as she instinctively recoiled. But there was no breaking the new bond between us.

A roar like the sea filled my head, and bright strands snaked away from me in all directions, like the afterglow of a child's sparkler hanging in the air. I knew instinctively that each strand represented one of my Vipers. I could feel them all, however distant, the way I was always subtly aware of all the people in a room, even the ones behind me. At the end of each ribbon of light, a Viper awaited my orders. I knew who each of them was, tasted their thoughts and dreams in my head. We were inextricably linked.

It was almost too much. Too many people, too much noise. Too much power. I was drunk with it. My heart began to pound with the enormity of the experience.

The snake-haired woman—her name was Umarenthe, and she was indeed a great Air mage—spoke. *"You will learn control. We will help you."*

Understanding flowed between us, and suddenly, the

noise abated. She was in my head, helping me, showing me how to sort through the bright strands and tug on the ones I wanted while leaving the others to fade into the background.

"Sage," Raven croaked. "Don't just stand there. Get out of here!"

I glanced down at my hands, almost expecting to see them glowing with the power pulsing in my veins. I was sure that any minute, it would burst through my skin, my body too frail to contain it all.

"Sage! What's wrong?"

Raven's words rolled over me without making any impact. I felt ... I felt *alive*, for the first time. I could do anything, now. The world was not only my oyster but my whole damn ocean. I could fly if I wanted to, cast any spell. This was what I had dreamed of all my life.

The shadow people pressed around me with proud smiles, welcoming me. Almost every Realm was represented among their number. Their powers—Ni'ishasana's power—were a gift beyond measure.

Pitch blackness descended on the clearing again, and a hand grabbed at mine. Not Ash—I would know his touch anywhere. Raven.

"Let's go," he whispered.

Impatiently, I blew his darkness away, Day magic bursting from me with such ease that I smiled even as I squinted against the glare. Raven grunted in pain and let go of my hand, subsiding into an untidy heap. The watching birds cawed and flapped in alarm.

Atinna joined us, hesitating a step behind Ash. Her

rage and hatred roared through our link, and I turned a frown on her.

Immediately she knelt, head bowed, though her outer obeisance did nothing to hide the turmoil within. Did she realise she couldn't hide her reactions from me? "Lady Serpent."

"Just *Serpent* will do fine," I said, and raised an eyebrow at Ash. His mind was a storm of anguish, but he was still a magnet that kept calling me to him.

He knelt, too. "My Serpent."

I stared at the top of his bent head, Umarenthe's words echoing in my mind. *Ashovar will be yours.* I stepped closer, inhaling his ironbark scent, and tipped his head up. He met my gaze expressionlessly, though unshed tears sparkled on his long lashes.

What was there to be upset about? I had it all. The power I'd always craved. Respect. My enemies were dead, and the man of my dreams was kneeling at my feet.

I flexed my fingers. They still tingled with the power surging through me. I gestured for Ash and Atinna to stand, rejoicing at how quickly they obeyed me. Raven hadn't moved, though I could see by the movement of his chest that he still lived.

I could kill him, of course, but his death hadn't been paid for. True, my fingers itched to try out my new powers in a bigger way. There were a dozen different ways he could die. I could boil him alive with Summer heat or stop his heart with Winter chill. I could choke him to death with the plants all around us or drag him deep into the earth and suffocate him. So many options. I had to take a few deep breaths to calm my sudden arousal.

Something far away clawed at my memory, and I paused, looking down at him. Raven lay on his back, one arm flung up above his head, the other over his stomach as if it pained him. He looked oddly vulnerable, and my lips tingled with the ghost of his kiss. It felt as if that moment on the dance floor had happened to a different person.

A tiny voice screamed for attention inside me, but it was buried too deep, too unimportant to bother with. I shrugged. He wasn't a Viper. What happened to him was none of my concern. No doubt his friends would find him eventually.

I walked away without a backward glance, followed by my Vipers, both the living and the dead. I was their Serpent, now, and I had other responsibilities.

THE END

Don't miss the next book, *Assassin's Dagger*, coming soon! To be informed when it's released, plus get special deals, behind-the-scenes info and other book news, sign up for my newsletter at www.marinafinlayson.com.

Reviews and word of mouth are vital for any author's success. If you enjoyed *Assassin's Blood*, please take a moment to leave a short review at Amazon.com. Just a few words sharing your thoughts on the book would be extremely helpful in spreading the word to other readers (and this author would be immensely grateful!).

ACKNOWLEDGMENTS

A big thank-you this time must go to Jen Rasmussen for her insightful comments and enthusiasm for the story. It was lovely to have a fellow writer to bounce ideas off when the story wasn't behaving.

Also to my editor, Isabella Pickering, whose suggestions made this a better book, and whose love for Raven knows no bounds.

And, as always, to my husband, Mal. Love you with broccoli on top.

ABOUT THE AUTHOR

Marina Finlayson is a reformed wedding organist who now writes fantasy. She is married and shares her Sydney home with three kids, a large collection of dragon statues and one very stupid dog with a death wish.

Her idea of heaven is lying in the bath with a cup of tea and a good book until she goes wrinkly.